MW00605471

Table of Contents

THE GRAY CLOAK OF RESPONSIBILITY

"What did you find?" asked Sumo.

"Canned fish, canned meat – some vegetables. Couple of candles."

"Perfect! At least we'll be full tonight."

They turned toward the beach to go back to the tree house – the sun low in the western sky.

"Shouldn't we leave some money to pay for the stuff?" asked Jessica.

"Jessica," said Aeala gently, "there's no one to pay – the wave took them all."

The words struck her like a hammer. The blonde hair trembled and she shuddered then broke into sobs.

"My father...he's gone," she choked.

Aeala waved the others toward the beach indicating they should go to the tree house. He then waited silently for Jessica.

"I'm sorry," she apologized between sobs, "it's just the reality of it all finally hit me."

"Not a problem."

He looked out to sea hoping to see his own dad's canoe returning from Puna – hoping for guidance from someone wiser than he. The sun sank lower turning the sky red and the water to blood. The words of his uncle Ko returned – trust your instincts; have faith in your intuition.

He looked at Jessica then at the others far down the beach. In his heart he knew the truth – he had known it from the beginning – since the first fissures opened in the earth and spewed poison into the air – they would have to leave the island or die; and it was he who would have to lead them. He did not want that responsibility but none of the others knew how to escape the island – to navigate the open sea. The gray cloak of responsibility had been laid before him and now he, perforce, would take it, embrace it and place it on his shoulders – he would walk in the world of adults as a peer and not as a child – for he *was* the last kahuna.

THE LAST KAHUNA

It was but yesterday I thought myself a fragment quivering without rhythm in the sphere of life. Now I know I am the sphere, and all life, in rhythmic fragments, moves within me.
Sand and Foam
Kahlil Gibran

When he was four his grandfather took him to sea in a canoe and had him slap the water with a paddle until the great black shark came. The grandfather spoke with the shark and it did his bidding, herding schools of fish into his nets. The shark came day after day, month after month, year after year to help his human friend.

When the grandfather died the shark came to the boy in a dream and led him toward the horizon. But the boy feared the unknown and turned back. Thus the shark swam away, never to be seen again.
from the chant: "The Way of the Kahuna"

CHAPTER I – THE TREE HOUSE

Aeala awoke and rolled over on his straw mat. The shutters on the tree house window rattled for a moment as a breeze blew through. It was a cool breeze with the smell of rain in it—different from the usual warm air on the island. Aeala gazed from his perch in the banyan tree toward the banana fields and the beach beyond. There were clouds on the horizon and a halo around the moon. It was not a full moon but a half moon, yet it lit the ocean with silver. He sniffed at the salt air, recognized the portent of rain, closed the shutters tightly and fell back

3

to sleep. The island itself waited quiet in the moonlight, tall ancient mountains wrapped in flora, dark seas with waves that churned on the shore and dissolved to foam.

The land waited – but not the underworld; it seethed and fumed restless after a long sleep anxious to taste the dark of night and light of day.

Aeala awoke several hours later to the drum of rain on the tree house roof. There was no sunrise but the dark of the sky slowly faded to gray. He stretched, rolled up his sleeping mat and climbed down the ladder from the tree house. The rain, cold and raw, splattered on his bare arms and legs. Coconut trees bent by the breeze leaned toward the sea and their fronds whipped about like the spray of waves on a windy day. The bungalow where his family lived sat on a small hill in a clearing in the center of the banana patch. As he approached, Kako the dog climbed out from under the steps and barked a greeting. He was a speckled mutt, a poi dog, with a short snout and pointed ears. By the time Aeala arrived at the bungalow Kako had already crawled back under the steps to keep dry. The tap of rain on the corrugated tin roof was thunder.

"Aeala, you look so cold!" It was Kaela, his mother, with a towel and hot bowl of porridge. There was always warmth about her, a softness, beauty that radiated from a joyous spirit. She had long dark hair, deep dark oval eyes, a slender body and grace that reminded him of bamboo swaying in the breeze. Mia, his thirteen-year-old sister, peered into the kitchen still in her nightclothes.

"Where's Dad?"

"Oh, he left early for Puna with the others to pick up hardware, and fish hooks."

"I hope he brings me something."

Kaela smiled. "Knowing your Dad he would never forget."

"You guys want to stay home today? It's really raining hard out."

Aeala shook his head. "No can – I got tests today. So does Mia – but she doesn't have to give a speech. She can make up her tests."

"Yeah, Mom – I like to stay home today," said Mia.

"Okay Mia. And you – my big guy, my big fourteen-year old – you go but be careful: falling coconuts and tree fronds, you know."

Aeala smiled, went to the bathroom and washed up. He pulled on some shorts and a kapa forest cape and gave Kaela a kiss. As he stepped out on the front porch Kako barked from under the steps.

"What's the matter, boy?" said Aeala.

It was then that the earth shook. Aeala looked around, not sure what to think. It was so slight that he thought it might be just the wind blowing him sideways. He ignored it and started out down the muddy path toward the beach. The way through the banana patch was strewn with puddles and little rivulets as the rain had saturated the earth and the runoff had nowhere to go. The rain slowed to a fine drizzle as Aeala rounded the last bend in the path and approached the beach. The waves marched toward shore in odd shapes with deep troughs and thin peaks. He noted this strange formation of sea surface, thought it strange, but put it aside for a later time, as he was concerned with his tests and speech. His sandals sank deep into the damp sand and its coolness nipped his toes. He passed the big mansions where green lawns extended to the seashore then looked back at his own footsteps – they were the only ones on the beach that morning and stretched in a straight line for a quarter of a mile. The drone of the surf on the shore was soft music and the gray of the morning reached far out to sea and merged with the horizon. The boat pier to his left stretched seaward for about thirty yards, the piles and planking bleached by the sun stood gray and cold in the morning mist. He finally turned inland toward the little town with the wind blowing in his face.

There was not much to the town – a church, a general store, a tavern, a cannery and a few dilapidated warehouses. A timelessness surrounded the town as if it had been built old, and endured year after year through heat, wind and storm. Over the years the salt air had permeated the rough timbers and planking and shingle and preserved them like tanning does leather. In ancient times it was a simple marketplace for the natives where the fisher folk could bring their daily catch and barter for taro and sweet potatoes and implements. When the white men arrived and discovered rare forest woods and other natural resources, the warehouses were erected to store the goods until the merchant ships could load them aboard and sail them away to the mills of Europe. In the 1880s a small canning company was formed and limited canning done to preserve the fish and domesticated pig of the island. Although it was only a few years old it was built with used timber already weathered by the elements and thus it also appeared enduring and ancient. Hence the little town stood like an uncultured bonsai tree clinging to the windward side of a cliff, gnarled and stunted by the elements – enduring, enduring, enduring.

As he walked up the street the rain grew intense and he had to seek shelter under the porch overhang of the tavern. He waited there for several minutes, the rain pummeled the earth, wind lashed the treetops and nature howled. He bowed his head and muttered a short prayer to the angry gods.

When he looked up three umbrellas appeared ahead of him in the distance. He could not discern who was under them but suspected they were other students. There was a junction to the east where the main road and the trail from the mansions met. The umbrellas appeared on that side trail, the one the kids that lived in the mansions took to get to school. The rain let up, and he continued on the street through town to the junction. He saw footsteps in the mud, large and deep, and figured Simon Webster and his group had passed earlier with the umbrellas.

There are some souls in the world that are so dark, so distanced from the rest, that they cannot stand the presence of other individuals. The mere idea of someone else occupying a place nearby is distasteful to them. They squelch speech and, when unable to do so, use less obvious methods such as ridicule and scorn to undermine the dignity and joy of the rest. Simon Webster was one of these souls. He and his minions attempted to lord over the schoolyard like sharks over the deep blue. His poison infected others and they in turn became unwittingly seething and sour.

Aeala continued up the path past the ginger fields. Planting had just begun and nothing was showing above the rich dark earth. The field was pitted with little pools of rainwater and a small gully had cut its way along the edge of the field and was running with water. Earthworms lay bare on the path and Aeala wondered why in times of rain they burrowed to the surface. Ferns and ti leaves grew along the sides of the path and on several, spiders weaved their webs. Raindrops clung to the strands of webbing and twinkled in the morning mist. He turned the bend in the path and the school came to view. It was beige with a red roof and a canopied porch. Above the front door hung a big brass bell; Bell of the Blue it was called and Miss Tucker, the teacher, had told them that it was a bell from a whaling vessel. It was named Bell of the Blue because whenever blue whales were spotted the lookout rang the bell.

"Hey Kanaka – you look like a drowned rat!"

Aeala looked up – it was Simon Webster and his cronies with their black umbrellas. "Kanaka" literally means "The People" but Webster used it derogatorily.

"Morning, Webster," said Aeala, "I see you didn't get lost on the way."

"What's that supposed to mean?"

"Just that you made your way here in the rain without getting lost."

Aeala couldn't resist a little jab of his own but didn't want to get into anything with Simon – especially when there were three of them and only himself. The bell rang and ended the conversation.

Aeala walked into the large one-room schoolhouse that was once a church. It even had pews, and in front of each pew a table, which the students themselves had made. He spotted the back and fine blonde hair of Jessica Goodroad, one of the new students, whose merchant father had recently uprooted her from Europe and plunked her here while he availed himself of the abundant natural resources. She, like most of the other foreigners, lived in a mansion by the beach. Although she had been at the school for three months she had never spoken to Aeala. He wanted to approach her but whenever he drew near something in his stomach knotted up, the primeval attraction of male and female had pinched him but apparently its vector extended only one way – from him toward her.

He had dreamed of her on occasion but they were dreams of mist and foam and shadow – things he could not clutch to his bosom, things that were not palpable. She had befriended those of her own kind, the foreigners, the sons and daughters of missionaries, merchants and businessmen that had come to the island to harvest copra and hardwood and save the souls of the "savages."

"Hey Aeala – you ready for your speech?"

He wheeled about. It was Miki, with a big smile. Her dark eyes twinkled and pearly teeth gleamed. She was fourteen with a button nose and cute smile. He'd known her all her life and valued her friendship and intelligence. She reminded him of the shade side of the cliffs, cool and pleasant and charmingly interesting. "Yeah," he said, "pretty much."

"What are you doing it on?"

"Well, since it has to be done on 'How to Do something,' I thought I'd do it on canoes, you know – how to sail them. And you?"

Miki grinned. "Medicine: kahuna medicine – mountain herbs and all that."

7

"Good choice," said Aeala, "you are smart about that."

"Hey, how's it?"

They glanced at the door – a short, dark haired boy with broad shoulder stood by the threshold and grinned.

"Sumo – you made it!"

At that moment the bell rang twice indicating the start of class and for everyone to shut up. Aeala seated himself in his pew behind Jessica and watched her blond hair shine in the morning light. The speeches started, many of the students timid and nervous as they spoke in front of the class. Miss Tucker benevolently encouraged them as best she could. When it was his turn Aeala stood calmly in front of the class and gave his speech, ignoring the scornful antics of Simon Webster and his minions. His knowledge and certainty of the subject pulled him through without the slightest flinch. Jessica sat passively, neither smiling nor frowning, without exhibiting any response to his words and when he sat he felt a touch of disappointment. Her reactions to the other speeches were similar and thus he decided he should not feel affronted.

CHAPTER 2 – THE LITTLE SAVAGE

"Listen not only to the lips but to the heart for it often whispers a different tune."

The Way of the Kahuna

Class let out at 1:00 PM, a whole hour later than usual, but they did not have to return for the remainder of the day. Aeala exited through the front door and stretched his back and shoulders as he stood on the canopied porch beneath the brass bell.

"You did well," said Miki.

"I take that as a compliment, coming from you."

"Oh, why's that?"

"Well, you know a bit about sailing too."

"Yeah, but nothing like you."

"I liked yours on medicine. I knew aloe healed burns – but not that it was good for you when you ate it. And ginger – good for upset stomachs. Will it cure seasickness?"

8

Miki smiled. "Well, we'll have to try it the next time we go sailing."

"Hey, you guys – come eat my house."

Miki laughed. "I'd love to have lunch at your place, Sumo."

"Me too," said Aeala.

The rain stopped and in its place vivid rainbows loomed above the mountains to the east. Stringy clouds, like floating dragons, wound their way among the peaks. Waterfalls, not there the day before, tumbled into pools of fine mist.

"Look – double rainbow," said Sumo. "Good luck, no?"

"I hope so Sumo – after all, our fathers all went to Puna this morning in the storm."

"Oh, yeah – that's right!"

Footsteps from inside the classroom echoed.

"Such boring speeches." It was the mocking voice of Simon Webster. "What do you think of their descriptions?"

"Which one?"

"You know the one about how to sail."

"It was okay. I don't know much about boats so who knows if what he said is true." She shrugged.   "No matter he's just a little savage." It was Jessica's voice, but it may as well have been a dagger.   Aeala stepped off the porch onto the path and quickly left the schoolyard.

Jessica noticed him as he walked away down the schoolhouse steps and immediately felt ashamed of her words. She did not believe them herself, but her father and friends did and after a while she began to mouth their opinions. She watched as he walked up the rain washed path toward the mountains, his lean body bent forward in the wind as if bearing a heavy weight.

"Don't mind her," said Miki. "She doesn't know our ways."

"Yeah," said Sumo. "She's with the foreigners – they poison her mind."

The wind howled from the east and slapped at their faces. A tear welled up in Aeala's eye and he wiped it away. He caught Miki glancing at him. "Wind in my eyes," he said.

She nodded and looked away.

Sumo's home lay tucked away in a small valley near the mountain cliffs. It was a bungalow like the one Aeala's parents had with a corrugated tin roof and banana plants that shaded the front porch. A large Koa tree stood like a lonesome sentential just outside the front yard watching over the home beyond. Orchids and red anthuriums lined the way to the front of the house, a hammock hung from the porch ceiling suspended by rope. Aeala always felt welcome here whether or not anyone was home. An aura of friendship and aloha surrounded the place.

"What is your father getting at Puna?" asked Aeala.

"Hardware, I think," said Sumo. "You know, nails and screws and patches for the roof."

"Seems like a long way to go for that," said Aeala.

"Yeah, I know. But my dad likes to go out to sea every once in a while."

"Miki, what is your dad getting?"

"I'm not sure – I suspect tools and bolts of cloth so my mom can make clothes."

"You ever been to Puna?" asked Aeala.

"No," said Miki, "but I'd love to go. It would be exciting."

"What are we having?"

"Pork and rice and dry fish – that's okay?"

"Oh yeah, of course."

They stepped in. Sumo grabbed a big frying pan, poured some oil in it and put it over the hearth. He fanned the coals until they burst into flame then added kindling. The flames leaped and fluttered – he added a couple of logs and waited for the pan to heat up. Aeala and Miki went to the family room and seated themselves on the bamboo couch. It was covered by a soft mattress and colorful comforter – but the softness went further. It permeated the whole room and made it feel cozy and comfortable. The candle on the coffee table, the painting of Sumo tossing a throw net and the vase of ferns and anthuriums in the corner all added to the comfort.

"Dig in," he smiled.

"You got a really nice house," said Aeala with a smile.

"Yeah, my mom keeps it really clean and chews on me when I mess it."

They laughed. The smell of fried pork wafted into the family room from the kitchen and Aeala's stomach growled in anticipation.

"Come help set the table," said Sumo.

"No problem," said Miki and jumped up from the couch and scurried into the kitchen.

"Lemonade?"

"Yeah," said Aeala.

Sumo, with a wooden spoon dumped rice and fried pork on each of the three plates on the table.

"Dig in." He smiled.

They did. The fried pork seasoned with rock salt and garlic was so tasty that Aeala chewed for as long as he could, not wanting to surrender the pleasure. It was as they finished their meal that the thunder roared, and their lives changed forever.

CHAPTER 3 – THUNDER

"In the darkness of chaos foresight lights the way."
The Way of the Kahuna

At first it whistled like the wind, a far away screech that grew louder and louder until like thunder it boomed through the valley. Aeala saw the dishes on the kitchen table begin to shake and rattle and stood up, startled. Cups and plates from the shelves fell from their perches and crashed to the floor. The walls themselves rocked and twisted and the whine of nails pulling free from their mounts echoed through the room.

"Quick – out the front door!" cried Aeala.

They scrambled through the kitchen, threw open the door and entered the porch. The canopy over them shuddered back and forth and a portion of it ripped away from its mounting. It sagged to the left and creaked ominously. Aeala grabbed Miki about the waist and lifted her down the stairs away from danger. Sumo followed in a blur just before the remainder of the canopy crashed down in a pile of splintered fragments on the porch. Boulders dislodged from the cliffs above bounced past spewing dust and rock fragments into the air. The earth itself undulated in waves as if it were no longer solid but doughy. The pigs from the pen behind the house had broken through the fencing and ran about the yard in terror, squealing wildly as they went.

Run!" cried Aeala. "Behind the Koa tree! – It will protect us from the rocks!"
He clutched Miki in his wiry arms and carried her to its protection, out of harm's way. Sumo hesitated, looked back and to his horror saw the earth continue to roll, large chunks of dirt and rock fell from the cliffs and collapsed to the valley below. A tree that had clung to the rock

walls for years toppled over and only its roots, raw and exposed, stopped it from crashing onto the front yard.

Aeala stared from his cover in a fork in the koa tree as a huge rockslide pulverized the little house. Sumo stood panting and sobbing behind him. The earth continued to undulate and long ugly cracks opened up in the ground. From these fissures mud gyred out as if the ground were a whale, injured and spouting blood from its blowhole. A stink from deep in the earth fouled the atmosphere as it rose from the cracks in the ground and spread across the land, carried by the wind. Like flotsam in a wild sea they clung to the koa tree as the earth continued to shake. Miki lost her balance and fell from the shaking. Aeala quickly grabbed her and set her upright. He noticed the panic in her eyes and laid a gentle hand on her back.

"It's okay, Miki. It will stop," he said. "Things will be okay."

After what seemed an eternity the earth settled. Aeala thought of his mother and sister in the bungalow near his tree house then remembered his other classmates and Miss Tucker back at the school. Thinking the school was much closer he decided to investigate that first.

"Let's head to the schoolhouse," he said. "They may be needing us."

They staggered down the path, Aeala in the lead clutching Miki's hand with Sumo following close behind. As they rounded the bend and approached the schoolhouse devastation confronted them. The south wall had collapsed and the roof lay demolished. Vertical timbers, cracked and splintered, jutted from the wreckage. The canopy over the porch hung from a couple of nails and the Bell of the Blue lay cracked on the porch steps.

Aeala rushed forward. "Miss Tucker! Miss Tucker!"

But the wispy schoolteacher did not answer. They searched the ruins as best they could but the aftershocks of the great quake raked the ground and created new cracks and sand geysers – the canopy over the porch caved in and the west wall of the school house collapsed with a loud crash. Aeala envisioned his schoolmates crushed in the chaos, Jessica her blonde hair bloodied, her face bruised and battered, her milky skin torn and scratched – he could not recall seeing her leave the schoolyard when he left. Regret swelled through him. He had been so hurt by her words that he didn't even bother to look back and see where she had gone. He could not even find the heart to wish Simon, with all his venom, harm, and hoped he too escaped. The shaking began again. Aeala swore he heard voices, swore he saw movement in the rubble and stumbled forward pulling aside four by fours and planking and dodging jagged fragments as he went.

Unconcerned for his safety, intent only on saving his classmates, he pressed on toward the spot; visions of torn bodies and gore racing through his thoughts. Sumo on the other side of the building made his way toward him.

"I heard something," he called. "It could have been just a movement or a sigh or a squeak, but I heard it."

Aeala sped up his course throwing splintered timbers this way and that, hopping over debris and dodging razor-sharp nails. Finally he was there. He took a deep breath and grabbed onto a massive joist and attempted to heave it aside. It did not budge. Again the horror or torn flesh and gore coursed through his mind.

"Sumo – hurry!" he cried. Sweat rolled down his brow into his eyes – but it was a cold sweat, the kind that develops from fear not heat. Sumo with only his powerful upper body above the debris thrashed and stumbled toward Aeala, furious that he could not make better headway toward the hapless victim. Aeala could not wait but again mustered all his strength focusing this time on his thighs and hips and gave a heave to the enormous joist. It moved upward, shifted, then pivoted clockwise as if attached to a hinge.

Aeala stumbled with the effort, fell and barked his knees – but he arose unconcerned – the pain and suffering of his classmates being of such vital importance that any discomfort to himself was insignificant. Then he spotted the source of the sound, bent down and began to sob – it was not the sob of grief but that of relief. Jaco the class rat peered up at him and squeaked, trapped in its mangled cage.

He waved off Sumo. "It's just Jaco, just Jaco," he called to a still struggling Sumo.

Sumo went lax and sat down on a half broken pew. "Thank the gods," he muttered.

"I'm going to let him go," said Aeala and pried open two of the bars until the terrified gray rat squeezed out and disappeared into the rubble.

They continued the search, hearts thumping fiercely, pulling up every timber and plank each new section a possible tomb of one of their friends – but they found nothing.

"Let's head toward town," said Aeala, "perhaps there are people there that need our help. As it's on the way home it looks like the best route." The three of them headed down the path past the ginger fields and toward town, the surface of the fields looked like grotesque ocean swells with jagged peaks and ribbed troughs mirroring the energy of the great quake. Aeala thought of giant pythons he had once seen in a book and imagined these had burrowed their way under the field and now lay all in a row sleeping, waiting for another quake, so they could burst forth and consume everything above ground. A large fissure traversed the path; gray and yellow gasses snaked forth, curling this way and that from its depths as if seeking victims to seize and suffocate.

"This way!" cried Aeala and pointed to the north where a stand of banana trees and ti leaves grew. They circumvented the fissure and returned to the path; the acrid smell burned at their nostrils. Aeala looked back and noticed the strands of fumes that had gathered near the ground had taken on the appearance of low-lying fog. His heart raced – old legends his father once told echoed through his mind and he recognized the fog – the fog his father had called *noe make*, the deadly fog, and how it had come once before a long time ago and poisoned many on the island. As they approached the town they found the mansion kids huddled up near a log. Several of the girls were teary eyed and weeping. Simon Webster and his minions stood milling about arguing as to what to do next. Simon flung his hat on the ground and stamped on it. He finally threw up his arms, sat down on the log in a tight ball and refused to say anything further to the others. They all looked haggard, dirty and confused.

"What are you guys doing?" asked Aeala.

Webster shivered. "None of your business," he muttered, "we're just waiting here like we was told."

"Miss Tucker went to town and told us to stay here as it was safer," said Dirk Kindal, one of Webster's minions. His lower lip quivered and his eyes darted back and forth. "She said she'd be back in a couple of minutes."

"Sounds like she knows what she's doing," said Aeala. "Is anyone injured?" No one spoke, a few heads shook side to side so Aeala assumed the answer was no. "Good then stay put until Miss Tucker returns."

"Where is your mom?" said Aeala to Miki.

"In the general store."

"And yours?" said Aeala to Sumo.

"Somewhere in the marketplace."

"Alright – let's go!" said Aeala.

The three of them started running toward town. Aeala noticed Jessica seated on a big log, her face streaked with tears. He had never seen her like that before and it unsettled him. He envisioned her as always perfect; always beautiful and seeing her in this state pained him.

"Look, it'll be alright," he said to her. "This is not the first time we've had quakes – so chin up."

They reached the general store. The whole building leaned toward the left but was still standing. Part of the roof had splintered and collapsed and many of the windows were shattered. Aeala burst through the front door and looked about.

It was chaos. Flour was everywhere; canned goods and bottles littered the floor. Most of the shelves were bare, their contents fallen and scattered about. Kaina Waha, Miki's mom, lay face down on the floor with a splintered rafter across her back. Aeala grabbed the rafter and gave it a yank but it was solid hardwood much too heavy to lift. He sensed her breathing and it came in gasps and pants, the sound of one struggling for life with the shrouds of death falling darkly about.

"Miki! Sumo! Quick!" he called and motioned Sumo toward the other side of the rafter and pointed at a wooden bucket for Miki to grab a hold of.

"We heave and you stick the bucket under the rafter to give your mom some relief." The two boys with great effort leaned to their task but even with the strength of two could not lift the rafter high enough to clear the bucket.

"Don't let go," snapped Aeala. "Miki – grab that two by four and shove it under the rafter when we lift."

She brusquely did so and Aeala then snatched the two by four and used it as a lever to relieve the pressure on Mrs. Waha's back.

"Put the bucket under the two by four and I'll lever the rafter." He prayed it would not break and pushed down with all his weight on the two by four.

The rafter slowly moved and as it did Mrs. Waha exhaled and coughed. Sumo and Miki gently slid her out from under the rafter, turned her on her back and she coughed and vomited. At least she's still alive thought Aeala, better than not breathing at all. Mrs. Waha let out a moan. Miki cradled her head and kissed her again and again and held her tight. The gasps came long and hard, but soon her breathing evened out. Sumo found a second bucket and disappeared. He

15

was back in an instant with water sloshing in it. He grabbed a towel from one of the racks and handed the bucket and towel to Miki.

"Thank you, Sumo," said Miki and began washing her mother's face with the water.

"Come on Sumo – let's get them out of here then find your mom," said Aeala. "I've got to head home soon to care for Mia and my mom!"

"Let's check the cannery," said Sumo, "she has friends there that she helps out."

As they ran toward the cannery Aeala glanced at the ocean and his jaw fell – he beheld the one thing that as a child he had always feared. In all his dreams, in all his dark nightmares this was the sign, the thing that made him shiver when the lights went out – and now it was nigh. The ocean had receded and the reefs and ocean bottom lay exposed – an omen of things to come. *Kai e'e*, the great wave, was on its way. Veiled by the vast sea in which it moved, it would rise up like a hideous monster from the depths and engulf the land. Once told the tale by his Uncle Ko, Aeala's had trembled at the image of the Kai e'e – when it last came and overwhelmed the island with waves so high that they obscured the coconut trees and horizon beyond.

"Quick! Quick! Quick, Sumo!"

They burst into the cannery but it was deserted. Machinery was overturned and portions of the ceiling had fallen to the floor. They rushed out.

"Sumo, there's going to be a great wave from the ocean – believe me it will be gigantic." He pointed toward the sea. The reefs were exposed – fish out of water flapped and twisted on the sand and the coral lay exposed to the open air.

"You've got to get to high ground! I'm going after Miki and her mom!"
He rushed back to the general store and to his surprise Mrs. Ka, Sumo's mother, was there with Miki and her mother. "Mrs. Ka! We were just looking for you!"

"I was down the beach looking for shellfish when the shaking started. I came here after helping some of the others."

"Mrs. Ka – the sea – the water is receding. There is going to be a great wave. We need to get Mrs.   Waha out of here and go to high ground!"

They helped Miki's mother to her feet. She appeared to have had the wind knocked out of her, her head hurt and she was still dizzy – but aside from that she did not appear to have more serious injuries.

"Have you seen Sumo?" asked Ms. Ka.

"He's right around here. I just left him."

As they stepped down the stairs of the general store another aftershock struck. The ground shook violently and the roof of the cannery down the street collapsed with a nauseating roar. The Timbers within the general store creaked loudly.

"Hurry!" cried Aeala. He spotted Sumo in the street a distance away.

"Sumo! We found your mom!"

With Miki and Aeala each holding an arm they helped Mrs. Waha through the street and up the path toward the school and high ground. They met up with Simon Webster and the other students who were still waiting for Miss Tucker.

"Everyone, listen up," said Aeala in a low and steady voice, "there is a tidal wave on its way. The sea has receded and will soon return. We need to get to higher ground, now!"

"That sounds stupid," said Simon Webster. "How can you be sure it's going to return as a giant wave?"

Aeala's eyes were ice, his countenance stone.

"Do you want to risk the chance? Is taking the advice of a little savage that bad?" Aeala couldn't resist the jab. Simon hawked some phlegm and spat it on the ground but never looked up at Aeala.

"Dirk, Obie, Jessica – the rest of you, let's go," said Simon. It was not a request.

Aeala loosened up, glad the confrontation had passed. "Let's head for the school – there is a trail behind it and it goes inland to higher ground. It will take us through the banana patch to my tree house, which is on a hill. That should be plenty high," said Aeala.

Simon said nothing but started up the trail to the school. The others followed. The odor of sulfur was strong in the air and they passed many fissures in the earth from where the fumes escaped. The noxious gas made their eyes water and their lungs hurt. They hurried up the muddy trail, past the school and turned east.

The foliage changed as they entered a tiny area of rain forest that bordered the banana patch. At the sides of the trail grew large ferns, ti leaves, red anthuriums, elephant ear monsteras and moss. Everything was damp from the morning rain; the pungent smell of rotting vegetation wafted through the forest.

The pace of their hike slowed as they began to tire – it had been a long day. Finally to the west a vista opened in the forest and a narrow valley, lush and green, revealed itself. The view extended all the way to the sea; however it was then that the first wave struck. Aeala noticed it – long and gray and ominous – as it swept toward shore. He stopped in his tracks and stared spellbound. The sea rose up and enveloped the land.

Gray sea mingled with mud turned the color of the water tan as it made its way inland. Aeala thought of blood and the End of Days, as told in the myths of the island, where the waters of the ocean would rise up and overwhelm the land as fire rained down from the heavens. He sensed the pain of the land itself. It was a primeval feeling, a deep silent ache that heralded the end of many beautiful and joyous things and the beginning of something very different. The moment seemed to last a long, long time as the great wave overwhelmed the land and turned it into shard and splinter and chaos. After what seemed an eternity it churned to a halt leaving its soiled waters, foam and debris upon the land. Aeala turned to his companions.

"You can all stay at the tree house tonight – it is too dangerous to return to your homes. There may be other great waves before the night is over." It was more a prophesy than an invitation. No one objected.

They continued on the trail, entered the eastern side of the banana patch and finally approached the tree house; it was sturdily built, large and set in the heart of a huge banyan tree. Four thick boughs cradled the joists that supported the foundation and structure above. His father, his uncle Ko and himself had built it when he was ten and he had lived in it ever since. Aeala's anxiety mounted; he knew not what had happened to his mother and sister. Guilt grabbed him, a cur dog at his feet, yet hadn't he done the right thing? Or had he misguidedly saved the others before looking after his own? He'd done what he thought was logical yet perhaps not what was loyal. He had saved those nearest in vicinity and worked his way back home, yet in his heart those closest to him had been ignored. Should he have immediately run home? Should he have left his friends and schoolmates to fend for themselves? The questions beat at him like a rain on a windy day. The slough of despair ran its callous fingers across his soul. The burden of the great wave, the weight of all this destruction squeezed him.

"Aeala! It's you!" It was Mia's voice.

"Are you and mom alright?"

"Yeah we're fine. She's here too!"

He stumbled forward then knelt for a moment in relief, head toward the earth, eyes blinded by tears. After a moment he settled himself and turned to his friends. "Okay, careful you guys – the steps to the tree house are a bit treacherous."

Chapter 4 – THE WAY OF THE KAHUNA

"Nature wears many faces, and one must recognize these… or perish"
The Way of the Kahuna

Sumo and Miki helped the injured Ms. Waha up the ladder and into the arms of Mia and Kaela. The rest of the party followed. Aeala waited until they were all safely aboard then grabbed a machete wedged in a fork of the tree and headed back up the trail into the banana patch. His Uncle Ko had showed him how to harvest the fruit and it took him but a moment to locate a large clusters of ripe yellow bananas. Instead of cutting the stalk he chopped through the soft trunk. As the plant slowly toppled he quickly stepped forward and braced the trunk top with his shoulder then lowered the truncated plant gently to the ground. He seized the cluster of ripe bananas and cut the stalk. After examining the individual bananas he was satisfied there was no damage to the fruit. Aware that the stump of the plant would grow back in full he did not bother to treat it in any way, but with a struggle flung the cluster of fruit over his shoulder and packed it back to the tree house.

"Sumo! Some help!"

Sumo appeared on the deck that surrounded the tree house and looked down. It was a large structure that could easily house a dozen people.

"Oh, Aeala – I wondered where you went!"

Sumo scrambled down the ladder and helped Aeala drag the bananas up.

"If anyone is hungry there are bananas."

He glanced at his schoolmates and the mothers. They all looked weary and worried and he felt empathy for them – and responsible for their physical wellbeing, for he had invited them into his home.

After setting the banana cluster down on the kitchen floor he grabbed a bucket, climbed the small ladder leading to the roof hatch, opened it and scrambled out onto the roof. The bucket he dipped into an open water barrel secured to the roof. It was full from the rain that fell the night before. He glanced at the vista in front of him before stepping back down – the bungalow of his parents, the western edge of the banana patch, the road and the beach beyond. It was then that the ocean again seized up – a long gray wall of water, frothing and boiling like dragon fire, as it sped toward land. It rose higher and higher with dark shadows shifting before its approach. Almost in slow motion the ridge of the wave feathered then folded over and crashed with an explosion of foam and spray and thunder. He watch transfixed as it consumed the land, overwhelming it, rendering it to waste and chaos.

Aeala's mind ran wild with images of those trapped by the wave, their bodies tumbling this way and that, torn and battered by the force; trees and buildings shattered and crushed by the sheer weight of the sea as it swept inland inexorably, relentlessly, devouring everything in its path. Aeala's stomach wrenched and he gagged for a moment, unable to control his muscles.

The smell of death wafted on the breeze – or was it just his imagination in view of what he had just witnessed?

A low roar thundered through the valley and along the mountain cliffs – the howl of a merciless predator consumed with the kill. And the earth cried out; it howled its anguish at the wind and sky and heavens. Aeala shielded his ears with his hands as if trying to block it all out yet its agony touched him, raw and painful, as the earth was despoiled and torn apart. Suddenly he was no longer in the flesh, but part of the elements themselves – part of the earth and rock and trees and sea. It was not a bodily sensation but the pain of unearthed and splintered trees, the agony of earth tossed and turned askew, the tumult of sea so violent it felt as if one were tearing one's own limbs off – and the agony grew with each fragment of nature crying out, tortured to the limit by the mayhem. He wrenched and twisted until his soul broke free of the bedlam and he was back in his body feeling the thrust in his throat, the knot in his stomach and the cold sweat on his brow. He staggered down the ladder back into the tree house, the memory of the wounded land still raw upon his soul. The others watched in shock through the spacious tree house window. Jessica and one of the other girls broke into tears – the long fingers of the sea reached far into the banana patch almost to the little bungalow perched on the hill nearby.

Aeala placed the water on the counter in the kitchen.

"If anyone wants food or water it's in the kitchen," he said softly. The house was a tomb, no one spoke, a mood of mourning permeated the space like a pall. Aeala looked around. Several of his guests sat heads down, eyes closed. Others stared blankly at the walls or out the window.

He did not speak again for some time but settled near the large window, trying to make sense of everything that had just happened, searching for some bit of wisdom, some scrap of adage that he could grasp onto and hold until the shock subsided. The old chants of his father and his uncle Ko began to pulsed through his memory – The Way of the Kahuna – *stay in tune, do not spurn the ways of the universe, for it is neither good nor evil but simply obedient to the will of gods. Learn its ways, for through knowledge one can become truly whole. Observe, know. In everything there is a lesson – even great misfortune.* He chanted silently, swaying side to side, the words dredged up from the bowels of his soul, words never forgotten or paled by time. The words of the chant flowed through him as if whispered by the gods until he regained his peace and composure. *The path to survival is through inner strength, through intuition, through observation and accomplishment.* The sun dipped red and fierce in the western sky until it touched the horizon and turned the waters to blood.

Chapter 5 – SANCTUARY

"To observe, to truly observe and trust what one sees, is a path to the gods – for the gods see all and do not doubt."
The Way of the Kahuna

Jessica seated on the straw mat next to the window stared at the scene lost in thought.

"Water?" She looked up. It was Miki.

"Yes, thank you."

Miki handed her a cup of water and an oversized banana. "When you get a chance you should take your shoes off. That way the mat will stay clean."

"I'm sorry," she apologized, "I was so caught up in other things…"

"Not a problem," said Miki. "We all have a lot on our minds."

Aeala and Miki had been kind to her. She had seldom spoken to them in school as her father had warned against the uncivilized ways of the natives. Simon Webster despised them and called them heathens. Due to these attitudes she had adopted similar ones toward the local kids. It was not that she hated them, for they had never treated her ill; it was just that she was unfamiliar for she had never made an effort to communicate. The conversation with Miki troubled her. Miki was always nice yet she had been cool to Miki over the last few months, unthinking even to the barest of social graces. Jessica observed her, really looked her over – her dark oval eyes, her long shiny hair, her flawless tanned skin, her high cheekbones and lean figure. But more than anything she radiated a soft steady energy like the trade winds in spring. There was nothing forbidding about her, nothing corrupt or demeaning. Jessica dropped her stare to the lauhala mat she sat on, and sighed.

"I want to apologize for what I said this morning," she said.

Miki looked at her, bewildered. "Tell that to Aeala – not me."

Jessica nodded and in her heart smiled. She realized Miki felt no affront to her words and had not taken it personally, yet she understood Miki's loyalty to Aeala and how the insult may have influenced him. She couldn't help but admire Miki's loyalty – and she was right – she needed to apologize to Aeala. He had been kind to them all – in fact he probably saved their lives. She appreciated his command and competence.

"I will," she said. "He was very brave today – as were you."

"We did it for friends," said Miki, simply.

That struck home with Jessica and she nodded and tried to smile in acknowledgment, but it fell short. Instead, her eyes misted and a long tear rolled down her cheek which she quickly wiped away. She felt alone among the youngsters for she was not like them – not like the natives and not like the others. The others were pompous, preferring to stay with their own kind until their parents grew powerful enough or wealthy enough to leave the island. Even the missionary kids felt the natives were beneath them and treated them as uncivilized brats.

The natives were mysterious and perplexing. They all had accents which were difficult to decipher. They had strange beliefs and customs. Worse, many were not Christian. She had heard rumors of their strange rituals—the sacred places and secret rites—and this had alarmed her, for she had been brought up to shun paganism in all of its aspects. By fate she was now thrown into their circle and although she personally witnessed nothing untoward about them, her upbringing and the opinions of her associates disposed her toward caution in their presence.

She grew up in Paris before coming to the island with her father, an ambitious French merchant. She loved it there, with its winding cobblestone streets, quaint manicured parks with marbled statues, outdoor cafes, chic basement apartments and old stately buildings. Everything was soft and mild, like warm summer rain or fog in the early morning, and she loved to walk through the streets with her friends, stop at the outdoor cafes and sit in the lattice-backed chairs and sip hot chocolate or sweet tea. The pastry in the shops were always sweet-smelling and delicious – croissants, éclairs, fruit tarts and cookies and the laid back, civil ambience of the shopping district just added joy to the whole experience. But her father had brought her here to a land of wild wind and water, a land of humid weather and harsh sun; nights filled with the relentless roar of crashing surf, flying insects, chirping lizards and the scents of salt air and rotting seaweed. Even when she walked the beach between the sand and foam her feet felt assaulted by rough sand and sharp coral and little creatures buried beneath the surface. The skin of her nose peeled as did that on her shoulders from the torrid sun and dried out her hair until it appeared the color of straw instead of that of fine gold. She feared the ocean, its depths and moods and the things below. And she grew weary of the effort, struggle and threats.

Jessica watched as the sun dipped below the horizon and the blood colored sky turned to indigo. Miki had gotten up to attend to the others and left Jessica to her own musings. The evening was warm and the wind off the ocean mild. The straw mat under her was strangely soft as if it were covering a thin mattress. The first star appeared in the sky. It was strong and bright and just above the horizon.

"Would you like a blanket?" She looked up – it was Aeala his face partly in shadow.

She nodded. "Thank you. I want to apologize for what I said this morning – it was stupid." He placed a blanket about her shoulders. "Don't worry – I know our ways may appear a bit different..."

"Still, I had no right."

"Then I accept your apology. I will go with you tomorrow and help you search for your father."

"You will?"

"Yes, of course." Tears began to well up in her eyes.

"You are crying. Is it something I said?"

She shook her head. "No, no – it's just that no one has been so kind."

He knelt next to her. "The earth is quiet again. I hope the worst is over and that you find some peace."

His words were more hope than truth for the acrid smell of the fumes from the fissures still filled the air and appeared to be getting worse. He sat there next to her until the moon came out and lit the ocean with its silver. His wish was simply that the calm of the tree house would heal her spiritually, at least for the moment and bring her some solace. He considered her the most beautiful creature he had ever seen but the feelings she elicited in him were strange and new, feelings he preferred to keep to himself, at least for the moment. There were more important things to put attention on and he knew the next few days would be hard for them all. Yet it was nice to sit in her presence for a few moments and even through the sweat and tears and smell of devastation he could still sense her essence – the fragrance of citrus and violets and things that hinted at a gentle softness.

She felt herself relax. His presence was warm and calm – different from the others, much like her father's – and she did not feel a necessity to talk or be interesting – that he was near was enough. Ever since she left Paris she had been at war – with this new environment, with the elements, with the missionary kids and with herself. For the first time in a long time she felt relaxed and at peace - for the first time in a long time she had found sanctuary.

CHAPTER 6 - KAHUNA LA'AU LAPA'AU

"To heal is not only a great responsibility but a joy for in the act one not only heals his patient, but the family, the group and life itself."
The Way of the Kahuna

After ensuring everyone had something to eat and drink and was comfortable Miki lay down next to her mother. She had watched her carefully throughout the evening to ensure she was alright. While Aeala was in the banana patch that afternoon procuring the fruit for them Miki had disappeared into the forest in search of forest herbs for her mother and the others. The forest was a good supplier of medicinal plants and Miki had come there often to gather medicine. Her grandmother had taught her which herbs cured which maladies, and which helped to soothe pain.

Her grandmother was a healer. Many people went to her for comfort and cures. She was known as the *Kahuna La'au Lapa'au* or medicinal master and kept a room full of herbs, barks and roots, which she dispensed as needed to the community. Although she would not accept money for "healing the spirit and body," they repaid her in many ways; it was not uncommon for a bag of fresh taro or several fresh fish wrapped in ti leaves to show up on her front porch.

She had taught Miki well, not only in the uses of herbs and natural medicines, but also in the ways of the spirit. She had said many times that the spirit always suffers before the body goes ill, and that a gentle conversation about any upset just before the illness does wonders to unburden the soul and start the healing.

Miki sighed and rested her head on her shoulder not wanting to look at what lay ahead, the agony of what they may find on the beach or in the village come the new day. She alone among those in the tree house could heal – yet she lacked full confidence in her ability. Perhaps there were no other survivors. Perhaps the others were all swept away. This would make her task easy but the alternative... she could not bear to view their faces – Miss Tucker their teacher, Mr. Kaah the warehouse manager, Jessica's father, the tavern owner and his little boy and so many others. Would she find no one to listen to? No souls to unburden, no cries of agony to comfort, no injured arms and legs and heads to heal? She squirmed trying to keep the images at bay.

Her grandmother had passed to the spirit world the summer before and Miki still felt the ache of the loss. She was close to her mother, but they were different in many ways—her grandmother was very special, a kindred soul, a wise and benevolent elder in the community. Grandmother Kaanananoa had passed the responsibility of the healer on to Miki, who accepted the burden but was not yet comfortable with it. She had not the confidence which comes with result after result, success after success, cure after cure – for she was only fourteen and had been healing for only a short time.

She listened to her mother's breathing. It was deep and rhythmic—a healthy sign. Miki lay on her back and stared at the ceiling, listening to the chirp of geckos and crickets outside. The animals had returned to normal, no longer panicked by the violence of earth and sea. She smiled for the first time in hours. The warmth of the tree house, the palpable spiritual calm that reigned within made her feel that all would work out. Her confidence returned and she drifted off to sleep.

CHAPTER 7 -- SUMO

"Dreams are the yearnings of the gods bestowed upon men to create great things."
The Way of the Kahuna

Mia, Kaela, Mrs. Ka and Sumo lay near the south wall of the tree house. From their vantage they could see the moon glow through the tree house window. Sumo lay on his right side, listened to the chirp of the geckos and wondered about the fate of his father.

They had been up early that morning and had eaten breakfast together. It was still raining when Paulo Ka left for the pier. Sumo gave him a big hug and closed the door behind as he left. He and the fathers of Aeala and Miki were going to Puna, an island to the west, to trade for goods they could not find on their home island. Sumo wondered if they were still alive – a big knot throbbed in his stomach and he felt chilled although he was wrapped in a blanket. He was thankful to Aeala for the lodgings but even more than that for his wisdom in saving them from the great waves. They were close friends and often went canoeing together – they would bring back fish and sea urchins and other things from the deep.

Once, Aeala spotted a giant sea turtle and jumped overboard after it. He finally caught the animal and rode on its back for an hour before letting it free. Sumo thought this was the most extraordinary and powerful thing he'd ever seen – his friend hugging the back of a green turtle that would sound and surface, and like a horse take him to places he'd never before seen. Under Aeala's direction it took Sumo a year to get up the courage (and skill) to do the same thing, but when he did it was one of the memorable events of his life.

His father was a pig farmer, but Sumo looked toward greater things: to go to sea and catch on with a merchant ship and see the world. Yet even that was not big enough – he hoped to someday become a merchant and bring goods to far away ports to exchange for exotic treasures. That, he felt, was his calling, and his shining dream danced each night in his head before he drifted off to sleep.

He rolled over on his back and listened to the soft breathing of his mother and the *peahi* (gentle breeze) that had just come up. After a while he drifted off to other worlds, safe in the sanctuary that was the tree house.

CHAPTER 8 - THE LAST KAHUNA

"To survive, everything must bloom – whether ready or not"
The Way of the Kahuna

When Aeala awoke his throat was dry and his eyes hurt. The view from the tree house window was the stuff of Hades – a red sun rose over a devastated island, milky fumes climbed from the fissures in the earth, extending out to form a brown layer that blanketed the land. It reminded him of pictures he had seen in a book called The Bible and in the last chapter "Revelations". He wondered if this was that time, when the gods would do battle and scorch the earth, and the god that won would reign forever and cast all his enemies into the fire.

He noticed disheveled blankets by the door and saw that Simon and his two buddies, Dirk and Obie, were gone. Jessica stirred – her long golden hair shrouded her face and she brushed it back with her hands. Miki was already up, had fetched water from the water barrel on the roof and had washed up. She crushed herbs in a cup of water, allowed it to steep for a few minutes and administered it to her mother. Mrs. Waha sipped the potion and appeared more comfortable than the night before. The other two girls—Emily and Robin—were also up and making ready to leave.

"Does anyone know where Simon and his friends went?" asked Aeala.

"They went looking for their parents," said Emily. "They left at dawn."

Aeala nodded. "Why don't we get ready and together we'll search for your families?"

"My mother looks better – she's recovering," whispered Miki, "I'd like to go with you."

"Mom – can you and Mrs. Ka care for Mrs. Waha?" said Aeala.

"Of course," they said together.

Aeala peered out of the tree house window at the sea. The water had receded from the land and looked as if nothing had happened. The land, on the other hand, was ravaged. Aeala decided it was safe to return to the low lands and made ready to leave. He secured water for himself and anyone else who cared to wash up. After washing they headed down the path past the bungalow and into the western section of the banana patch.

The ground was still damp with puddles here and there. A large crack in the earth lay across the trail, and from its depths spewed the acrid yellow fumes. Although he tried to deny it, Aeala recognized the omen – he sensed the danger and knew that the others did not. He knew the legends all too well which described the signs in great detail. The deadly fog had returned; it would soon engulf the land and the suffering would be gruesome. He thought of his father and uncle. They had sung the chants and told the tales about the land and sea. They had shown him the signs and shared the solution – a difficult one; one so difficult he did not care to consider it. They had showed him the old fissures, the ones from ancient times when the earth moved and explained what happens thereafter – the coughing, the gasping, the writhing and finally the dark blood that would seep from the nose and throat shortly before death. They had relayed the images well, etched the signs and symptoms in his memory, until the roars of the angry gods both on land and sea echoed in his nightmares. He thought of his mother and the other adult women but they were of no help for they were not privy to the knowledge or histories, they had their own special knowledge, child bearing, homemaking, mat and clothes making and others. The knowledge of the land and sea, the history and technology was handed down from father to son through the chants and tales, for their ears only, as was the custom. He wanted someone else to make the decision – an adult with more experience, with more wisdom than he – for if his belief was correct their lives would change forever.

He gestured for the group to circumvent the fissure, avoid it by a wide margin, yet he stood transfixed at its maw, the vaporous opening to the underworld, unable to tear his gaze away. Again his attention drifted to his father and uncle, kahunas both, masters of nature, experts of the earth and sea. They had taught him well – showed him the signs and what to expect. They had explained the solution, which was to leave their home and sail the open sea, find another island more hospitable, and carve out a new life. They had sailed with him to Puna, the island to the west, showed him how to find the way and pointed out the guide star in the sky, how to navigate with it and how to use the swells as well. But he had never gone it alone, never fully trusting his own observations, his own decisions. Although his elders had carefully explained the signs and lore, he knew there was a big difference between being a spectator and being a participant; a big difference between being a kahuna and being an apprentice.

And, then there was the certainty that went with it – the intuitive aspect of the lore. His uncle Ko had once sat with him and explained the nature of the universe: *Before the earth there were the Great Ones and they knew all. But they became bored, as they had no travail, and thus created light and space and matter and energy. And they arranged the chaos into forms and created the heavens and the earth and all that lives therein. But many were still dissatisfied, as they could not walk among their creations. And thus they took the form of their creations and walked upon the earth as men. But now being men they followed the laws of men – and the laws that dictated the behavior of matter, energy, space, time and form.* And, thus the contests of life began – the contests of survival and acquisition and defense and procreation – each defined by its own physical laws. But behind it all was the knowledge of the Great Ones – the original creators – and their primordial knowledge was never wholly forgotten that knowledge that has always gone by the name of intuition.

Uncle Ko had emphasized the use of intuition and encouraged Aeala to use it, for only through its use would it become stronger, more defined. Now it appeared time to employ it all, yet he hesitated. He was too young to shoulder the entire burden; too small to contest against the heavens and the earth and the sea; too inexperienced to be fully responsible for the lives of his family and friends.

Jessica's cough brought him back to reality – had she the first signs of the deadly infirmity?

"That way." He pointed and stepped into the banana patch to circumvent the fissure. It was a long crack, and they had to travel several hundred yards into the banana patch before circling back to the path. There they found the edge of the destruction from the tsunami. Banana plants lay uprooted and crushed, covered with all sorts of muddy debris – scraps of wood, clumps of grass, displaced boulders, coconut fronds and dead fish.

As they continued on the path they realized a bend in the road and a hillock had shielded them from the full view of the ruin. The panorama of the beach opened up. The sand was gouged out in long vertical strips as if some sea monster had climbed upon the shore and with its sharp claws defiled it. Debris laid strewn everywhere – dead fish, seaweed, small sponges, pieces of displaced coral, driftwood and planking from god knows where. The milky morning made the beach appear surreal as if some artist had painted the Apocalypse in pastel colors. They continued slowly, dreamlike along the muddy shore. Aeala looked back. Long columns of their crooked footsteps lined the beach. He thought back to the day before; the day before paradise's end when only his footsteps marked the sand.

Uncle Ko had once told him that of the many contests of life there was always the continual one between order and chaos, between Man and the physical universe; Man with the mission of bringing order and the physical universe tending toward chaos, contesting Man's dominance in every quarter. This was the essence of the universal contest, the universal game – bringing order to chaos – observing nature, its facets and laws and learning its ways; then bending it to the will of Man, changing it in such a way as to be useful to Man yet not breaking its essence. He described it as similar to training a dog to herd pigs or a bird to return once freed.

Could Aeala dare? Would he dare? Dare take the path of the Kahuna, lead his people away from this hell, and bend the will of the earth and sea to his own spirit?

Jessica and the other girls suddenly broke into a run – the site where the mansions once stood came to view in the distance. Aeala continued at an even pace, stared at the sand expecting the worst. The sea was ugly – dark and muddy – and although not red, reminded him of blood. The mansions stood stripped of form, skeleton-like, without walls or windows, with only the bashed and beaten frames still standing—and even they stood crooked and crippled by the forces of nature. Mud, sand, gravel and debris blanketed the floors – a chaos of sea and earth and man-made creations all crammed together in a tumultuous soup.

The cries of the girls echoed across the beach and out to sea – they sounded familiar, like the cries of the earth he had heard the day before: the reaction to deep wounds that hurt to the soul. He hurried to Jessica who sat on the floor of her former home, head bowed, hands shrouding her face. She trembled and shuddered like the earth had done the day before – severely and uncontrollably. He inconspicuously sat himself next to her and waited for the flood of emotion to course through. Gradually the sobbing ceased.

"Aeala – Jessica – we should continue. Perhaps there are people still alive," said Miki softly. She stood on the beach, arm around Robin whose face was streaked with tears. Sumo and Emily stood a distance away staring at the carnage that was once her home.

"Come on, Jessica," said Aeala gently, "perhaps your father went inland to get away from the waves. We will look all over." Deep down below the surface he knew he lied – in his heart he hoped it was not so but in his head he knew different.

They continued down the beach to the road that led to town – there they found only foundations and timbers. The cannery was gone; in its place, splintered beams, mud and tangled machinery. The general store still stood listing badly toward the mountains, apparently saved by the stone wall that stood between it and the beach. The other buildings were nowhere to be found, swept inland by the rush of water. Odd objects – a doll, canned goods, a pocketknife, a ceramic bowl were strewn along the road half drowned in sand and mud. Torn coconut fronds and ti leaves, shards of glass, shattered roof tiles and piles of tangled planking, timbers and rusted nails littered the foundations where once buildings stood. A cat slinked by, cowed by the brutality of earth and water. But they found no one alive – the only voices were those of nature, the call of gulls, the bark of a lone dog, the dirge of the wind and the moan of the sea. After several hours of searching Aeala was convinced no others survived the disaster – at least not on this side of the island.

"Come," he called. "We should head back to the tree house. Tomorrow we'll check the other side of the island."

"Let's stop by the general store," said Miki, "perhaps we can find some food."

"Good idea." They returned down the path to town.

"You guys wait here." Aeala carefully stepped over the wreckage at the front door of the store and entered. Goods were strewn everywhere – cans of food on the floor, half soaked bags of flour in the corner, tangled rope, candles, knives and on and on. He waded through the debris and picked up several cans of meat and fish, threw them in a bag, found a can opener and carefully made his way back out.

"What did you find?" asked Sumo.

"Canned fish, canned meat - some vegetables. Couple of candles."

"Perfect! At least we'll be full tonight."

They turned toward the beach to go back to the tree house – the sun low in the western sky.

"Shouldn't we leave some money to pay for the stuff?" asked Jessica.

"Jessica," said Aeala gently, "there's no one to pay – the wave took them all."

The words struck her like a hammer. The blonde hair trembled and she shuddered then broke into sobs.

"My father…he's gone," she choked.

Aeala waved the others toward the beach indicating they should go to the tree house. He then waited silently for Jessica.

"I'm sorry," she apologized between sobs. "It's just the reality of it all finally hit me."

"I understand," he said.

He looked out to sea hoping to see his dad's canoe returning from Puna – hoping for guidance from someone wiser than he. The sun sank lower, turning the sky red and the water to blood. The words of his uncle Ko returned: *Trust your instincts; have faith in your intuition.*

He looked at Jessica, then at the others far down the beach. In his heart he knew the truth—he had known it from the beginning, since the first fissures opened in the earth and spewed poison into the air—they would have to leave the island or die; and it was he who would have to lead them. He did not want that responsibility, but none of the others knew how to escape the island—to navigate the open sea. The gray cloak of responsibility had been laid before him and now he must accept it, embrace it and place it on his shoulders. He would walk in the world of adults, as a peer and not as a child, for he was the last kahuna.

CHAPTER 9 – THE CANOE

"The Canoe bears within its essence not only the hopes and dreams of its riders, but of its entire people."
The Way of the Kahuna

He gently led Jessica across the sand to the others. As they turned up the path and into the banana patch they met up with Simon Webster and his group.

"Where have you been?" asked Aeala.

"None of your business," snorted Webster. "You're not the boss of us."

"We searched this side of the island early this morning then went to the other side," said Dirk calmly.

"Did you find anyone?"

"A few families – maybe fifteen people. None of our… families."

Aeala nodded. "You are welcome to come with us and stay at the tree house. We have food."

"Thanks," said Dirk. "We're hungry and tired."

Webster frowned but said nothing. He glared at Jessica and the other girls; they shouldn't be with Aeala and the local kids. They walked the trail in silence too weary to speak. When they approached the fissure in the road they took a wide loop around it as the fumes continued to pour forth into the atmosphere.

Sumo looked at Aeala and muttered something under his breath. Although he could not hear the words, he felt Sumo's intent: Sumo also was worried about the fumes in the air.

Kaela and the other women had left the tree house and returned to the bungalow. A lamp sat burning in the west window, a sign as to where they were. She wiped a tear from her cheek and tried to push the loss of her husband and friends far from her thoughts. She also was aware of their predicament and well aware of her own helplessness in the matter. She knew nothing of seamanship and realized if they left the island it would be up to Aeala and Sumo to lead the way. She had faith in her son and was aware of his abilities, but this was an extraordinary situation and she worried none-the-less.

When Aeala arrive in the clearing Kako emerged from the far side of the banana patch and began barking joyously.

"Kako! Kako!" called Aeala with a smile.

The little dog sprinted across the clearing and into his open arms. "Kako, I was so afraid you had been lost."

Jessica smiled for the first time all day, her face lit with the last dying rays of the sun.

"Come, let's all go inside and rest," said Aeala.

The interior of the bungalow was warm and cozy. The aroma of fried ham wafted through the living room. As Jessica entered, she slipped off her shoes and left them on the front steps. Miki noticed and smiled. The meal consisted of fried ham, forest vegetables and rice. Dirk and Obie sat on the floor with their legs crossed and silently devoured the meal. Aeala could sympathize with their hunger, but not with their etiquette. He took care to ensure everyone had food and was comfortable before he sat, grasped his chopsticks and with dignity, commenced his meal. His uncle Ko had traveled to far lands in his sailing canoe and once brought back the chopsticks from a distant port.

"You'll have to show me how to use those," said Jessica, impressed not only with his dexterity but also his decorum.

He nodded, glad that she had recovered somewhat from her grief. "Anytime," he smiled.

Simon Webster frowned and muttered something to Dirk.

After everyone was done Aeala stood and addressed the group.

"I have something to say," he began. He saw that he had their attention and continued. "As you all know there are cracks in the earth. The ground is throwing up fumes that soon will cloud the whole island. The fumes are poisonous – we have to do something."

He paused and observed their reaction. They sat attentive waiting for his words. "We have to leave the island or we will all choke and…"

Most of them nodded solemnly and understood the truth of his words.

"I have sailed to Puna with my father – I can get us there. He has taught me to navigate the open sea and Sumo and Miki know how to sail. I can teach the rest of you as needed. There are two large canoes in my uncle's shed on the other side of the island. I can lead the guys there tomorrow and we can sail them here. While we are doing that the others can gather supplies – food, water and blankets – and take them to the beach where we can load and leave."

"How do we know you can get us there?" said Webster. "Have you ever navigated the open sea without your father or uncle?"

"No," admitted Aeala, "however, our other choice is to stay here and die."

There was a long silence.

"I'm with you," said Miki.

The others, one by one agreed – all except Webster who sat in sullen silence. Aeala didn't push it. He decided whichever way Webster went was fine with him. If he decided to stay they were rid of him. If he came along his physical strength would help.

"Good, then," he said. "We will start at dawn tomorrow the two canoes on the other side of the island are in a shed on my Uncle Ko's land. We will hike over the mountains and sail them back here. We should be able to leave for Puna the morning after."

Miki stared at him for a long moment in the silence that followed. He seemed different, no longer a boy, sure and determined. She too determined to do her best.

They all decided to sleep in the tree house as they had done the night before, as it was roomier than the bungalow. The moon came out. Like a benevolent angel, it gazed down upon them from on high and cast its light through the tree house window. Jessica lay on a cushion and propped her head up with a wrist and elbow. She stared out the window at the banana patch and sea beyond. Through her fine blond hair she glanced over at Aeala who sat curled in a corner asleep. She had also noticed the difference in him – an aura of certainty, of gentle power that surrounded him. Miki watched her in the silence of the room and listened to her breath.

"That's the mana you see," whispered Miki.

"What?"

"The mana – the thing the spirit is made of. Some people have more of it than others. And only when one takes responsibility for himself and things around him is it fully revealed. He has changed because he is no longer a boy; he had to take on the burden of an adult in order to help us all. His job is very difficult. He will have to guide us across open ocean and protect us from the sea."

Jessica nodded. "I had such a wrong view of him, of all of you. I mistook the gentle and calm of his personality for…"

"For being uncivilized?"

"Yes. I hate to admit it, but yes."

"He likes you, you know."

Jessica looked over at him. He lay serenely in the corner fast asleep with a faint glow about him.   "He does?"

"Yes. When you called him… you know, a little savage… he was hurt. He tried not to show it, but he was."

"I know, and I apologized to him. He seemed to accept it. He seemed to be a friend."

"We better sleep now. We have a long day tomorrow."

"I would like to learn more about the mana."

Miki nodded, "I will show you tomorrow."

Dawn broke red and cool. There was moisture in the air as a soft mist had arisen overnight and blanketed the ground. The window of the tree house sat just above the mist layer, and as Aeala awoke he peered out the window. A few banana fronds peeked above the blanket of mist, as if they were searching for the dawn.

He yawned and stretched, catlike, until his muscles were fully extended, then rose to wake the others. His mother had once told him that in sleep sometimes the spirit leaves the body; if one is awoken suddenly then the spirit jams back and the person is uncomfortable the whole day. He therefore gently touched each sleeping person on the temple and whispered their name until they awoke.

35

It took them an hour to wash up and eat but they were ready shortly after sunrise. The boys headed out toward the east up the trail and through the banana patch. They passed several fissures in the earth, which still spewed gray and yellow fumes. A mixture of wet sand and mud leaked from the fissures and every so often spewed a stream of the hot mixture into the air. The trail wound through a pass and down a steep grade to the east side of the island. Moss and grasses clung to tall cliffs that towered on either side of the rocky trail, which was littered with shards of rock from the recent earthquakes. Once through the pass the south wall fell away and a deep gorge appeared on their right. The sound of rushing water echoed. Aeala and the others peeked over the cliff and into the gorge.

From a crevasse in the cliff water churned out and down the gorge into the valley beyond. Aeala had never seen it that violent before and hoped it did not damage anything further down the valley. They continued down the steep trail, past stands of teak and sandalwood and through a small bamboo forest. It was then, as they circumvented several large boulders in the trail, that the earth shook again, a mighty jolt, then a long slow shiver. There was no sound of thunder this time before the shaking – no warning of nature's wrath. The north cliff of the mountain they had just passed through collapsed with a roar. Huge pieces of rock careened down the mountainside, bounced high into the air and fractured into sharp jagged fragments toward them.

"Run!" cried Aeala. He sprinted down the path toward a stand of thick sandalwoods with the others on his heels. As he approached the stand he looked back to ensure everyone was close behind. Dirk tripped over a root in the trail and fell to his knees. The rock fall closed in quickly on him. Aeala raced back, jerked him to his feet and half carried him down the last few yards of trail as boulders and shards of rock bounced past. Aeala dove behind a thick sandalwood and pulled Dirk down with him. A large boulder struck the tree and ricocheted to their left. Several other large shards of rock struck the tree but Aeala had pulled himself and Dirk up and they positioned themselves between the trunk and rock fall.

"That was close," muttered Dirk. He staggered back and fell again.

"You okay?" said Aeala and extended a hand.

"Yeah," said Dirk, "yeah, I'm okay. Thanks."

"No problem," said Aeala, and pulled him to his feet.

"The rest of you guys okay?"

"Yeah, we're okay," said Simon. "The danger's gone now."

"Good – then follow me," said Aeala. "The boathouse is not more than a couple of miles up the road."

They continued on hot and tired until the winding trail opened up and revealed a small beach no more than a hundred yards wide. There were shady coconut trees and a small spring of water. The spring was about three feet across and bubbled up from underground. They all fell to their knees and sucked up the clear liquid. The boathouse stood on the south corner of the beach about fifty yards from the water.

"The canoes are in there," said Aeala and pointed toward the little shack by the edge of the beach.

"Look!" said Sumo and pointed to the beach in front of the shack. Footprints and two long ruts extended out from the front of the boathouse and disappeared in the surf.

Aeala rushed to the shack and peered in. He breathed a sigh of relief as he spotted a large double-hulled canoe in the shadows.

"They took one but I'm sure we will all fit in this one," called Aeala to the others.

"Wonder who took the other one?" said Sumo.

"Probably the people that live on this side of the island," said Aeala calmly. "They know what the score is with the fumes."

The canoe sat on a small-wheeled platform, and on shelves in the back of the shack was a tall mast, sails and paddles.

"It was nice of them to take only what they needed," said Aeala, "or our trip here would be useless."

"Let us rest a few minutes before pushing this thing out," said Dirk.

Aeala nodded. "Good idea."

The group lay in the shade under the coconut trees and relaxed for a few minutes. It was pleasant except for the faint smell of brimstone from the fissures.

"We don't know anything about sailing," said Dirk. He was a tall boy with blonde hair and small freckles on his nose. His father was a lumber merchant that harvested sandalwood and teak and shipped it across the sea to far away lands. Aeala often wondered why he hung around Simon Webster as he did not seem to be Webster's type; neither obnoxious nor confrontational.

37

"Don't worry – I'll show you," said Aeala. He slowly rose to his feet and walked over to the boathouse and peered inside.

The tall mast lay on a shelf in the shadows. Aeala slowly marched over to it and dusted it off. The thick heavy wood felt good under his hands. A few rays of sunlight entered the boathouse from cracks in the planking and illuminated a small portion of the mast. The wood instead of being tan or brown had a silver gray patina and a course linear grain. It emitted a slightly aromatic odor. He then went over to the canoe and ran his fingers across the bow. The smooth koa wood felt cool to the touch. It was as if his touch penetrated to the heart of the wood and he felt its strength, its weight, its fine tough grain and its essence, its life. He felt safe with the double hulls – confident in their substance and construction.

"They are beautiful." Aeala turned. It was Sumo, admiring the hulls.

"Yes they are, Sumo, and I touched their essence and they are strong. They will take us where we want to go."

They pushed the canoe out of the boathouse with relative ease as it was on a platform with small wheels. The double hulls gleamed in the sunlight like a deep brown jewel. The hulls were connected by thick koa wood cross-booms that fit onto gunwale stakes and over the booms gray teakwood planking was fastened to form a platform. In the middle of the platform was a hole for the mast and below the platform hole was another smaller cross boom to accept the mast base. Around the edges of the platform were metal eyes screwed into the platform for the attachment of the shrouds and stays. Two grooves on the planking ran parallel to the hulls.

"What are those grooves for?" asked Dirk.

"They hold fast the shelter base," said Aeala. "I believe the shelter itself is somewhere in the boathouse. Would you mind looking for it?"

Dirk headed back to the boathouse happy to have something to do. The rest of the boys pushed the canoe the last ten yards to the water's edge.

"Stop here," said Aeala. "We'll mount the mast and hook up the shrouds and stays before we launch her."

They turned and headed back to the boathouse after Dirk to fetch the mast and cordage. The mast was heavy, being about twenty-five feet long. They struggled to lift it but finally ended up dragging the masthead in the sand to the canoe.

"Now what?" asked Simon?

"Now we haul it onto the platform and mount it in the hole."

"How we going to stand it on end? —It's too heavy."

"Watch," said Aeala.

He strung the cordage through the metal eyes attached to the masthead. "Alright – help me lift the mast onto the platform and we'll lay the base right over the hole. They heaved and pushed and finally slid the base of the mast over the hole.

"Well done!" said Aeala. He strung the line attached to the masthead through the eye on the front edge of the platform.

"Okay… three of you lift the masthead up and try and walk toward the hole. Sumo you steady the whole thing so it doesn't fall over. I'll be pulling on the line on the other side of this metal eye which will add upward force to the mast head and it'll go straight up."
They all struggled to do exactly as they were told and the masthead was hoisted skyward and the base slipped into the hole – it slid three feet down until it caught in the hole of the cross boom below the platform hole.

"Perfect!" cried Aeala. "Now we'll secure the rigging and be off!"
It took another hour for them to secure the rigging and connect the boom to the mast. Finally they attached the sail with Aeala patiently giving the others directions on how exactly each detail was to be done.

The wind blew gently out of the east and created a slight chop to the surface of the water. "Grab the paddles from the boathouse and we'll launch," said Aeala. Dirk and Sumo jogged back, picked up the paddles, ran back and dropped them in the hulls – four in the starboard and four in the port hull.

"Okay, everybody – push!"
They all grunted and groaned and pushed the canoe – it slid slowly from the low platform onto the wet sand and into the water. Webster complained that there should be an easier way to launch but he didn't offer up any ideas.

"All right, everybody – hop in," said Aeala. "Except you, Sumo. Help me push it out."
They splashed and pushed and the canoe started to bob in the surf. "Jump in!"
Sumo leaped, and his head, arms and torso disappeared over the gunwale into the canoe. His bottom and legs flailed for a moment then slid over the side and vanished. Aeala, water to his armpits, pushed his toes into the sand, secured a toehold and gave one last mighty push. The

canoe slid forward on the water, responding like a well-trained horse. Aeala grabbed the starboard gunwale and pulled himself out of the water and into the hull. The canoe sat for a moment and bobbed gently.

"Grab a paddle everybody and let's paddle out a ways."

"I ain't paddling all the way to the other side of the island!" said Webster.

"Don't worry!" said Aeala. "In a few minutes I'll get the sails going."

They paddled until the canoe was away from the shore and into deep water. Aeala then climbed onto the platform and shifted the boom on the bottom of the sail until the wind caught it and the sail billowed out. The canoe responded and shot forward the twin hulls slicing through the water with a soothing grace.

"This is called running before the wind," said Aeala. "The wind is directly behind us and the boom is at a right angle to the hull."

He held on tight to a line at the end of the boom and aligned the bows of the canoe with a point of land at the far end of the island. The sun was low in the sky a fiery red globe against a gray backdrop. After a while he tied the boom line fast to a metal eye on the perimeter of the platform. The canoe raced forward propelled by the wind and cut a sharp line through the water. Except for the wind on the sail everything was quiet. Aeala noticed a familiar relaxation creep over him – the feel of spacious freedom; the feel of running with the elements.

"See that point of land," he said to Dirk and Obie, "I've aligned the bow of the canoe toward it and we're moving in a straight line in that direction."

They nodded from their positions in the port hull. Dirk climbed onto the deck between the hulls and observed carefully what Aeala was doing and the way the canoe responded to him.

"Remarkable!" he said. "If I wasn't so damned tired I'd ask you to let me run this thing." Aeala grinned. "They'll be plenty of time for that."

The sun set red and angry as they rounded the point and headed back toward the beach by the tree house.

CHAPTER 10 – THE MANA

Within the land, life; within the sea, life; within the sky, life; within thought, life – and that life invested in its people is the nation.

"We need to get everything ready for the trip," said Miki. "We have a lot to take – food, blankets, water – all of those things."

"And when we get to town we can pick up more food at the general store," said Jessica.

"Good idea," said Miki. She was starting to like Jessica – her willingness, her appreciation.

They gathered up blankets from the bungalow and some from the tree house – leaving enough for the following night. Emily and Robin found a wheelbarrow in the banana patch and helped load it with the blankets and cooking utensils. Kaela pulled out an old wagon from under the stairs and they loaded that with large jars for drinking water. The girls and Kaela headed down the trail toward the beach with their loads. It took them about an hour to reach what was left of the pier.

"Let's leave the stuff here on the beach," said Kaela," and go into town."

"Jessica and I will go to the general store and see what we can find," said Miki.

"Okay, then Emily, Robin and I will go to the cannery and tavern and see what we can find. Be careful, now."

Miki headed for the general store with Jessica close behind. "Tell me more about mana."

Miki looked over her shoulder. Jessica's large gray eyes stared back at her. Miki shrugged. "What would you like to know?"

"Well, you mentioned that it was the stuff the spirit was made of ..."

"Yes. That, and magic, too. There is mana in many things—not just people. There is even mana in things like water and earth. Have you ever been to a place that just seems alive—full of joy or excitement or beauty?"

"Yes, of course."

"Well, that's mana—the thing that makes things be alive. There is a big koa tree that we passed on the way to the tree house. I have sat under it and leaned on it. You can feel the life in the tree; even feel its thoughts."

"It's not that I don't believe you. It just seems so strange to me—the idea of non-living things having life or trees having thoughts."

Miki hesitated. "I will show you a place—a place only the locals know about. I will take you there and you can feel the mana. It is near the trail by the banana patch, but it is sacred ground, so you must be respectful."

Jessica nodded. "I will do my best."

They arrived at the general store, which appeared ready to collapse. The walls all leaned toward the hills; sections were already split and fractured from the forces of the earthquakes and great waves.

"Be careful," said Jessica. "Everything looks very flimsy."

They tiptoed in as if floating on the wind and carefully gathered canned goods, taking great care to displace as little as possible. Jessica found some large clay jars, gently picked them up and took them outside. She also found leather ponchos, which she gathered up. Miki collected canned goods: pickled fish, vegetables and meat. There were many boxes of these canned items and it took them quite some time to pack them out of the store. Jessica spotted two beautifully crafted pistols in the corner, several boxes of ammunition and what appeared to be a keg of black powder.

"Should we take these?"

Miki examined the pistols. The handles shimmered with mother of pearl, and the barrels gleamed grimly in the light. She was enthralled with their beauty.

"Yes, we may need them for hunting."

Jessica picked them up. They were cool to the touch, like the marble of the inner walls of a mausoleum, beautiful yet lifeless: statuary, not flesh. Jessica wrapped the pistols in cloth, and took them with the ammunition and keg of black powder out of the store and laid them beside the rest of the goods. There was also an axe and machete on one of the shelves which she wrapped in cloth and packed out.

It was then that the earth shook again. Miki raced to the door in terror. As she scrambled down the battered steps the roof collapsed with a roar. Jessica, already outside, gasped and grabbed her friend's arm.

"Are you okay?"

Miki nodded, "Yeah – but that was too close. We need to check on Kaela and the others."

They headed for the cannery but Kaela and the girls were already walking back to them with sacks of canned goods.

"We're fine," she called. "Let's get this stuff to the beach and head back."

Once all the goods were stacked on the beach they headed toward the tree house.

"We will be back soon," said Miki. "Jessica and I are going to pick some herbs first."

"We'll meet you at the tree house then," said Kaela.

"Come. I'll show you the sacred pond, but you must keep its location a secret," whispered Miki.

"I will—I'm just tired and hot, and it would be nice to stick my toes in the water."

Miki grinned. "Yes, I agree."

Instead of turning inland at the path to the tree house they continued down the shore another two hundred yards. A faint trail snaked into the banana patch and they followed it. It wound inland and opened up into a streambed full of boulders. Grass and moss grew along the edges, and an occasional ginger plant clung to the rocks and fertile soil. The water slowly gurgled down the streambed toward the sea. At first Jessica didn't see them, but Miki pointed out the freshwater shrimp near the bottom, wiggling above the streambed gravel, attempting to hold their position in the current.

"Opae!" said Miki. "They are freshwater shrimp and good to eat. You barbecue them and they are really tasty."

Jessica paused and watched them, glad to be near the cool water. The movement of the water at first obscured her view but she stared awhile and was finally able to make out the stream bottom and what lay on it. The opae were large, nearly colorless, with whiskers and tails like shrimp.

"How do you catch them?"

"You use a little scoop net. You can catch lots of them in a short time."

They continued up the streambed for about half a mile. It wound around boulders and over small rapids, and even over a small waterfall. Finally they approached a second waterfall that dropped into a little green pool.

The pool was partly shadowed by a big coconut tree, but the sunlit portion glittered like an emerald. Ti leaves and maiden-hair grew around the edges, and the fragrance of ginger plants sweetened the air. Every leaf, every blade of grass, every colony of algae, every pebble and stone and every drop of water, even the air itself exuded energy. The colors, distinct and vivid, gleamed with the purity of new life. The ambience was that of a great cathedral—timeless calm, the illusion of limitless space, the joy of goodwill and welcome. Jessica, engulfed in this atmosphere, stood trembling awed by the view. She noticed the faint breath of orchid and ginger on the breeze and with each sniff the powerful grip of awe relaxed until it fell and crumbled at her feet and was washed away; in its place a serene calm. In all her life, through all her experience, she had never felt this soft-cool exhale of life, this infusion of energy into her body and soul. She wondered if this was not the fundamental difference between the natives and her own kind—this awareness of that part of existence beyond the physical form, beyond the rock and clay and buildings and gates; this spiritual awareness of nature and the world. She was Christian and believed in the tenets of her religion, but wasn't there mention of the goodness of men and the world, of the search for awareness of truth through ones own efforts?

"Do you feel it?"

Jessica nodded. "Yes."

Her skin tingled, she could feel the aliveness of her inner organs, her muscles, her joints, her stomach and her bones; but more than that, her awareness expand across the pool to the splashing waters of the waterfall, to the algae growing on the wetness of the water's channel as it tumbled down the rock face into the pool, to the plants growing beside the water's edge, to the air itself. She sensed these elements, not from a distance, but from the intimacy that was the substance contained in each. She quivered with the excitement of insight, unable to utter anything further. Her forehead beaded with tiny drops of perspiration, and she realized her body had warmed up considerably as she had hiked the trail to the falls. She slid off her shoes and waded in up to her ankles. The cool waters enveloped her feet and calves.

"If you acknowledge its life, the pool it will let you in and soothe you."

Jessica could see no harm and whispered a short greeting. She took another step and immediately felt welcomed. The pool, a host, invited her in.

She stripped to her underwear, leaving her outer clothing on a big boulder and waded deeper. The cool waters were soothing and the fine gravel on the pool bottom gently massaged the soles of her feet. As the waters enveloped her thighs and hips she felt the soft buoyancy lift her body and relieve her tired muscles. She looked up at the waterfall on the far side of the pool and noticed a vivid ribbon of rainbow that extended across the foam where the falling water met the pool.

"Anuenue," said Miki, "that's the name of the ribbon of colors."

The two of them swam in the waters as time hesitated—what seemed an eternity may have been just a few moments—yet they were fulfilled. Their weariness dissipated as the pool infused their bodies with new energy.

Jessica drifted like mountain mist, floating at first on the surface, the cool spray of the waterfall cascading down about her, then ascending gently, ghostly, perceiving the falling water, cool and pure and sparkling, flowing smoothly along the stone channel as she went. Finally she rose above the falls, suspended in the ether, and glanced down from her perch as the flowing stream tumbled over the edge of the cliff and down the moist rock face into the pool. There in the pool below stood two girls bathing in the green waters, one with fine blonde hair and the other tanned with dark hair and eyes. The magic of the moment filled her and she felt a soft joy in her heart—not the ecstasy of victory or accomplishment, but the gentle joy that was all life: the life of the water and the stones, of the plants, insects, animals and her own essence, the distinct difference between the awareness that was Jessica Goodroad and that of her body.

Long moments drawn out by the company of mana passed. Finally the magic, like haze in the early morning, dissipated. She found herself standing in the pool of water up to her armpits and Miki, a few yards away, smiling.

"That... is the mana," said Miki.

"I felt..." Jessica fell silent. There was radiance about her, a radiance that matched the vividness of the pool and its surroundings. Her hair, delicate strands of gold, shimmered in the warm fire of the sun. Her face, milk-white and blushed with rose, bobbed gently in the water, a lily of youthful beauty. Nearby an orange butterfly flittered then caught by a mild updraft soared above the waterfall. Jessica pointed, Miki chuckled and nodded.

"The mana helps you do many things—makes you see many things—makes you understand. This is a sacred place. There is much life here; the spirit is very strong."

"Yes." Jessica smiled, eyes lucid. She scrambled out of the pool, onto the boulder where her clothes lay and put them on. She still thought of her vision – she had seen the two girls from a distance and knew that one of them was her. But if that were so...

She stared at the waterfall a long time and knew its essence. She beheld the pool itself and understood its beauty.

"I am not sure how this happens," she said, "but I feel wiser—more intelligent—after being here."

Miki again smiled, turned and started down the path the way they had come.

"You see much. You are a bright person," she said.

CHAPTER 11 – THE DREAM

Within dreams rise the voices of the gods. It is the realm where mortals and gods meet, where they share their hopes, and visions, and futures.
The Way of the Kahuna

The first stars had just appeared in the night sky—specks of diamond set in the vault of heaven—when the canoe broke through the surf and foam and beached itself on the sand.

Aeala jumped off the bow and grabbed a line fastened to it. He lashed it securely about a tree stump in anticipation of the tide receding. Then with the help of Sumo they pushed the canoe back a few feet until the rear of the canoe was afloat.

"It's high tide now," said Aeala, "if we load the canoe on the sand it will be too heavy to push when the tide ebbs."

"Does it have a name?' asked Dirk.

"You mean the canoe?"

"Yeah."

Aeala thought about it for a moment. His uncle Ko had never mentioned a name.

"No, but that's a good point. We should think one up."

"Hey, look!" said Sumo and pointed toward the stack of goods and equipment on the beach about thirty yards away.

"Looks like the girls have been working hard." Aeala grinned. "Let's load the stuff. We need to get an early start tomorrow."

"Why do we have to leave early?" said Webster. "Why can't we sleep in and leave later?"

"Because of Hoku-loa and A'a." said Aeala. "That's Venus and Sirius in your language: stars in the sky."

"What does that have to do with anything?"

"Hoku-loa is the morning star: it appears in the east before sunrise. A'a is a stationary star: it doesn't move much except in a straight line in the heavens. In order to find our way I have to align our path with a point of land on the island and A'a. The canoe must travel in a straight line with A'a—preferably right under it. Hoku-loa, I can use as a reference. It will always be at the same angle in reference to A'a."

Aeala knew this was much too brief an explanation of what he would do to navigate their way to Puna, but it was sufficient to answer Webster's question.

Webster grunted, apparently satisfied. They loaded the twin hulls and platform with supplies and equipment, Aeala taking great care to balance the weight properly so the canoe would not list to one side, or be too heavy in the bow or stern. They filled the clay jars that Jessica had found with fresh water for drinking. When the job was done Aeala plopped down on the beach, satisfied – and looked at the stars. A'a was now out looking down on them from its perch in the heavens.

"There!" he said. "That's A'a – the really bright one."

They rested a few minutes then Aeala got up and made certain the canoe was secure on the beach. The bows of the twin hulls sank deep in the wet sand from the weight of the load they had just put on the canoe.

Satisfied, he turned toward the southern shore.

"Come on – let's go home."

They trudged down the beach toward the trail. The footprints of the girls were still distinct in the sand ahead of them. When they approached the trail the moonlight on the beach, golden over the sand and water, revealed the divergent paths the girls took. Aeala wondered where the two sets of prints that continued down the beach went. He put it out of his mind as he turned east onto the trail and entered the banana patch.

The fumes were strong where the fissure crossed the trail – where warm gas still rose like a ghostly specter from the underworld. After circumventing the fissure and returning to the trail Aeala looked back. The gas diffused the moonlight; like a golden shroud it obscured the view of the trail back to the beach.

They continued until they neared the bungalow. Candlelight lit the interior and an oil lamp burned as a beacon on the front porch.

"They must have moved from the tree house to the Bungalow," said Sumo.

Aeala nodded. "I hope there is something hot to eat."

When they entered, Kaela was there to greet them with a hug and a smile. The kitchen was warm from the wooden stove. The aroma of cooked fish, onion and spice permeated the space.

"Smells good! Where is everybody?"

"They're in the living room."

Miki peeked in. "Hi, you guys. Did everything go okay?"

"Yep, just fine. The canoe is down by the beach and we loaded all the stuff in."

"Oh good! I wasn't looking forward to doing that in the morning."

"You girls also did a good job—there are enough supplies for three weeks down there. It's only a two day trip, you know."

"Well, we didn't know if we were ever coming back so we thought we should take as much as we could."

Jessica entered the kitchen and immediately Aeala noticed something different about her. She seemed lighter, less solemn, with a glow about her—nothing physical, but she was definitely different.

"Hi!" she said.

"Hi. How are you?"

"I'm fine," she said. "We had a good day and got a lot done."

"That is good. Have you eaten?"

"Yes. Thank you for asking."

Aeala turned to Kalea. "How is Mrs. Waha?"

"Recovering well. She wanted to help us get ready but we told her she should rest. She's in the living room."

"I am fine, Aeala." It was Mrs. Waha's voice.

"I am glad to hear that Mrs. Waha," said Aeala. "We all love you very much."

The three families had lived together on the island for as long as Aeala could remember, and he considered them all family. Mrs. Waha and Mrs. Ka were like aunties to him.

"Why don't you all go in the living room and I'll bring in food," said Kalea.

Aeala kissed her and headed into the other room. It was a big room with two low-lying beds and cushions on the floor. There were low tables with plates on them. The girls had already eaten and their plates were stacked on one table ready to be taken into the kitchen and washed. Aeala seated himself on a cushion and sighed deeply.

"Long day," he said.

Jessica smiled. "How big is the canoe?"

"It's about thirty feet long—maybe a bit longer—but there are two hulls."

"What are hulls?"

"Oh, they are the canoes themselves. There are two hulls connected by booms... ah... logs, and there is a platform between the canoes that holds them together as one. That way we do not have to sit in the hulls all the time. We can climb onto the platform, which may be more comfortable."

"Do we have to paddle?"

"Not all the time. There is a triangle sail that will help us along."

"That is good to know," she smiled. "I was afraid it was just a little boat and we'd be out at sea and..."

Aeala grinned. "I can see your concern, but it's not like that. The two hulls make the canoe very stable, and there will be plenty of room for everyone. When we got there the second canoe was gone. We figured the people on the other side of the island had taken it."

Jessica looked up quickly. "I wonder if my father..."

"I have no idea, Jessica – I suppose it's possible. Perhaps they also headed for Puna and we'll find them there."

She nodded. "Did you see anyone on the other side of the island at all?"

He shook his head.

The food was hot and tasty but Aeala sat preoccupied. He wondered if Jessica's father may have survived after all; but if so, then why would he not come looking for her, unless he was injured and couldn't do so. Had those on the other side of the island taken him with them and escaped into the open ocean to get away from the poisonous fumes? He didn't want to get Jessica's hopes up, but there was that possibility.

When he was done eating, he brought everyone into the living room.

"I have something to say," he said. "We must leave before dawn tomorrow. I don't want to explain all of the reasons why but it has to do with navigation. I need to see the stars upon our departure. It is about a two day trip to Puna. We should be able to find help and shelter there."

They all nodded their agreement except Webster who simply sat there with no reaction at all.

"We should get some sleep. I'll wake everyone when it's time to leave."

He headed for the tree house. Miki, Sumo and Jessica followed with Webster and his friends bringing up the rear. Mia, the older women, Robin and Emily stayed in the bungalow, finding it more comfortable there.

The crickets and geckos cooed and chirped noisily that night. When they arrived at the tree house the geckos clung to the outside of the shutters as if bidding farewell to the occupants. Aeala lit a lamp then gave each guest a blanket, and a cushion to use as a pillow. He set himself near the north wall so he could look out the window at the stars.

"Miki showed me what mana is," whispered Jessica.

"Oh?"

"I understand now," she said.

"I saw the footprints in the sand…"

"Yes, those were ours. We went to the pool."

"And did you feel it?"

"Yes – very much so. Miki said it is the stuff the spirit is made of and that you have much of it."

Aeala was silent for a moment then continued. "It is more than that. Mana is as much a decision as anything else. One may possess a potential, but until he decides to be and do something the energy does not show itself. Once one decides to be—be a man, or a woman, or a teacher, or a healer, or a kahuna, or anything else—the decision acts like a trigger and brings the mana into the universe. That is how I see it, anyway."

"But what about inanimate things?" asked Jessica.

"You mean like rocks and pools and such?"

"Yes, exactly."

"I suppose there are spirits that inhabit rocks, and pools, and trees, and such."
She nodded.

"I think we should sleep now. We have a long day tomorrow," said Aeala.
He gazed out the window toward the south and spotted A'a, the brightest star in the heavens.

As he drifted between the realms of consciousness and sleep he saw the star above him, guiding him westward. The great swells of the sea slipped under him, and when he looked closer he beheld a canoe with a boy and his party, surrounded by golden light, headed toward the setting sun. On the horizon to the west was a great pearly light that emanated, not from the sky, but from below the horizon. As time passed the little canoe approached the light and a beautiful rainbow appeared in the sky, soft and pastel as if viewed through mist. Then from the light rose a green island with tall mountains, lustrous white sand and gleaming waterfalls and pools. The sea about the island was not blue but emerald, with long breakers that dissipated upon the shore in bursts of spray and foam. From the waters a shark surfaced and approached the canoe. It was black, with a white belly and a tall dorsal fin. As it swam closer Aeala noticed the black of its back was actually a coat of tiny black pearls so fine they appeared as sand. It raised its massive head toward the bow of the canoe and Aeala could see that the white of its belly was sand, pearly sand, a mixture of mother-of-pearl and powdered coral.

"I am Kuula-Kai, god of the fisherman," it said. "Your father is a fisherman, is he not?

"Yes," said Aeala.

"I reside within him, within all fishermen and their fathers before them, on and on to the beginning. I am the god of fishermen. I am part of you—your strength, your wisdom, your mana. You have a great burden to bear, for you must lead your people into an open and often angry sea. You are their only hope, their only light. You must lead even when you cannot see, and then hold to your dream, your vision. Take them across the sea to the land of light where they will be safe to flourish and prosper. You will not be alone; I send my brother with you. He will guide you, comfort you, council you and watch over you. You will know him when you see him, both in the flesh and spirit. You voyage to a new land, a land called 'Āina Le'a Nu'i – Land of Great Joy.' The gods bestow it on you. It is yours to care for, to nurture. Be good to it, and those that walk its shores."

"But if I fail?"

A great wind arose. It blew across the still waters and they rose in great waves, high and furious. The shark disappeared beneath the waves and the question was left unanswered. The great star that had guided him settled over the island and shone brightly.

CHAPTER 12 – IKE PONO

Certainty, not courage makes the strong what they are.
The Way of the Kahuna

Aeala awoke before dawn with the dream, like orchids in bloom, still vivid in his mind. In the dark he knelt silently and contemplated his future. One must define what he wants and who he is—then one must be who he is and no less.

He awoke his friends and they washed up. There was fog over the banana patch when they climbed down the tree house ladder onto the path to the bungalow. Kaela and the girls were already up when they arrived, and in the cool of the morning mist they headed down the path to the beach. Long strands of fog floated above the land like strips of fine silk. The stench of the fumes hung thick in the air especially as they approached the fissure in the trail. Once to the beach, it was only a short way to the canoe. The tide was low, the wind gentle and the surface of the water glassy. The sound of the surf on the sand was but a murmur.

"Do you have enough herbs and medicine?"

Miki nodded. "Two bags full, including ginger root."

"Good."

"We should all push until the canoe is off the sand and floating. Then the girls and women board and find comfortable seats. Not everyone in one hull—we need to balance the thing. There are blankets near the rear of the canoe if you want them. The guys will board last after the canoe is floating free and easy."

Aeala realized he might not see this land again, that this could be his final goodbye. His stomach tightened, his heart ached and he felt as if a great giant had placed its hands on his breast and pushed. The pressure was that of loneliness, of a spirit adrift in the sea of emptiness, of a man wandering without a home.

They all pushed the canoe, the hulls tracing long grooves in the sand. The girls and women climbed aboard the canoe with some difficulty as the sides of the hulls stood high out of the water. The boys, water to their waists pushed mightily until the twin hulls slid smoothly through the surf and across the ocean surface. Aeala felt the bow of the canoe lift with the surf, and bob on the water, completely freed from the land.

"Jump in and paddle!"

As they did so Aeala waded back to the beach reached down and grabbed a handful of wet sand. It was cool and course between his fingers and he felt as if it was part of himself—part of his thigh or back or heart. He tucked it in his pocket as a last reminder of his home. He then ran through the surf, gave the canoe one last heave and jumped on. The gunwale was high and it took some effort to pull himself into the hollow of the starboard hull, but once accomplished he quickly headed for the stern with his paddle.

"Only those on the left paddle!" he called. With his long arms he dipped his paddle in the water and held it there like a rudder, resisting the torque of the opposite side. The canoe rotated clockwise until the bows pointed seaward.

"Okay stop paddling!"

He climbed onto the platform, untied the boom lines and set the sail. The wind caught and the canoe began to move forward.

The wind was blowing from the east and thus they were downwind with the blow coming from directly behind them. The sail billowed tightly against the wind and the twin bows cut a fine line through the glassy water. Aeala tied down the boom line and searched the sky for Hoku-loa (Venus), which had just risen above the mountains. Noting its position he then searched for A'a (Sirius), found it near Orion's Belt and then aligned it with a point of land on the island. He carefully noted the angle between that line and Hoku-loa, untied the boom line and positioned the canoe on a course that followed A'a and the point of land he had chosen as a reference point.

Kako began to bark. He had been securely tucked away in the starboard hull by Mia but now came forth, trying to look over the gunwale into the sea. Aeala looked at the surface where Kako's attention had gone. A single dark fin broke the surface and followed alongside the canoe. "Kuula-Kai!" thought Aeala. "The god of the fisherman, or his brother." Then he thought better of it. "It's just an ordinary shark escorting us out to sea."

"Have you thought of a name?" Aeala looked down from the platform into the port hull. Dirk's bright eyes peered back at him from out of the shadows.

"You mean of the canoe?"

"Yeah, of the canoe."

Aelea hesitated. Before him, the dark fin sliced through the surface of the shadowy morning sea. His little group, silhouettes on the far horizon, for a moment stood motionless against a great wide and unpredictable world. His qualms dimly reverberated from somewhere deep within.

"Yeah, I've thought of one—Ike Pono. It means 'to see clearly, to know.'"

CHAPTER 13 – THE CROSSING

It is by action, and action alone that the vapors of dreams are transformed into the pith of the real world.
The Way of the Kahuna

Dawn arrived an hour later, red and rough, with the island still in sight. The wind had picked up and the surface of the water turned from glass to grit, the chop feathering with foam. The pitch, yaw and roll action of the canoe as it rode the swells became more pronounced as the seas rose. Aeala held the steering paddle steady and kept an eye on the sail to ensure the canoe was running before the wind.

Webster sat near the stern of the port hull, head bowed, and appeared to be pouting. Aeala reflected on him: never satisfied, never happy, always in contest with someone or something. Had he ever had a moment of happiness? A second without "attitude" galore? He envisioned Webster's universe—a universe of contention and venom, of hate and hostility; a universe devoid of pleasure or beauty or love.

He wondered what the future would hold for all of them if their lives became truly dependent on each other. He reckoned he could count on Dirk and Jessica, but Webster and Obie were a different season in the sun. It concerned him especially when they reached Puna. He had not been there in two years, but the last time he visited it was not the safest place to stop over. There were thieves about. Pirates arrived occasionally to hide out or pick up supplies, but if you stayed away from the seamier parts of town things remained calm. He hoped the earthquake had not changed life on the island so that it was now a thieves' world, rife with barbarism or anarchy.

Jessica sat in the center of the starboard bow on a fixed canoe seat, her back to the gunwale. She appeared to be dozing, swaying bow to aft with the canoe's pitch and roll, long blond hair flitting in the wind. There was still a certain feeling that seized him whenever he beheld her—a wholeness, a magic, a joy, like the fragrance of fresh flowers that lingers even after you've left the field. He wondered if she was feeling seasick, and looked over at Miki in the bow seat of the starboard hull. Miki felt his attention on her and looked up, eyes bright and clear.

"Just wondering if you have any ginger?" he said.

"Feeling seasick?"

"No, not me. But perhaps some of the others?"

She reached into one of the bags at her feet and pulled out a large ginger root. "Hope this works," she said and flipped it up to him.

He broke off a little knob for himself, secured the steering paddle with rope so it would not move, walked over to Jessica, leaned down over the platform, tapped her on the shoulder and handed her a small piece of the root. "If you get seasick – chew this."

She smiled up at him. "Thanks."

Robin sat near the bow of the starboard hull of the canoe, the sea breeze buffeting her dark brown hair about. She was slender and pretty with an oval face, dimpled chin, smooth forehead and pouty lips. Now and then as the canoe pitched she caught glimpses of the ocean swells from her seat deep within the bowels of the canoe. The loss of her father and mother was still raw in her mind, a deep wound oozing sorrow; a wound deep enough to turn her attention away from the present, away from the living and toward the void of death and despair. She reminded herself that she could not live in the past; in order for her to survive she would have to move forward with the others. Her stomach grew queasy from the roll of the canoe and she searched about for something to do to distract her attention from the discomfort. She, like Jessica, had come from Paris with her parents to make a new life in the South Pacific. A natively curious person, she had explored the island from seashore to mountain trail as far as was feasible without placing herself in serious danger. This she had done with others, always able to procure the cooperation of her friends in her adventures. They had stayed away from the native children, curious but never trusting, observing them from a distance and realizing the natives had knowledge about the island and the elements which was beyond the ken of her and her friends. Once, while on the beach, she had spotted Aeala and Sumo in the surf with boards of light wood riding the waves to shore. She stood fascinated for an hour as they road wave after wave moving in perfect harmony along the wave faces in rhythmic accord with the breakers' energy. It was then that she realized they possessed a knowledge and lore that she longed to partake of.

The orb of the sun climbed above the horizon and Aeala made careful note of its position. He now had four reference points on which to navigate. He noted the angle between the rising sun and the island, which was now but a dot on the eastern horizon. Sumo climbed up on the platform. Aeala untied and handed the steering paddle over to him, then went to the stern of the starboard hull and took close note of the character, angle and strength of the ground swell that approached them from the west. He noted the angle as it intersected the bows of the canoe and the direction the wind blew in relation to the swells. He then sought the location of his home island Pa'ai. This he could not see physically for it was now below the horizon. Even so, in his mind's eye it burned in memory and he slowly turned and pointed to its location. Satisfied, he scrambled to the stern of the starboard hull and hopped in.

There were blankets and other equipment neatly stacked on racks. He sat with his back against the rear of the hull, draped a blanket over himself and settled in. His uncle Ko had said one could feel the surface of the water, the swell and the bottom of the sea by sitting naked on the floor of the canoe—the vibration would speak to one.

The vibration was very faint, like the purr of a cat or the feel of a gentle breeze. After a few minutes he was able to distinguish the difference in the vibrations, and decided the longer, fainter ones marked the sea bottom, and the stronger, quicker ones the sea surface.

"What are you doing?"

He looked up – it was Jessica come from amidships to the stern.

"Navigating."

"Can you show me?"

"Sure—Sit."

She did, in front of him with her back to him. "Now feel the vibration of the hull on your backside and legs."

"Okay?"

"There are at least two types of vibrations – a quick strong one and a slower fainter one. Can you feel them?"

She hesitated for some time, trying to feel and distinguish the motions. "I – I think so."

"The long faint ones, I believe, are the bottom of the ocean and the quicker ones are the surface."

"How does that help to find our way?"

"Well, when we left I memorized our path in relation to the island and several stars. When the stars are gone it is harder to keep on a straight path. By observing the swells in the ocean and the angle they make as they pass under the bow one can keep on course. If the swell itself or the angle of the swell changes, I have to recognize and compensate for it by changing the direction of the canoe. By knowing the depth of the water I can tell if we are nearing land."

"I see," she said, still puzzling over what he'd just said.

"You don't really understand, do you?"

"No," she laughed, "I guess I don't."

"I will help you little by little and make sure it's all clear."

"Thanks," she said. "You've changed a lot."

"Changed?"

"Yes. In school you were always so shy. For three months we never spoke yet you sat right behind me."

"Well, I didn't feel you were interested in talking to me."

She was quiet for a moment. "I was ignorant."

"I am glad we talk now," he said.

"Yes. Me too."

Kako began to bark. Aeala stood and looked about. Kako was on the platform between the hulls looking down into the water. "Excuse me," said Aeala.

He climbed out of the hull and on to the platform just as a big swell struck the canoe. The bow lifted out of the water and rose toward the sky – foam and spray exploded. Kako scrambled to maintain his balance but slid backward off the platform, his little legs thrashing in the air. As he struck the surface of the sea a dark fin ascended from the depths. Aeala saw his pet, his life long friend, paddling frantically to keep his head above water, struggling to survive, a look of dismay and fear in his eyes.

In that moment, all that was important, all that was good, all that he loved surfaced in his mind. He saw himself in the little dog's terrified eyes, himself struggling, fighting, not only for himself but for that he embraced—his friends, his family and all that was life. His emotion was not fear, but vibrant certainty that he would overcome. He leaped—a long graceful leap—and landed in the cool water several yards from the struggling dog. The dark fin circled, then sank beneath the waves. Aeala swam toward the little dog while the dread of the shark and ocean coursed through his mind. Another swell struck the canoe and threw foam into the air. He saw Sumo lower the sail and scramble toward the stern. The little dog whined in terror, and at that moment the black fin surfaced. Aeala dove under the waves in an attempt to shield the little dog from the jaws of the shark. He could see the white belly and dark fins as the beast circled. The eyes stared back, dark and intense, but without the predator-like viciousness which Aeala expected. Instead the eyes reflected his image, the image of a young warrior ready to defend his friends; determined, no matter what the circumstances, to act.

Aeala blinked, not believing what he saw, startled that the creature had not immediately struck. Perhaps it was mocking them: two pathetic life forms floundering in a windswept sea. Within him anger suddenly flared. It was not the anger of combat, but that which stemmed from mockery. His lungs were bursting and he surfaced for a breath of air. The waves towered above him and he caught a momentary glimpse of the canoe. The black fin slid by, unconcerned. He struggled to keep his head above water and headed toward Kako, keeping an eye on the circling shadow just below the surface. A large wave engulfed the little dog and he disappeared. Aeala plunged into the depths determined to save his friend before he perished. The salt stung his eyes but he forced himself to keep them open. He saw movement several yards away and reached with all his strength in a desperate effort grasp hold of his friend. His fingers closed on one of the dog's hind legs and he pulled him to his chest. When he surfaced the canoe was about forty yards away; the dark fin slightly closer. He held tight and dragged Kako toward the canoe. Sumo was there on the stern and heaved a rope toward them. His aim was true and the end struck Aeala on the shoulder. They dragged them through the turbulent water, spray burst from the hulls of the canoe, the dark fin followed like a rear guard, protecting them from the deep. The strong grips of Sumo and Dirk grasped him under the armpit and by the arm and hauled him and the little dog aboard. Kako whimpered and whined and hopped into the hollow of the starboard hull and into Mia's arms. Aeala's breath came in long gasps – seawater in his nose and throat made him cough and vomit. He lay on the platform on his side with his muscles burning. Sumo threw him a blanket and he covered up, still wet.

"Sumo.— Sumo!" he gasped. "Haul up the sail and start us going again. I'm alright."

"God, we thought we lost you!" said Dirk.

"Thanks, both of you. You guys saved me."

Sumo grunted. "This may seem crazy, but I think that damned shark saved you. Did you see it circle as soon as Kako and you fell in? It was not trying to eat you. It was protecting you."

"We were so afraid!" It was Jessica's voice. She had climbed out of the hollow of the starboard hull and onto the platform. "We're—I'm so happy you're safe." She hugged him timidly for a moment, and tears rolled down her face. She wiped them away, embarrassed, and smiled at him.

After a few minutes the burning in his lungs and limbs ceased and he crawled over to the steering paddle where Sumo was standing.

"I can take over now. Why don't you get yourself something to eat?"

Sumo smiled. "Glad you still with us, Kahuna."

Aeala looked his friend in the eye. They glistened. A small tear rolled down his cheek and was swept away by the wind. Aeala nodded and took the steering paddle from Sumo. It felt different, familiar and warm to the touch, like a canoe-maker's adze or a warrior's spear.

The sea was rough but not angry. There was a chop on the surface, but with the wind directly behind them they made headway efficiently. By midday Aeala grew hungry and thirsty.

Kaela handed him some dried fish and bananas. He ate slowly, silently and drank some water from a coconut shell to wash it down. Miki took the steering paddle after Aeala carefully instructed her as to the direction and angle of the canoe in reference to the ground swell.

"We're headed directly west," he said, "when the sun sets tonight the bow will be exactly to the setting sun."

"What was that with you and the shark, this morning?"

He looked at Miki. "You saw it?"

She nodded. "It was remarkable. It circled you and Kako until both of you were back on the canoe. It was… looking after you, I think. That sounds so odd, but I can see no other conclusion.

"I had a dream before we left, Miki. The god of fishermen, Kuula-Kai, spoke to me and said he would take us to a land called ʻĀina Leʻa Nuʻi. It was not Puna, but a new land.

I saw it and it was beautiful, like a jewel in the sea. He said the gods had bestowed the land on me to care for, and that it was my responsibility to care for us all. He told me that he would send his brother to guide us. In the dream, I saw a black shark with a jeweled back and sand-white belly—a shark exactly like the one you saw today."

Miki was silent for a long moment and stared at the waves and far horizon. "I also had a dream – or more precisely a vision. I saw you on a tall mountain with your arms spread out as if you were blessing the land. Your mana touched everything and it thrived and grew. The land was very beautiful, full of vivid colors and pleasing scents. The winds spoke to me and said this would all work out and we would be safe. The vines and shrubs reached out and touched me and the wind said we must care for the land. It was up to me and you and the others to build a house of clouds and rain. I did not know what that meant and asked the wind, but it just laughed. I saw a beautiful palace tucked in a valley with a waterfall at one end and delicate mist and clouds above it. A little stream from the waterfall ran down the valley and through the palace. The winds called this the life of the land and from it—from this little spring—all life on the island would issue. It was water full of mana."

Aeala looked into her face and saw the righteousness of the spirit in them: a beautiful soul draped about the young dark body. "Thank you, Miki. I needed someone to believe in me—in us."

60

She smiled at him. "You are the Kahuna Kilo Hoku—the navigator."

"And you are the Kahuna Lapa'au—the healer," he said.

They knew they were both bourgeoning kahunas, thrown into a wild and unpredictable world, with nothing but the teachings of their former mentors and their own intuition to guide them, and due to the foibles of fate they now had to assume their places in the world. They would have to lead. They would overcome the forces of water and wind and rain and the powers of the gods themselves.

The seas calmed in the late afternoon and Sumo again took the steering paddle. The shark still followed them, its dark fin sliced through the water like a sharp knife through flesh. Every so often, a fish jumped and plopped back into the blue, its sliver lingering for a moment in the light even after it had disappeared. Not accustomed to seafaring, Jessica was seasick, as were several of the other foreigners. Miki had given them all ginger, but the herb's soothing properties had not yet taken effect and Webster heaved over the port gunwale.

Aeala sat on the bottom of the starboard hull and sensed the rhythms of the wind, swell and ocean floor through the vibrations they created on the canoe. In his mind he reviewed their journey: the location of their home island, Pa'ai, the reference point on it that he had chosen and their current heading. All seemed aligned and on course. He was anxious for sundown so he could again view the stars and crosscheck them against their heading. He started to doze, then shook himself back to consciousness. If he slept he might lose his bearings, and with that their way. He wondered how many, while on the open sea had done just that—lost their way—and perished.

His ancestors had come to Pa'ai from lands far across the sea—lands clouded in myth and legend, the routes of which had long ago been lost. Uncle Ko had told him the legends. They had sat on the beach under bonfire light on certain nights, nights dictated by tradition and festival, and the stories of their heritage were spun. The story of Haipule, the saint, cast out to sea by his enemies and left to die on the open ocean in a tiny outrigger canoe. Guided by the gods in the form of a flock of seagulls he crossed the wide ocean and arrived on Pa'ai. The first thing he did upon arrival was to build a temple to the gods that preserved him. The temple, built in the foothills behind Sumo's home, was called Hale O Manu, home of the birds.

There were many other legends, not only of brave sailors but of gods and animals too. Aeala understood the message in the legends, the importance not so much of the event, but of those qualities that enabled men to accomplish such feats—foresightedness, self-discipline, courage, faith, responsibility and the search for truth. He also understood the opposite—the path of incompetence and sloth—and how this would lead to disaster; either slow and drawn out, or quick and violent. Thus he struggled to stay awake, to keep his bearings, to navigate as the Kahunas of legend did.

The sun finally touched the horizon in the west. Again the sunset was blood, both sky and water turned to crimson. Aeala suspected the colors had something to do with the fumes and gases that came out of the earth and he hoped that the fate that had befallen Pa'ai had not touched Puna. The dream still bothered him, as the shark had not mentioned Puna but another land, 'Āina Le'a Nu'i. It was tough enough to sail to Puna, a voyage of only two days, but venturing further seemed a risky, risky venture.

A stiff breeze from the northeast, cool and moist, arose as the sun descended in the west. Sumo shifted the angle of the sail to accommodate it.

They sailed directly into the setting sun, with Aeala now at the steering paddle. To his right, near the horizon, something surfaced. He could not make out exactly what it was, but the shadow that ascended from the deep was undeniable.

"Miki!" he called. "Can you come up here?"

She scrambled over the gunwale and onto the sailing platform between the hulls.

"What's up?"

"Keep an eye out there," he said and pointed to starboard.

"What did you see?"

"I don't know… just a shadow of something."

He shivered, and a mild dread overtook him. He had heard the stories—stories from sailors and elders—about the monsters: great beasts that ate men alive and swallowed their boats, monsters so dark that even the great ocean itself quivered in their presence. He anxiously searched the waters close by, but they rolled dark and deep and concealed their treasures or terrors jealously.

"There!" cried Miki and pointed toward the horizon. Twilight, red and purple, obscured the forms and hid the motions other than the roll of the swells.

"I missed it. What did you see?"

"It looked like a hump. It surfaced then sank back into the waves."

"Yeah, that's what I thought I saw," said Aeala.

Miki stayed with him for a time and searched the surface but the waters did not give up their secrets. It was not till after the moon rose that it again emerged from the black depths, this time just off the starboard bow. A huge hump surfaced, water ran down its sides and suddenly seawater gyred skyward then fell like rain onto the canoe.

"It's a whale!" cried Miki with delight. "And look! There is a baby right next to it!"

There was a golden glow around the moon. Moonlight fell on the sea and illuminated the giants, turning their backs to silver. The distinct sound of water being sucked in resounded across the canoe – again the whale blew the water into the sky and it fell like gentle rain over the canoe. Aeala laughed with relief until tears rolled down his cheeks. He looked into the sea and now it did not seem so scary—like investigating a shadow and finding there was nothing there but shade. The night seemed close—friendly and benign—no longer a foe but a friend. Half an hour later A'a appeared in the heavens.

Aeala took his bearings and was satisfied that they were on course. The dark fin surfaced and glided alongside the canoe like a guardian angel accompanying its charge.

"That was so amazing," said Miki from the starboard hull.

"Yes it was. I learned something from that," said Aeala.

"Oh, what's that?"

"That what you fear you must face up to. If you do that, you find it is not so fearsome."

Miki smiled and nodded. "It's a beautiful night."

The night drew on with Aeala on the steering paddle and nearly everyone else asleep.

"That was stupid what you did this morning."

Aeala looked down into the port bow. Webster looked up at him a frown on his face.

"What are you talking about, Webster?"

"Saving that little dog. If you had drowned we would have all been lost. You should have let him drown."

Aeala understood that Webster did not like anyone, animals included, and would just as well see Kako dead. He did not respond to Webster's jab but was bothered by the truth of it. If he had drowned they all would have died.

"We'll be at Puna in a few hours, Webster. You can think what you want, do what you want there."

"You think all of these people are going to stay with you? You think Jessica is going to stay with you? They aren't kanakas. They don't care about you or your ways."

"Webster—enough!"

Webster was silent, and why not? — The venom had been spread; the hurt had been administered.

The night grew dark as A'a twinkled in the heavens and they followed it across the ocean.

The moon set in the early morning, before first light, and a fog gathered on the water. It was a thick fog that obscured not only the water, but the sky. Aeala woke Sumo and asked him to take the steering paddle, told him to keep it steady and not to worry about anything. He then went to the stern of the starboard hull and sat on the bottom. The vibration of the swell had changed in strength—had weakened, as if something had fractured its vigor—but he was not certain what had caused the phenomenon. The air turned crisp and moist as they went deeper into the fog. Visibility was nil, and Aeala again became uneasy. Like a dark dream, they slipped further and further into the fog bank until they were totally lost. Aeala sensed the angle of the canoe against the swell. That had not changed, and he was thankful that at least one indicator of their heading was still perceivable.

The echoes began imperceptibly, like the first drops of a new rain. Aeala failed to notice, his mind lost in other things. When he finally became aware, he wondered how long it had accompanied them and how long it had gone unnoticed. His tanned face slowly broke into a smile, and relief coursed through him upon recognition of the echo's source. The lonesome call of gulls in the distance meant land was near; perhaps not very near, but close enough so he knew he had been successful in his navigating.

He then realized what the change of the sea swell was all about. A barrier sat between them and the unbroken deep ocean swell, a barrier that caused the swell's strength to fade and dissipate. That barrier was Puna!

Dawn gently lit the eastern horizon and the fog, like silk cloth unraveling strand by strand, abated until it was no more than a thin blanket on the sea. The swells were glass, long and smooth, and sloped like gentle knolls as they marched in line toward the canoe. The flocks of birds soared and circled: some, high in the jet stream, but dots in the dome of heaven; others, closer to the sea, helter-skelter as they dive-bombed after fish just below the surface.

"Are you hungry?"

Aeala looked down from the platform toward the voice in the starboard hull. It was Jessica smiling up at him.

"No longer seasick?" he said.

"I think I'm back with the living," she grinned.

"Yeah, kinda' hungry—could use some water too."

"Well, there's canned fish and crackers, will that do?"

He nodded gratefully. "Yeah, that will do."

She bustled about in the hull and opened the canned fish and handed him a coconut bowl with crackers and sardines in it. She disappeared for a second and reappeared with a jug of water. He reached down and carefully grasped the jug and thanked her. The water was cool and sweet as if it had been drawn from a honeycomb.

"Where did you get this from?" he said pointing to the jug.

"There was a pool Miki took me to a couple of days ago. I drew some water from there."

He saw the image of the sacred pool with the coconut tree with moss and ti leaves encircling it and smiled. The vision itself breathed energy back into his tired body.

"It is good water—sweet like honey."

Dirk climbed onto the platform from the port hull.

"Hey, Aeala. Can you teach me…" He pointed toward the steering paddle.

"To sail this thing?"

"Yeah, that would be great."

"Of course—grab the steering paddle handle and keep it steady."

"I'd like to learn too."

Aeala extended his hand into the starboard hull and pulled Jessica onto the platform.

"Not a problem," he said. "I'll show you both."

The day wore on with Aeala giving careful instruction to the two novice sailors. He taught them that the wind powers the canoe, and that both its strength and direction are important in setting the sail. When the wind is coming from behind the canoe the sail must be trimmed perpendicular to the boat and when it is blowing from port or starboard the sail is set at an angle to ensure the sail is full of wind. He carefully explained the terminology: windward – the direction in which the wind is blowing; leeward – opposite the way the wind is blowing; mast – the vertical pole that the sail is attached to; boom – the horizontal pole attached to the mast and the foot of the sail; sheets – ropes that control the boom and sail; running – sailing with the wind blowing from behind and reaching – sailing with the wind side-on to the canoe. Then there was the matter of the steering paddle. With the wind blowing from behind, the paddle was simply used like a rudder to keep the canoe moving on a straight path but when the wind came over port or starboard the paddle was moved to the opposite side from the wind and held with the flat side of the paddle parallel to the hull itself. In this way the canoe was steadied and would move forward smoothly.

He taught them to observe the swells and note the angle at which the bow of the canoe crossed the swells. He warned them of the danger of aligning the canoe parallel to the swells, which could end in the canoe capsizing. He taught them thoroughly about the wind, the waves and the sail and how they all worked intimately together to propel the craft.

The day wore on. The ocean, a satin field of blue with long, wide swells and gently sloping toughs, unfolded before them. Ike Pono, like a giant gull gliding on the winds, gracefully negotiated the watery knolls, pitching and rolling rhythmically as they headed west. Aeala scanned the horizon and sky above, it was not clear, but milky. He worried, as it indicated the presence of smoke high in the sky. They were a day out of Pa'ai at sea yet the haze persisted.

Dirk had slowly begun to like Aeala. It was hard for him not to: Aeala had saved his life. True, he had returned the favor by pulling Aeala from the sea with Kako, but Aeala had grown on him. He was never obnoxious, always willing to help and wonderfully competent. Dirk's admiration grew. Dirk's father had been a prizefighter until he was blinded in one eye. He then made his living cutting timber in the forests of Europe and had come to Pa'ai to make a fortune with the harvesting and sale of teak and sandalwood. Now that was erased. In two days everything had changed. Dirk still grieved for his father, almost certainly drowned in the great waves, but he grieved alone, silently, unable to express his desolation. He considered it a miracle that he himself was still living, and he appreciated life in a different way now, realizing its preciousness not only for his own life but that of others.

He resolved to make the best of it and to break bonds with Webster. He realized Webster was trouble, lots of trouble, but when he had come to the island he knew no one and Webster was a convenient companion. However, after a consistent barrage of venom from Webster aimed at him as well as others he grew weary of the association, and, like Jessica, had withdrawn.

Dirk, an accomplished woodworker, a craft taught to him by his father, could turn a chair or table in his sleep. He had made the majority of tables in the schoolhouse and had taught the others how to do it. He was, in fact, a near master when it involved wood but did not acknowledge the fact to others or himself. Instead he considered woodworking a mundane endeavor not worthy of admiration—except for the canoe. When he had first seen it he was awestruck. The massive hulls, sleek lines and the gorgeous dark patina of the Koa wood—that, he felt, was a true treasure. He had asked Aeala who had built the canoe, but was told that it was built long before Aeala or even Aeala's father were born, and the story of its creation and creator had been lost. Perhaps, Aeala had said, his uncle Ko knew but Ko had never mentioned it.

Dirk now held the steering paddle that guided the canoe, and it came to life in his hands—the vibration as it slid through the water, the canoe's response to it as Dirk moved it left or right and the sail's reply to its every move. He felt free, and was thankful to Aeala for teaching the sailing lore to him.

Jessica, also on the platform, carefully observed all the little details and nuances that were going on, anxious to take the paddle. Aeala on her right explained the angle of the sail boom in relation to the wind's direction. Seagulls circled the canoe from above and looked for any fish or morsel to be had. Their calls, like wind through a mountain pass, resounded over the sea.

"It is a good sign," said Aeala. "The gulls indicate land is near."

She smiled at his words, happy to be there.

"Dirk, let Jessica take the paddle," said Aeala.

He surrendered the handle to her and stepped aside. She grasped it with two hands. It was thick and long, made of koa wood and set on a rectangular stand fitted with a pivot so when one pulled the handle of the paddle down the blade moved up and when the handle was pushed up the blade went down into the water.

"Feel the way the *hoe uli* moves through the water. It's all a matter of feel. You'll get to know it once you've been on it for some time."

"*Hoe uli?*"

"Yes, you know, the paddle."

"Oh—so that's what you call it."

She concentrated, and soon became familiar with its feel, its pressure, its vibration and the way it sliced through the water. It became an extension of her arms and she came to feel the canoe, the swells, the water, the wind and the *hoe uli* blade all working together to influence the movement of the canoe. She smiled to herself, secure in the lore which was now hers. Slowly it dawned that these factors, learned to total certainty, were what she saw in the locals—an aura, almost a swagger of certainty stemming from their confidence in the handling and conquering of their environment. It extended further, from specific skills such as canoeing, fishing, farming to a general confidence in life and knowing where they fit in. She saw the happiness in Aeala, Miki, Sumo and the others, an almost unconscious joy of living, and understood now the source of it. Competence in the handling of the environment, certainty in self and the belief that one could conquer and overcome barriers to accomplish one's work or goals—these were the grains of sand that composed the dunes of happiness.

It was shortly after the sun had reached its zenith that the dark dot appeared on the western horizon. It was Miki that saw it first. She had been on watch on the port bow for some time, scanning the sky and the cloud formations, the way they gathered in one area and dispersed out from there. At first she thought it was just a shadow on the water caused by the cloud cover, but after a few minutes it rose from the sea like the morning star in the heavens—a tall mountain peak with black cliffs that were lost in mist.

"There!" she cried, "there!" pointing to the western horizon. Aeala and the others stared at the shadow-turned-island and shouted their approval and joy. Kako barked. Mia clapped and danced. Kaela waved a kapa cloth and ti leaves then released them into the water as a sacrifice to the gods. Kapa was the fabric their clothes were made of, a bark from the *wauti* tree soaked in seawater and beaten into sheets until it was soft and pliable then dyed and designed with intricate patterns. Its release into the waves signified the life and effort of its makers. The ti leaves were thought to hold great spiritual power and bring good luck to the possessor. Jessica and Emilie hugged each other and cried. Webster spat over the side, muttered something to Obie, and frowned.

"I doubt we will be able to make landfall before sundown," said Aeala. "We will sail straight in then look for a beach where we can land."

"What will we do once we land?" asked Jessica.

"Look for my father and a place to stay."

She smiled and nodded. "I certainly hope we find them all."

As they drew closer they noticed a great plume of smoke rise from the far side of the island. Aeala worried, this was not a good sign as it indicated volcanic activity and more fumes, but he did not mention it so as not to worry the others.

Miki also sensed the truth and kept silent, except to point out the plume to Aeala. She sniffed the air to see if there was any scent of sulfur, but it was blowing in the wrong direction—from her back and toward the island with only the smell of sea salt in it. She started to pack things up and neaten the hollow of the port hull, folding the damp kapa blankets and gathered up the leaves, which they had used as plates. She checked the keg of powder and flints that they had brought along, to ensure they were moisture free. After seeing that the port hull was ship shape she climbed onto the platform and disappeared into the starboard hull. Sumo was seated at the stern talking with Robin. Miki observed them for a moment and decided Sumo had fallen for her. She smiled, and hoped it would work out for them all. Two of the mothers lay on benches amidships fast asleep, her mother being one of them. Miki wondered what it was like for them – their husbands missing, their children running a canoe with their lives in their hands. She smiled again at the prospect that they might feel perfectly confident in their children's ability and care. After all, they had taught them well in *malama* (caring for things) and *Kokau* (help). Everyone had contributed on the trip except for Webster and Obie, who disappeared into the port hull and stayed there the whole trip, isolated from the others.

Miki was pragmatic, and worried about their future on Puna. If they could find their fathers everything would be fine. If not... She did not want to think of the prospect. It would be hard enough to start a new life on Puna, but without the aid of the fathers—near impossible. And now with the smoke of a volcano on the horizon, she did not want to face that prospect—yet she knew she must.

"Sumo, could you tend the steering paddle for awhile? I'd like to speak with Aeala."

He was startled by her presence, not having noticed she had slipped into the starboard hull.

"Oh, sure, not problem. Be back in a bit."

Emilie nodded and Sumo climbed onto the platform.

"Aeala! Aeala!" Sumo's voice echoed. "Miki wants to see you."

Aeala slid into the starboard hull. "What's up?"

"I don't mean to spoil the joy but what's going to happen when we land?" asked Miki.

"Well, we'll search for our fathers and once we find them we'll follow what they decide to do next."

"And, if they're not there?"

"We'll have to find shelter and jobs."

"You saw the plume. What if Puna is as bad as where we came from."

Aeala was silent. Miki frowned. "We need a plan in that event."

"I will consider it," said Aeala, "and let you know."

"Webster and Obie?"

"I don't trust them," said Aeala, "one way or the other, once we reach Puna they're gone."

Miki nodded. "Agreed."

The day proceeded with the late winter sun crossing the sky in a low arc. They could see the tall cliffs of Puna, gray and wet, towering from the sea. Foam and spray burst from the cliffs base as tall waves crashed against it. They were still a mile from the island when the sun set against a red sky.

The moon, now nearly full, rose and cast its glow against the dark cliffs, which shimmered in the gloaming. The evening stars winked on over the horizon. Aeala decided he would seek help on Puna if the island became too noxious. He suspected the volcano on Puna began erupting at the same time the quakes on Pa'ai began. If this were the case the natives of Puna would have a sharp eye out for danger signs in the event they would have to evacuate. He also understood the reluctance of people to leave their homes and suspected they would stay till the very last ounce of hope had drained away before leaving. There must be navigators, he thought, that could guide them far away from the poisons to some land with fresh air and clear skies. The canoe was their only possession of value, but with it anything was possible. He suspected the spirit of aloha (welcome) did not hold sway on Puna the way it did on Pa'ai and there may be those that would want to steal the canoe. Aeala concluded they should find a deserted beach to make landfall and hide it as best they could.

It was just after midnight when Miki spotted the coconut trees and tiny cove tucked away between tall cliffs. "There! Aeala look!"

It was the first time in two days that Aeala had gotten any sleep and when Miki called for him he did not move. She went over and gently shook him.

"We've found a good place to land," she said.

Aeala shook himself awake and looked about – the small beach, only about fifty yards wide, shimmered in the moonlight. Aeala thought this strange and stared at it a long time. The ocean lapped at the sides of the canoe and the wind in the sails purred as he tried to perceive every sense – the smell, the sound, the sight and feel of his surroundings, searching for the source of the mysterious shimmering beach. He took the steering paddle from Sumo, guided the canoe through the outer reef, away from the breakers and into the small cove. Ike Pono glided gently across the surface of the dark water and the two bows touched the sand together with a soft jerk. With the landfall, Aeala felt something deep within him change. He had taken responsibility for his position and his people; this was the result of that responsibility, the product of his resolve, his belief in himself. Even more, he was proud of his crew, the way they had bested the elements, handled the sea

71

and faced the trials of the gods themselves. He had gained faith—not just a belief in things he suspected were true, but a confidence in what he knew: a confidence in himself, his environment and his group.

He again stared at the little beach and wondered if this were not something the underworld had vomited up, a place there demons and dark gods waited. But all was quiet. The feeling was not that of evil but of peace—the kind of peace one feels around a person endowed with mana, or a place saturated with it. He stepped from the gunwale on the starboard bow onto the beach. The sand glittered. At that moment he wondered if he had made the right move. Were his perceptions exact, his intuition accurate? He reached down and picked up a handful of the glowing water and sand half expecting it to burn. The glow clung to his fingers.

"Sea fire," said Miki. "I've seen it before on the north coast of Pa'ai."

"In Europe it's called plankton," said Jessica. "Sailors see it occasionally in the deep sea. It lights up the surface like fireflies."

When he looked closely Aeala saw the tiny organisms, glowing green and blue in his hand. He breathed a sign of relief. Sumo and Dirk hopped from the canoe and began pulling on the bowlines to beach the canoe. Webster and Obie also helped, and in a short time the canoe was securely on the beach.

The group was glad to be on land again. Aeala stepped into the shadows of a tall coconut tree, knelt and kissed the ground. It had been his first navigation – the first time he had taken a group across the open ocean. He whispered a short prayer to the gods then stood proudly and walked back out of the shadows to the beach.

"We can sleep under the trees," said Aeala. "Can we get some blankets from the Canoe?"

Mia and Emilie grabbed the blankets and the group spread them under the coconut trees. Aeala slept well, deeply and peacefully, and dreamed of the sea. In his dreams a great Kahuna—a navigator of the open sea—appeared. Young and strong and dark, with a thick beard and deep eyes, he spoke of the mana in all things, the life within the universe that animates even the tiniest of creatures and most insignificant of objects, that renews the world and all of its elements. He spoke of the illusions of time and space, and how to navigate, not by the heavens or the sea swells but by the heart, the knowledge within, the confidence that one can navigate through land and sea and life and change the universe for the better. He spoke of the ancestors—always with one, there to console or consult, there to watch over one and lend support; they who will always be with you as long as you care for your people, and your land, and your air, and your sea. And, even if you abandon that, they will not abandon you: always watching, always there to lean on. Around the kahuna's neck hung a great white pearl, and in the pearl, the universe, and in the universe the world, and in the world Aeala. The kahuna took off the pearl and placed it around Aeala's neck. "This is your compass," he said, "your heart—Keep it close and heed its bearings, for it shall guide you all the way to heaven."

CHAPTER – 14 THE WARNING

The duty of the wise is to warn but not to command, for commanding undermines freedom, and, finally, survival itself.

The Way of the Kahuna

When Aeala awoke there was a fine mist like gossamer on the water and over the land. The sun was above the horizon and rising into the morning sky. The air was cool and he threw a cloak over his shoulders to keep warm. The beach behind them gradually diminished into a tropical forest with tall cliffs on both sides.

At the edge of the forest was a small cabin with a tin roof and two tiny windows. To the left of the cabin was a small vegetable garden. An old Polynesian man, deeply tanned, sat on the front porch in a rocking chair and smoked a koa pipe. The pipe smoke curled and hung in the air below the overhang of the roof. He was naked to the waist except for a kapa blanket over his shoulder and wrapped waist down in a kapa loincloth. Aeala walked over to the cabin, smiled and approached the old man. The man waved back, the wrinkles on the side of his mouth creased as a slight smile appeared. The hair both on his scalp and face was peppered with gray and the eyebrows hung shaggy over the eyes. The body was thin but the skin was still tight and the flesh firm, and healthy. The eyes were dark and deep and full of life, with a friendly twinkle to them.

"Good morning," he said. "Did you sleep well?"

"Oh yes, very well thank you. We came in late last night."

"Yes, I heard you on the beach as you arrived."

"Oh, sorry. Hope we didn't disturb you."

"Not at all; I was expecting you."

"Expecting us?"

"Yes. The gods told me you were on your way after the earthquakes."

"The gods?"

"Yes, yes – come have a seat. I will get you a cup of tea. The water is already hot."

Aeala seated himself in a bamboo chair on the porch.

The old man returned with a cup of hot tea in his hand. He had a kapa blanket over him; a hole was cut in the center and his head poked through it.

"Here, drink this. It will give you strength." He handed the cup to Aeala. It steamed, hot and fragrant, and in the cup floated a vivid purple flower.

"What is it?"

"A special brew. The flower is from a plant that grows high in the mountains. To grow, it takes some of the mana from the mountain, and thus when we use it in tea it strengthens us."

"You mentioned the gods telling you that we were coming?"

"Oh, yes, yes. Many years ago I had a vision. The gods told me that after the great quake a canoe of children would arrive on Puna on their way to the light in the west."

"I am sorry, you are mistaken. We have come to Puna to live. But it sounds like a nice story.   What is the light?"

"Well, since you are not the ones it does not matter."

"That is true," said Aeala not wanting to pry.

"Can you direct us to the town?"

"The town toward the setting sun is gone – taken by the great waves. The town toward the rising sun is five miles that way." He pointed toward the mountains. "But you do not want to go there,"

"Why not?"

"Because the people there have no mana."

"I will go and see for myself," said Aeala.

74

The old man nodded. "If you must," he said.

"How do I get there?"

"Take the trail behind the cottage. There is a pass that will take you through the mountains to a waterfall. Go under the falls and there is a fissure in the rock that will lead you to the valley beyond. Be careful." The last words reverberated even after the old man had finished.

"What is your name?' asked Aeala.

"Ka Mano."

"The shark?" said Aeala. "I am Aeala of Pai'a"

The old man nodded. The smoke from his pipe drifted in the air in front of his face then curled upward into the milky morning.

"Thank you for the tea, sir. May we use your beach for a few days?"

"As long as you please, and I will care for those that stay."

"Thank you again," said Aeala.

Chapter 15 – PUNA

Beware of beginnings, for though they may dawn brightly they do not all lead to the day.
The Way of the Kahuna

Port Ka'au was a stench, a thief's world, a squalid flophouse, and a dingy supply depot for the remainder of the South Pacific. It was the first stop (or fortieth, depending on the way you went) on a long trade route that extended all the way to Asia. The town sat on the northeast coast of Puna, unprotected from the trade winds and pirates that blew in. There was a large outdoor marketplace and a row of warehouses where everything from flour, to barreled pork, to nails, to canvass sails, to cumshaw weapons were stored. The warehouses fed the marketplace and the marketplace fed the South Pacific.

Bartoldo Akers the bar tender at *The Crow's Nest* tavern wiggled his loose tooth then buried his tongue in the gap between it and the tooth next to it. His gums had been bleeding for a couple of months and he suspected he'd lose the tooth in another week or two. He washed the last of the dishes from the night before and set them to dry on a towel spread out on the bar. The bar itself was an impressive piece of koa wood, twenty feet long, as dark as the night itself and three inches thick. It was polished to a deep crystalline sheen. The heavy wooden tables and thick captain's chairs had just been cleaned and stood in the shadows awaiting fresh customers to occupy them. He stared out the window for a moment at the black sand beach and pier beyond. No trading ship had been to the island in a month and he expected one any day now. The sun was still climbing in the morning sky and the day was warming up.

The heavy door swung open and the smell of brimstone wafted through the tavern carried by the trade winds.

"It's about time!"

The thin tawny haired girl frowned. "Sorry – I was here late last night and overslept."

"Well, the floor don't sweep and mop itself – so get started."

Honeycomb Dunn nodded – her long hair flopped back and forth as she did so but her heart flared with anger. She had worked in The Crow's Nest since her father's death when she was ten. Now sixteen she had Tom-tom, her little brother, to care for and a dreary future to look forward to—at least for the next two years. Bartoldo had been her father's "friend" and had taken them in and "cared" for them. He had other motives than altruism, she suspected, as when she turned eighteen she would inherit her father's fortune and he wanted part of it. Her mother had died giving birth to Tom-tom eight years ago, so she worked to support them both as the barmaid, clean-up maid and supply purchaser on behalf of Bartoldo and the tavern. In return she received a place to sleep for her and Tom-tom, food and little else. Bartoldo had never struck her but he was inclined to drink, which led to fits of rage that he oft-times took out on her.

She went over to the side door and out the back of the tavern to the water pump. After cranking the handle several times the water coughed out and she filled her bucket. Back in the tavern she dipped a mop in the water, wrung it dry and stared mopping the floor. The front door creaked open and a large bearded man stood in the doorway blocking the light.

"Jackson – what you doing here so early in the morning?" said Bartoldo.

"Lookin' for you, Akers." The bushy eyebrows furrowed and the dark eyes glared intensely.

"Oh – and what might that be for?"

"Perhaps to make a deal. Me and the boys found some rum in the ruins on the west side after the great waves."

"Good rum or lousy stuff?"

"Oh, it's the good stuff—barrels of it."

"Found it in the ruins, eh? No one's goin' to come lookin' for it and sayin' it was stole?"

"Course not! Who do you think we is?"

"Don't trust you, Jackson, except from a mile away."

One Eyed Jackson frowned and tugged at his beard. His dreadlocks fell over his ears like snakes. The scar on his cheek and chin stood out in shadow, the rest of his face highlighted by the sunshine outside. He was a big man with powerful arms easily able to crush a rib or nose with one blow. He stared down the bartender.

"Have it your way, Akers. The next ship will be in a week from now and we'll sell it to them for much more. Just givin' you the courtesy of first dibs; but obviously you can't recognize a deal when you see it."

"Ain't seen it yet. Where are the barrels?"

"At the Sandy Point warehouse — the boys are guardin' it."

"How many barrels?"

"Eight… and one half. Me and the boys did a bit of drinkin' last night."

"So they are at Sandy Point sleepin' it off?"

"They are guardin' it – I told you that." Jackson's eyes flared with irritation.

"What you want for it?" asked Bartoldo.

"Twenty five in gold."

"You're nuts – that's three a barrel!"

"Take it or leave it." The bushy eyebrows again furrowed.

"Twelve – for the whole thing if it's okay after my inspection."

"Twenty."

"Fifteen – and that's final!"

Jackson, grunted, hawked up some phlegm and spit it in the spittoon near the bar.

"Gold now – only gold."

"Yes, fifteen gold pieces if it's good rum and nobody's after it."

"Well, you can pay me in three days. That'll give anyone that's after it plenty of time to find it, if'n you believe we stole it."

"I'll be by at noon to check it out." Bartoldo turned, grabbed a bottle of whiskey poured a shot and handed it to Jackson.

"It's good stuff—a change from all that rum you drink."

"I also got some guns too," said Jackson.

"Forget it. No market for guns here," said Bartoldo.

Jackson turned, stared at Honeycomb for a moment, put the glass on the bar and walked out.

"He gives me the willies," said Honeycomb.

"Shut your mouth, girl," said Bartoldo with a scowl, "we stand to make more money in two weeks than we have in the last six months.—Sell that rum to the next ship that comes by for three times what we buy it for."

"Where you going to get 15 gold pieces?"

"I got my stashes."

She returned to her mopping. The gloomy tavern began to brighten as the sun rose and peeked through the large latticed window.

"When you're done with that go down to the market and get us three chickens. They'll be lots of customers tonight."

"You mean refugees from the great wave?"

"Yeah, the west side of the island was hit bad. — You're going to have to kill and pluck the chickens yourself. I have some barrels of rum to check out."

"You want to give me some money?"

"Oh, yeah – here's some silver." Bartoldo reached into his apron, pulled out some coins and laid them on the table.

"Get whatever else you need to make a chicken stew – potatoes, carrots – you know."

"No problem," said Honeycomb. "I know the routine."

She was glad to get out and about, and liked going to the outdoor market. On the way she'd pick up Tom-tom to help carry the groceries. It took her ten minutes to finish the mopping and the wood floor sparkled in the limited sunlight. Satisfied, she looked in the mirror which hung behind the bar and located her reflection. She straightened her hair, as she didn't want to appear disheveled in public.

"Get out of here," called Bartoldo from the corner table, where he had set himself with a bottle of whiskey.

She stepped out into the street and squinted until her eyes adjusted to the bright sunlight. The distance from the tavern to the flophouse where she lived was only a couple of hundred yards, but the street was still muddy from the rain two days ago. There were many holes in the street; standing water had set in there after the rain and had not yet evaporated. Children played in the street, and when Honeycomb approached the flophouse she spotted Tom-tom in the street chasing after two other children.

"Tom-tom! Come here," she called.

The fluff of brown hair swung back and two piecing dark eyes peered up.

"Sis. What you doing here?"

"Going to the market, and you're coming too."

"Darn – I…"

"There's a piece of candy in it for you," she said, before he could finish.

A smile broke out over the tanned little face. "As I was saying – darned glad you showed up!"

They walked together side by side past the rundown warehouses and stores, until they came to a wide open area with stalls, carts, tables and makeshift shelves of planks set on boxes. The wares were numerous and varied: apple carts, flower carts, stalls of sweet potatoes and taro, grapefruit and breadfruit, jars of candy and dried fruit, planks with fish and meats and tables piled with pineapple, papaya, guavas and mountain apples. In the center of the market were slatted boxes with animals in them—chickens, pigeons, goats and small pigs—each emitting its own characteristic sound.

They walked over to a stall with large jars of nuts and candies. The jars were light blue and wide at the bottom, with tiny bubbles in the thick glass. Tom-tom peered over the top of one of the candy jars. Hard candy, red and green and yellow, lay in the jar. Tom-tom smiled.

"I want a green one – please."

"One of the green ones," said Honeycomb to the old man in the stall.

"Its three for a copper," he said.

She smiled. "Three, then."

The old man reached into the jar and retrieved three green ones and handed them to Tom-tom.

"Thank you, sir! And you too, Sis!"

He popped one into his mouth and put the other two in his pocket.

"Alright, let's get the vegetables and chickens," said Honeycomb with a smile. She handed the old man a silver piece and he returned nine coppers in change to her. The marketplace was crowded with women who had come from the town to buy goods and children with nothing better to do than gawk at the goings on. As they walked toward the vegetable stands Honeycomb spotted a group of three large men whom she did not recognize. They were dark, barefooted and dressed in ankle length canvas pants. Her intuition told her to give them a wide swathe and she grabbed Tom-tom by the forearm and headed toward the clothing and tool stalls.

"Where are we going?" asked Tom-tom.

"Away from those guys," said Honeycomb. "They look like trouble."

"I think they're from the other side of the island," said Tom-tom.

"Oh, how do you know that?"

"Oana's mother said a big wave ruined the other side of the island and people had come here looking for food and stuff."

"We'll just keep away from them."

They approached a canopied stall with potatoes, white onions, carrots and celery laid out on planking. Honeycomb pointed to the potatoes and carrots.

"May I have eight of those and eight of those?" she said to the woman behind the planking.

"The woman smiled up at her. "Of course, dear."

It was then that the shrieking started; it came from the location they had just left. Tom-tom was off like a startled lizard running down the aisle way toward the commotion. Honeycomb followed, anxious for his safety. They arrived to a crowd around the candy stall. The jars of nuts and candy were overturned with their contents lying in the mud about the stand. One of the jars was broken and the old man behind the counter was bloodied by a slash on the forehead and hand.

"They're worse hurt than I! That'll teach them to try and steal!"
A bloodied machete sat on the counter where the candy jar once stood. Honeycomb shook her head and frowned then found a rag and some water from one of the stalls and washed out the old man's wounds. The one on the forehead was long but not deep, the one on the hand was much worse. Honeycomb was very careful to wash it out well then found some honey and applied it to the wounds.

"That'll keep out any infection," she said.

"Thank you," said the old man still shaking from the encounter, "you're the barmaid at *The Crow's Nest*, ain't you?"

Honeycomb nodded. "Yes, yes I am."

"You Amos Dunn's girl?"

"Yes, he was my father."

The old man smiled exposing the wrinkles around his mouth and his dark eyes sparkled for a moment. "Thank you, I won't forget this. Your father was a good man—a real good man."

"Not a problem," she said. "Hope you're feeling better."

They walked back to the vegetable stall where Honeycomb picked up her vegetables and paid for them.

"I've got to pick up the chickens," she said.

"Are they going to kill them first?"

"I'm going to ask them to."

They headed for the center of the market where the boxes of animals was kept. As they walked down the aisle they crossed a trail of blood – small droplets splattered on the mud.

"He must have cut 'em bad!" said Tom-tom.

Honeycomb nodded, disgusted. "You don't have to be so enthused about it."

Tom-tom made a face at her. "I ain't enthused, whatever that means. It's just they got what they deserved."

"The old man was just trying to protect what was his. It's just a shame it had to get violent."

Tom-tom shrugged. "They got what they deserved," he muttered under his breath.

They approached the center of the market where the boxes of live chickens were stacked, the heads with the dark beaks and red cockerels extending out between the slats. The eyes flicked this way and that.

"Three large ones please," said Honeycomb to the stout man with the dirty apron.

"Want em' slaughtered and cleaned? Cost a couple of coppers more."

She nodded. "Yes, thank you."

He opened one of the wooden boxed and grabbed a chicken by the feet. It cackled as he did so. He displayed it up side down to her.

"That one's good," she said.

He did the same for two other chickens. The three birds were then bound by the feet and placed on a table where the clerk slit their throats and let the blood run down into a large pot. At first the chickens hardly moved and Tom-tom was fascinated.

"It's almost like they didn't feel it," he said.

Then their eyes changed from placid to panic and they began to flap their wings and struggle wildly. The clerk held them down. They shook their heads back and forth as if trying to stave off death, the droplets of blood from their wounds sprayed about then soaked quickly into the ground. Within a couple of minutes they no longer moved and the clerk took them to a big pot of hot water nearby. The pot was heavy and black and sat on a fire of hardwood logs. The water was not hot enough to boil but it bubbled and steamed. The man dipped each chicken in the hot water several times then picked the feathers off the birds and handed them to Honeycomb. In exchange she gave him a silver piece and two coppers. With Tom-tom carrying the vegetables they headed back for the tavern.

The tavern was locked when they returned, and they had to go around and enter through the back door. It also was locked, but Honeycomb reached into the crook of an old tree in the back alley and retrieved the key.

"Take the vegetables inside and lay them on the counter in the kitchen," she said. Tom-tom took the key and disappeared into the tavern. Honeycomb laid the chickens down by the water pump and followed him. She returned with a long knife and dressed the chickens – chopping off the heads and feet and taking out the entrails. After washing them she headed back for the tavern as an old dog sniffed at the entrails and started to feed.

"Go out back and draw some water in a pail and wash the vegetables."

Tom-tom snickered at the order but when Honeycomb stared at him sternly he obeyed. She cut up the chickens and started a fire in the stove. She normally liked the smell of burning wood but since the earthquakes and eruption four days ago the town had been inundated with a blanket of fumes from the volcano on the far side of the island. She put a big pot on the stove and smeared some lard in it. The lard crackled as it melted and began to sizzle. The back door flew open and Tom-tom entered with the wet vegetables in his hands. She laid the chicken parts in the pot and stirred them with a wooden spoon.

"Cut up the potatoes and stuff and throw them in the pot," she said, "while I fix you something to eat."

"What you got to eat?"

"Bread, cheese, olives… and some jam."

"That sounds good," said Tom-tom, "I haven't eaten today."

After the stew was made and set to simmering on the stove she and Tom-tom sat down at one of the tavern tables and took their meal of bread and cheese.

"I like this jam," said Tom-tom.

"The guavas are just ripening and that's the first batch," she said.

"That was an exciting morning."

She looked at the little brown eyes. They sparkled again and after the fright from the earthquakes. It was nice to see him happy again.

"There's too much violence and thievery," she muttered, "I wish… I don't know what I wish."

They ate in silence until everything was gone. The aroma of the chicken stew wafted into the dining room area from the kitchen and Honeycomb went into the kitchen to look after it.

"Are we going to have that tonight?"

"Well, it's for the guests but, of course, you can have some. Why don't you go outside and play; but stay near. I don't want you wandering, especially with all the strangers from the other side of the island coming over here."

"No problem – see you later."

Tom-tom headed out the back door and down the alley. Honeycomb sighed and stirred the stew and wondered if Bartoldo had found the rum to his liking.

Aeala walked back to the beach with the impression he had just spoken with a ghost. The old man was different: full of mana, full of things to say, yet withholding them intentionally. If there was one thing that Aeala knew, it was that knowledge was much more than knowing facts. Ambience was as important a part of knowledge as facts, and above that, certainty. Certainty was knowledge and supreme certainty was certainty in self. From what he perceived the old man was withholding because Aeala wasn't ready to know. He determined to keep his mind clear and his senses aware: the truth might be right before him. If he wasn't ready to accept it, it would be lost to him.

The old man called himself the shark. Aeala wondered if there was a connection.

"What did the old one say?" asked Kaela.

"He said we were welcome to stay on the beach for as long as we needed."

"Do you have a plan?"

Aeala nodded. "Let us gather everyone up and I'll go over it."

Kaela nodded. She had a new respect for her son. In a few days he had grown into a man—a man she trusted, a man she loved and admired.

It took a few minutes for all to assemble, as some were on the beach or in the water.

"Listen up everyone. I have a plan and I would like to run it by you to see what you think."

Webster grunted. Everyone else was silent.

"I do not know how safe it is in town. The town to the west was destroyed by the great wave.

The one to the east is about five miles away. Several of the guys and I should go and find out what's there. The rest of you stay here till we get back. There is plenty of food here."

"I'm going," said Webster, "and Obie, and Dirk too."

"I think you, Sumo, should stay," said Aeala.

Sumo looked up in protest. "I will speak with you alone," said Aeala. "Webster – you and your friends get ready. We leave in half an hour."

"Do you know how to get there or are we going to wander about the island?"

"The old man has given me directions."

Aeala put his hand on Sumo's shoulder. "I need you to stay. Protect the women. There is a gun and ammo in the stern of the starboard hull. If I am not back by sundown tomorrow you'll know something is wrong."

Sumo nodded. "Be careful."

Aeala went to the canoe and found the two pistols and ammo. He wrapped one in a cloth with some ammo and put the other in the inner pocket of his forest cloak. He grabbed a gourd with fresh water in it and some dried fish. He saw Dirk approach.

"How are you doing?"

"Good," said Dirk tentatively, "I think I'll take a weapon or two."

"Oh, didn't know you had any."

"Couple of long knives – my father taught me to use them."

"Take some water and food too."

"I will. — Thanks."

Aeala walked over to Sumo and discreetly handed him the pistol wrapped in the cloth.

"Thanks," said Sumo with a nod.

"Go speak to the old man when you get a chance. Take him some canned food. He will enjoy it," said Aeala.

"I will," smiled Sumo.

Miki gave Aeala a hug and buried her face in his shoulder. "You come back quick, huh?"

"I will."

Mia and Kaela hugged him. Their eyes said all that was needed.

"Aeala, I…" Jessica stuttered. A tear appeared on her cheek. He wiped it away and kissed her on the top of the head. Her hair smelled of bouquet and the sea and it reminded him of the beautiful island he had seen in his dream.

"I will be fine and back here in no time," he whispered.
She nodded, turned away and wiped her eyes.

"Let's get out of here," muttered Webster and started off toward the cottage. Aeala and Dirk caught up with him.

"It's that way," said Aeala and pointed to the narrow trail behind the cottage that disappeared between tall cliffs.

"Yeah, I picked that up," said Webster. "It's the only way out."
The trail wound between tall lush cliffs, damp with spring water. Bordering the trail grew moss, ferns and ti leaves; the fragrance of wild ginger nipped at their nostrils every so often. A green iguana far up the path turned and stared at them for a moment then scurried off into the shrubbery. They passed rabbit droppings, and once spotted a little white tail disappear into the ferns. Aeala expected bird song but strangely there was none, only the sound of gurgling water and their footsteps. The trail switched back and forth as it wound through the mountain range until finally the echo of falling water roared in the distance. As they approached, a fine mist enveloped them and the colors of the rainbow drifted about.

"Smooth move, kanaka. The trail ends at the waterfall. Now what are we going to do?"

"Don't worry about it, Webster. The old man told me what to do."
Aeala continued down the trail to the pond where the water from the falls cascaded, and, hopped from boulder to boulder until he was just feet in front of the sheet of falling water. He set his feet firmly on a large boulder and stepped through the sheet. It was cold and powerful but his position was solid and his balance true. He passed through and found himself in a small cavern with a large fissure on the far end. The lighting in the cavern was dim as the sunlight from outside penetrated the sheet of falling water and made it appear translucent. The sun rays entered the cavern but were fractured by the cascade and appeared like a thousand flickering candles against the cavern walls. Aeala scrambled through the cavern to the far end and carefully entered the fissure. It extended

about fifty yards into the rock and at the end a thin beam of sunlight shimmered. He stumbled through the fissure, which was almost totally in shadow to the opening on the other side. The opening was a sliver just wide enough to slip through without rubbing against the sharp rock edges. Aeala pictured Sumo trying to squeeze though and grinned briefly.

He was met with a view of a verdant valley below. The fissure was situated high on a rocky outcrop, on the side of a mountain that gradually descended to the valley floor below. The town lay near the far edge of the valley, tucked away between a thick forest and a grove of coconut trees, beyond it a black sand beach and the endless ocean. A thin fog blanketed the valley like a shroud over a corpse.

"Aeala!" It was the voice of Dirk.

Aeala turned and headed back to the waterfall. The sunlight danced on the cavern walls as it shone through the cascade. He took a deep breath then stepped carefully through the falling water.

"Come on – it's safe!" he called.

He then stepped back into the cavern chilled to the bone by the cold sheet of water. Dirk was the second to enter the cavern with a yelp as the cold water burst over his head and shoulders.

"Wow! That really wakes you up!"

Aeala laughed at his expression. "It certainly does."

Obie was next and burst through the sheet into the cavern with his hands over his head to shield his face from the falling water. Webster was last to enter and he simply scowled as he exited the sheet of falling water as if it were not even there.

"Let's move kanaka. We still have a ways to go."

"There appears to be a shallow trail on the side of the rocks which gets broader as it descends down the mountain into the valley," said Aeala.

"Well, lead on," said Webster.

Aeala carefully stepped out of the fissure and onto the rocky outcrop. There was a steep cliff and a narrow lip that disappeared about thirty yards to the right. Aeala followed the lip until it disappeared. He then sat down and slid for about ten yards down the side of the outcrop. Tiny chips of stone slipped and scraped at his bottom as he slid which made his descent all the more precarious due to the slippery nature of the chips. He extended his right leg as far as he could until the muscles could stretch no more and began to tremble with the effort; he was finally able to touch the earth at the bottom of the outcrop.

Once on the narrow trail the going became easier. The trail wound back and forth down the mountainside. Short grass and stunted trees clung to the side of the steep mountain, and often the trail would disappear and the party would have to make their way over rocky terrain until the trail again showed up. Lush undergrowth began to appear—deep green shrubs, gnarled windblown trees and further down, moss and ferns. A small spring bubbled from a depression in the earth and drained down the mountainside in a shallow gully. Aeala was glad to cool himself with its waters. The party rested for a few minutes under the shade of a koa tree and cooled themselves by throwing water from the gully on their heads and shoulders. Obie slapped at a mosquito and Dirk wiped the perspiration from his forehead.

"It's getting hot and stinky," said Dirk.

"Better we stayed on Pa'ai," muttered Webster, "the smell here is just as bad."

The smell of brimstone was thick in the afternoon air and a stifling fog hung low to the land.

"We only have another couple miles to go," said Aeala, "we can cover it in a short time."

His spirits faltered with the noxious atmosphere and he wondered if what Webster had said was not the precise truth: that they were no better off here than on Pa'ai. If it was, then he had no solution for their survival. He did not know of anywhere else to go except what his dreams told him and that was but fantasy. He put the dilemma out of his mind and focused on the job at hand – to get to the town and find out where they could safely stay. They passed cattle grazing in a meadow the lush grass up to their ankles. Aeala glimpsed what looked like a large bird running on two feet, its tan and jet feathers fluttering in the wind.

"Did you see that?" he said and pointed toward a stand of koa trees and brush.

"Yeah," said Dirk, "It looked like a big bird."

"Stay to the trail," said Webster. "We ain't chasin' no birds."

The trail flattened out and grew wider. They hiked down the mountain and were now on flat land at the bottom of the valley. A stream, several yards wide with large boulders jutting from its waters, bordered the trail and wound through the valley. A small cloudbank moved in from the sea to the north and dumped a rain shower on them. It was warm and lasted only ten minutes, then moved south in the direction they had hiked from. The sun broke through the ragged cloud cover and dried the land almost immediately. They rounded a bend in the trail and in a small clearing to their left sat a small shack. The tin roof was rusted and patches of leaves from a nearby tree lay on top of it.

As they approached a little boy opened the door, peered out with big brown eyes then slammed it quickly.

"Not a good sign," said Dirk. "We may not be welcomed."

"These are native people," said Aeala. "The custom is to be hospitable."

The door opened again, a young man and an older woman stood in the doorway smiling.

"Aloha," said the young man. "Are you from the other side of the island?"

"No," said Aeala, "we recently arrived from another island."

"Oh, did you hear about the disaster?"

"Tell me," said Aeala.

"Oh, come in first – sit down make yourselves comfortable. I'll get us some drinks – you guys look hot."

"Mahalo," said Aeala.

"See, I told you," he whispered to Dirk. "'Mahalo' means thank you."

"Yeah, I picked that up," he said, "I'll remember that one."

He brought five cups of coconut juice and set them on a low table. There were cushions on the floor and a large reed mat under the cushions.

"My name is Moko," said the young man. "A few days ago the volcano on the island erupted. Just before the eruption there was an earthquake.

It was not a very big earthquake but it brought the great waves and they destroyed everything on the west side of the island. There are rumors that there was fire from the sea and a great plume rose up just before the great wave."

"What do you mean by a plume?"

"Like when fire touches water there is a cloud – except this one rose very fast and violent… at least that's what I was told."

"I am Aeala - and this is Dirk, Obie and Simon. We are looking for my father and a place to stay. His name is Kulo and he was with two other men."

"I have not seen them. I do not go into town unless it is absolutely necessary."

"We are also looking for a place to stay and jobs."

"You can stay here for the night."

"Oh, I meant a permanent place to stay."

"The volcano has erupted. I don't know how much longer any of us will be here." said Moko.

"Why?"

"When my father was living he told me of a time the volcano erupted and killed nearly everyone on the island. This was a long time ago and it was the fumes that killed not the lava."

Aeala's spirits sunk further. "Where will all the people go?"

Moko shrugged. "Who knows – there are only legends of other lands. The foreigners come and go on their sailing ships and they tell tales of lands far, far away – but it is too far for us to travel in canoes."

"There are no other islands close by?"

Moko shook his head sadly. "No, only legends – no one has ever been there."

"What are the legends?"

"Islands below the horizon – my grandfather once told me that our ancestors traveled there and one, Ko Laa, returned. He told of a beautiful island full of plants, and waterfalls and fish in the sea. It was deserted but only a few on his canoe made it. He said there were other islands but he had not explored them before returning to Puna."

"What happened to him?"

"He picked up his girlfriend and sailed over the horizon – he was never seen again."

"Do you think the legend is true?"

Moko shrugged. "As a child I was never interested enough to question my grandfather further. By the time I was grown he was dead."

"Did he say where the island was?"

"He said it was under A'a, the bright blue star in the night sky. That is all I remember."

"Thank you," said Aeala. "Please take some of this dried fish we have."

Moko understood he would be honoring his guests by accepting the gift. "Mahalo," he said.

"We should be going. Do you know of anyone that we could speak to regarding a permanent place to stay?"

"For you four?"

"No, for twelve."

"There is a man in town – he is the owner of *The Crow's Nest* tavern – he can find you something. His name is Bartoldo."

"Where is the tavern?"

"Continue on this trail – it will take you to town. There will be a cross street – go left on the cross street. It is the third building on the left."

"Thank you again," said Aeala. He stood and gestured for the others to do the same. They exited the home.

"Oh, one other thing," said Aeala, "we saw a giant bird?"

Moko chuckled. "They are Emu. Supposedly Ko Laa brought back the eggs of the bird from the island he found – they hatched, and here they have lived ever since."

Aeala smiled and waved a farewell at Moko and the little boy who peered out from around Moko's leg.

They continued down the trail. "We ain't staying all together," said Weaver, "soon as we find a place to live me and the others are leaving."

Aeala looked at him but said nothing. He had expected this from Webster. They reached the town as the sun began to set in the west. The sunset like the ones on Pa'ai was blood. They turned left on the cross street and the tavern with shake roof and heavy wooden columns, loomed in the shadows of dusk. Oil lamps lit the interior and the soft golden light flooded out the windows onto the street.

"You guys hungry?" asked Aeala.

They laughed. They hadn't eaten since morning.

Aeala stepped through the front door and looked about. In the far corner was a huge elephant ear plant in a pot. It cast a shadow on the table adjacent to it where two men sat their faces obscured by the dark. Behind the bar to the left were oil lamps that illuminated the heavy wooden bar and made it shine. Tables and captain's chairs partly in shadow were spaced comfortably about the area. To the far end by the elephant ear plant was a staircase that led to the second floor of the building. The aroma of chicken stew and whiskey permeated the tavern. The hum of low voices drifted about and behind the bar stood a young girl and an older man.

He had a two days growth of beard on his face with grizzled disheveled hair and dark beady eyes. She was thin with straight tawny hair, large gray eyes and a thin nose. Aeala thought she would be pretty if it were not for her sober bearing which made her appear unapproachable. As the others in his party entered the two behind the bar looked up and took notice.

"Hey, strangers." It was the bartender's raspy voice – it reverberated through the tavern.

"Good evening," said Aeala.

"What'll you have?"

"What do you have for dinner?"

"Fresh chicken stew with potatoes and vegetables."

"That's fine for four."

"We'll have it to you in a moment. It's two coppers apiece."

"Also four juices."

"Another copper."

Aeala reached into his leather purse and pulled out a silver piece.

"Your change," said the bartender and handed Aeala a copper.

They settled themselves at a table near a window and relaxed.

"It's nice in here," said Dirk, "but that smell of brimstone seems to be getting worse." Aeala nodded. The door opened and several men walked in. They were tall men – foreigners looking for riches or a place to hide, thought Aeala. The tawny-haired girl brought a platter with four plates on it each steaming with chicken stew.

"Thanks," said Aeala with a smile.

"I'll get the drinks right away," she said.

She was back in a moment with four mugs and a pitcher of red liquid. "Its berry juice," she said.

"Thank you again," said Aeala.

This time she smiled. "You're welcome."

"When you get a chance I'd like to ask you a question," said Aeala.

"In a moment," she said, "let me just take the orders of the customers that just walked in."

She was back in a few minutes. "How can I help you?"

"We're looking for a place to stay for the night."

"You can stay here. There are rooms for rent upstairs."

"By any chance is the bartender named Bartoldo?"

"Yes. How did you know?"

"A local farmer told us. One other question – several days ago three men left Pa'ai and sailed here. One was called Kulo - about six foot tall, thin, dark hair? Have you seen them?"

"Many strangers came here after the great wave. Let me think a few moments and I'll get back to you. If you want to speak with Bartoldo I will send him over, but he is one that … that has his own interests in mind. So beware." She turned and walked back to the bar where several full mugs of ale sat, their heads overflowing, ready to be distributed to thirsty patrons.

"I like her," said Dirk.

Aeala looked up at him. "Do you think we can trust her?"

"We shouldn't trust anyone," said Webster with a scowl.

"I think we can trust her," said Dirk.

"What's wrong with you," said Webster, "you use to be with us, not the kanakas."

Dirk just shook his head and said no more.

Bartoldo walked over to their table and wiped his hands on his apron. He smelled of sweat and liquor.

"The barmaid said you had something to say."

"We're looking for a permanent place to stay. She said you may know of something."

"You got money?" The beady eyes stared piercingly at him.

"Not much but I can get some."

"From where?"

Aeala had a bad feeling about this fellow. "Never mind – I've changed my mind - we'll search elsewhere."

"Didn't mean to put you off," said the Bartender, "but have it your way." He turned around and walked back to the bar.

"What's wrong with you?" said Webster. "I thought we came here to find dwellings."

"You said we shouldn't trust anyone.—I had a bad feeling about him," said Aeala.

"So what are we going to do, live out in the open?"

Aeala saw there was no reasoning with Webster. "Do as you please, Webster. I don't trust him and won't deal with him."

Nothing more was said. Webster simply shut up and dozed in his chair. Honeycomb returned to their table after serving the other customers.

"I seem to remember serving three strangers that came in together. It was a day or so after the great wave. There were so many people in here at that time. They said they would be leaving the next morning for some other island – they didn't say where. They looked worried."

Aeala's spirits brightened. "Did one have a small tattoo on his cheek?"

She nodded. "They left the next day. At least I never saw them again."

"Can we get a couple of rooms for the night?"

"Yes, of course. When the crowd leaves in a couple of hours I'll make up the beds. Is that okay?"

"Perfect," said Aeala.

The two men in the corner by the elephant ear plant had been joined by several more and they spoke in low voices and laughed loudly. Unlike the other patrons, Bartoldo himself served them, and brought to the table bread and cheese and chicken stew and mugs of frothy ale. The night passed slowly with patrons entering and leaving, many just staying for dinner while others lingered, attracted by the company and liquor. The men in the corner by the elephant ear plant seemed to have settled in as they had not moved for hours except to use the outhouse, out back. The tawny-haired girl worked hard – refilled mugs, cleared tables, and brought the chicken stew in big bowls to hungry patrons. The tavern began to empty as the night wore on and finally she disappeared for a few minutes upstairs, and then was back.

"Your rooms are ready," she said. "If you are done then follow me."

"Thank you," said Aeala. They stood and followed her across the room to the stairs near the elephant ear plant. As they passed, one of the men at the table looked up – Aeala noticed he was a large man with a patch over his left eye. It was just a glance before he turned back, his face again in shadow, but Aeala shivered at the chill of his presence. They ascended the stairs to the top floor lit by a single oil lamp, which radiated a pale yellow light.

"Stay away from that one," she whispered pointing down the stairs. "He's bad news all the way."

Dirk and Aeala nodded. "Thanks."

There was a row of four doors on the second floor – she went to the one to the far left and opened it.

"Two of you can sleep here and two in the next room. My brother is in there," she said and pointed to the door directly above the stairs. "He should be asleep but if he makes any noise just bang on the door and he'll shut up."

Aeala gestured to Dirk. "We'll take the one closest to your brother's room," he said to the tawny haired girl. "By the way. What is your name?"

"Honeycomb," she said with a smile.

"This is Simon, Obie and Dirk. I am Aeala."

"Dirk like the dagger?"

Dirk nodded. "Honeycomb like the bee?"

She laughed. "Sleep well."

There were two beds in the room with a big window. Aeala threw it open, took off his sandals and flopped down on the bed.

"You like her, huh?"

"Yeah, somewhat," said Dirk, "but we got lots of other stuff to deal with here."

Aeala smiled. "Yeah, but it's a pleasant distraction."

"Thanks for all you done," said Dirk.

"Not a problem," said Aeala and slowly drifted off to sleep.

Chapter 16 – THE DAGGER AND THE BEE

What is a friend worth? Time, money – or much, much more?
The measure of an individual is in how he treats his friends.
The Way of the Kahuna

It was around 1:00 AM when Dirk awoke. He was not sure what roused him but as he lay in bed he heard the sound of whispering. It seemed odd, and as he was already on edge from the recent events he opened the door and peeked out. The door above the stairs where Honeycomb's brother slept stood open. Dirk pulled on his pants and boots and cautiously stepped out of his room. He was met by Honeycomb with Tom-tom in her arms.

"Oh, didn't mean to wake you," she said.

"Where are you going?"

"Home," she said, "we don't live here."

"You going to carry him all the way?"

"Yeah – I do it whenever he won't wake up."

"Let me do it," said Dirk.

"Oh, you don't have to bother."

"Oh, I couldn't sleep anyway – do me some good to take a walk."

She looked into his eyes and saw no guile. "Thanks – I appreciate it. I live just down the street."

She handed the sleeping boy over to Dirk and he cradled him in his strong arms. They turned and headed down the stairs. The tavern was dark except for a single candle that burned on a small plate at the bar. As they passed the elephant ear plant Dirk noticed the two men were still at the table near the plant fast asleep. Honeycomb turned into the kitchen behind the bar and Dirk followed – she opened the back door and stepped out into the night. Dirk closed the door behind them but made certain it was unlocked so he could get back in. The moon was nowhere to be seen and Dirk recalled one of the lessons Aeala taught him about the night sky—that in its first quarter the moon set around midnight. He also recalled that he had seen the waxing crescent of the moon a few nights ago and that it was growing larger each night. He thought Aeala was the smartest young person he had ever met: smart in a practical way. He understood the night sky and the tides and the winds and other elements and how they all worked together. He wondered how one so young could know so much.

He could hear Honeycomb's footsteps ahead of him and the soft breathing of the little boy in his arms. Although it was early morning it was not chilly and the walk was pleasant. They passed a couple of dark buildings and approached a three-story structure with many windows. A light burned in one of the windows on the third floor.

"That's Mr. Stephenson – he always leaves a light burning at night. I think he's afraid of ghosts."

Dirk smiled. He was familiar with the feeling.

"What floor do you live on?"

"The third – if you want I'll take him from here."

"Nah, I'm okay. I'll take him up and lay him in his bed."

They entered the flophouse, climbed the stairs and Honeycomb produced a key from her blouse and unlocked a heavy wooden door. She entered, struck a flint and lit a candle. The room was extremely neat with two small bunks in one corner, a dresser, a table and chair and a large straw rug on the floor. A mirror hung from the east wall and the candle flickered in its reflection. A bowl of fruit sat on the dresser along with a pitcher of water.

"Would you like some?" she said.

He wanted to stay a moment and this provided him a means to that end.

"That would be nice. Let me put Tom-tom down."

She handed him a banana.

"Do you really plan on staying here on Puna?"

"Well, we did. The reason we left our home was because there were poisonous fumes leaking from cracks in the earth – but it's worse here."

"What are you going to do?"

"I don't know. Aeala is our leader – he has the answers."

"I see - Tom-tom and I…"

Her voice trailed without finishing. She simply looked up at Dirk then out the window.

"I will keep in contact with you while we are here – I cannot tell you more than that at the moment," said Dirk.

She said no more but nodded.

"I should go," he said. "Thank you for the banana."

"Thank you for carrying Tom-tom—and I know I woke you although you said I didn't, but I appreciate your help anyway."

Dirk laughed, he liked her verve and honesty. "Good night."

. .

The turning of the doorknob and the squeak of the hinges roused Aeala. He saw only shadows at first but as he sat up in bed he realized what he was looking at. The two shadows grabbed him and pinned him to the bed.

"Where is the money, kanaka?"

"What?" Aeala said choking.

"The money! The money you brought with you."

Aeala smelled the putrid breath of his assailant. It was the odor of liquor and stewed chicken. He stared into the face inches from his own; there was one large eye and a black patch on the other.

"Where is the money?" The voice was drunken and threatening.

"Here!" cried Aeala and thrust his middle finger into the one good eye. One Eyed Jackson howled with rage and tried to strangle Aeala with his powerful hands.

"Kill him!" cried the second shadow. But Aeala was too quick. He rolled out of bed onto the floor to get away from the two men. The second one grabbed his leg. Aeala kicked at him to shake him off, but the man clutched a knife and raised it ready to thrust it into Aeala. He rolled under the bed and found the pistol he had brought with him mixed in with his clothes and backpack. He deftly drew it and cocked the hammer. The second man was on him like a giant cat. The pistol boomed. There was a flash of light, a howl. Webster and Obie scrambled into the doorway as the second man fell to the floor. Aeala was up quickly, grabbed the metal pitcher on the side table and slammed it into the side of the head of the man with one eye. The man fell backward still grabbing at his wounded eye, which Aeala had nearly plucked out.

"What the heck?" It was Webster's voice confused and angry.

"They attacked me!"

"I think this one's dead!" said Obie.

The one eyed man was still blinded from the finger Aeala had put in his good eye and crawled about the room in a panic howling.

"Let's get out of here," said Aeala.

"You're not going anywhere." It was Bartoldo and he welded a flintlock pistol. "Drop that gun, young-un."

Aeala had already put the pistol down so he threw up his hands to show that he was unarmed.

"Alright – the three of you get out of here and walk slowly downstairs"

As they approached the first floor Dirk entered from the kitchen. "What happened? I heard a gunshot."

"Stay right there," said Bartoldo, "your friend just shot and killed someone."

"It was self-defense – I was just defending myself. He was going to stab me with a knife," said Aeala.

The kitchen door opened and Honeycomb burst through. "What in the name? I heard a shot."

"One of your guests shot Willie in the upstairs room."

Honeycomb gasped. "He must have gone in there to rob them. I saw Willie at the table by the elephant ear plant just a few minutes ago."

"We'll see," said Bartoldo. "I'm taking them to the constable."

"We weren't involved," said Webster. "Only that one was," he said and pointed to Aeala.

"Don't matter," said Bartoldo. "The constable will sort it out. Honeycomb, attend to One-eyed Jackson. Appears there's something wrong with him."

It was a short walk to the constable's office, which was on the far side of town. When they arrived the building was dark. Bartoldo rapped on the door and someone inside stirred.

"Who is it?" The voice was raspy.

"It's Bartoldo Akers. Open up!"

The front door creaked open and a young bearded man in overalls peered out, the fog of sleep still about him.

"Where's the constable?" asked Bartoldo.

"Ahh, he's at home. I'm on duty tonight."

"Yeah, well – we got a killing."

"A what!" The eyes of the young deputy grew wide.

"You heard me," said Bartoldo. "Get the constable!"

The young man bolted down the street toward the constable's home.

"Wait a moment," yelled Bartoldo. "Put these guys in jail first!"

The young deputy stopped in his tracks. "Oh, yeah – I almost forgot. By the way, who got shot?"

"Willie Boy."

The deputy nodded, threw the cell key at Bartoldo, and was off like a covey of flushed quail to find the constable. Bartoldo put all four of the boys in the cell and locked the door.

"Look what you got us into now," said Webster.

"It was self defense. They broke in and he pulled a knife on me."

Dirk could stand the guilt no longer. He was not accustomed to withholding the truth and in a situation such as this it became intolerable.

"Aeala. It was me. It was my fault. I left the door unlocked when I sneaked out to take Honeycomb and Tom-tom home. The two thugs went upstairs after we left, found the door unlocked and attacked you. I suspect Bartoldo is connected with this somehow. Remember when he asked you if you had money to pay for a permanent place to stay?"

"Yeah, I remember. He thought I was lying about not having money and sent those two to steal what we had. Then it went bad, and now he needs to cover himself."

"I'm sorry," repeated Dirk.

"Forget it. We'll get out of here fine and everything will be okay."

"Okay? Okay? We're about to be hanged and you think we're okay?" screamed Webster.

"Calm down Simon. No-one's hanging no one. We'll simply explain what happened and everything will be okay."

"When we get out of here, kanaka, you're on your own. We're leaving."

"Have it your way Webster."

It took twenty minutes for the constable to arrive. The high voice of the excited deputy chattered away. The constable poked his head into the jail room area, took a look at the prisoners and left. They heard the office door slam then all was quiet.

"They must be heading back to the tavern," said Aeala. "We may as well make ourselves comfortable; we'll be here till morning."

"What a dog's breakfast you got us into, kanaka."

The bunk beds in the cell smelled of vomit and liquor. Aeala suspected they had been used in recent times to confine drunks who had gotten out of hand and disturbed the townspeople. He turned the mattress over and sat down and sighed. It was shortly after dawn when the tapping began. It was a short low sound as if someone were hammering on metal. The cell window was no more than a foot across with vertical bars implanted into the rock frame. After a short time the tapping became more frantic which roused Aeala from a fitful sleep.

"Aeala! Aeala!" The whisper carried through the cell.

He started to stand up, hit his head on the bunk above and grabbed for the spot on his head that hurt.

"Aeala – it's me, Honeycomb – come quick!"

He again attempted to stand, this time managed to do so and stumbled to the window.

"They're going to frame you. I heard them talking. They are going to say the shooting was your fault."

"Who?"

"Bartoldo, the constable and One-Eyed Jackson. They're in it together. We got to get you out and…"

"Are they going to let my friends go?"

"I think so. They want your money and someone to blame the death on. I guess if they blame you, then they figure your money is theirs."

"When they let Dirk out, find him. I'll tell him to look for you. Perhaps the three of us can figure something out.—And thanks!"

"Tell Dirk I'll either be at the tavern or in the flophouse. He knows where that is. Do you guys have a boat?"

Aeala nodded.

"Are you leaving?" asked Honeycomb.

"Yes."

"I and my little brother want to go."

"There's room, so go and prepare your belongings and some food. Once I escape it will be a fast flight."

She was gone. Aeala thought how foolish he was to bring all his money with him to town. Then again, how was he to know it was so thoroughly a thieves' haven. The old man at the beach had said the people here had no mana; apparently this is what he meant. Everyone that was, except the tawny haired girl known as Honeycomb, and her little brother.

He shook Dirk on the top bunk then remembered what his mother had told him about the spirit leaving the body at sleep. He touched him gently on the temple and he sleepily opened his eyes.

"Aeala?"

"Yeah, it's me. Listen up: Honeycomb came to the window a few moments ago. She said the constable and his bunch are going to frame me and keep me locked up. You and the others will probably be let go. You are going to have to make up your mind!"

"About what?"

"Whether you are with me and the others back at the canoe, or with Webster."

"Why?"

"Because Webster is not going to help and if I don't get out of here no one is going to help the people back at the canoe; but if you help me, you'll put your life in danger."

Dirk was taken aback. It had not occurred to him that he would have to take sides, and, more surprisingly, that Aeala would think that he might choose Webster. He was of the opinion that after Aeala had saved his life things had changed between them. He owed Aeala everything. That his life was in danger was a given—it had been that way since the earthquake. The only dilemma he had was that Aeala would not be there to lead until he was freed, and the responsibility to free him now fell on Dirk's shoulders. He had always been the follower, not the instigator, and he was not confident that he could pull it off. But if not him, then who? Sumo? Miki ? Obie?

Two of them weren't here, and Obie simply obeyed Webster like a trick-dog its master. He looked at himself and his life—his own habits and reactions to difficult situations—and recognized the pattern: he would take the easy way out, the way that afforded the least exposure to danger and blame. But after what Aeala had done, not only for him, but for all of them, he saw that it was possible to act in a different manner. There was the possibility that he, too, could act nobly and honorably.

He looked up at Aeala standing before him. "I'm with you, Aeala. I'll do anything to help."

"Good. I thought you would say that. You and the others will probably be let out today. Find Honeycomb. She will help you. We need a plan. Do not tell Webster anything. He can't be trusted."

Dirk nodded. The morning outside was just awakening; it would be a long day. Dirk drifted back to sleep for a couple of hours and dreamed of peace—an island without criminals, where people respected each other and life; all of life. He saw the emu, the great spirit-bird of the land, that roamed the hills and fields and beaches; he saw the shark, the great spirit-creature of the sea; and he saw the land, and sea, and air and the breath in them: the life resident in all things under the dome of heaven.

Then it all shattered, and in its place the empty eyes of Willie Boy, the thug that had been shot and killed by Aeala; the leering face of Bartoldo Akins, and the struggle between One-eyed Jackson and Aeala. And then death itself—the dark cold shroud between this universe and the other. The shroud appeared before him like an impenetrable barrier, and on the other side, everything he believed in—Aeala, Honeycomb, Miki, Sumo, light and love itself. He struggled to break through, frantic and furious all at the same time. He saw a tear in the shroud, a small narrow breach, and when he peered through he beheld its shining light, all white and clean and pure. When he looked closer it twinkled, and in it his own reflection: innocent and uncorrupted as if relieved of sin and doubt.

"Dirk! Wake up!"

Dirk rolled over and opened his eyes. It was Obie.

"We're free... me you and Webster that is. Let's go!"

The cell door was open and Webster was already out. The constable with the key held on to the cell door. "The three of you are free to go. He stays." The constable pointed to Aeala.

Dirk looked at Aeala, turned and walked out of the cell. The steel door clanged behind him.

"We're out of here," said Webster. "You coming with us?"

"Where you going?" asked Dirk.

"Going to see Bartoldo. The constable said he wanted to see us."

"I'll catch up to you."

"Where you going?"

"To see the constable, see if I can get Aeala released." Dirk lied.

"Good luck. Serves him right for getting us all in trouble."

As soon as the two disappeared, Dirk took off through the alleyways to the flophouse where Honeycomb lived. He found her closing up a sea bag.

"Honeycomb!"

She turned and gave him a big hug.

"What's in there?"

"Food and clothes. Aeala told me to pack. We're going with you. We got to get Aeala free."

"We don't have much time," said Dirk. "Webster is on his way to the Tavern. I think he'll tell Bartoldo about the canoe and the others. Bartoldo may go, or send someone to the cove where my friends are to steal the canoe, or worse."

"What shall we do?" asked Honeycomb.

"I have a plan. We must go back to the cove and get help. You and Tom-tom come with me. Bring your bag. We'll hide it on the way and pick it up later."

"Whatever you say. I know how to get out of town without being seen. Where are we going?"

"Toward the mountains."

"I'm ready," said Honeycomb.

"You lead. I'll carry the bag," said Dirk.

She went down the staircase, followed by Tom-tom and Dirk. They entered a cellar at the bottom of the flophouse, and in the shadows at the far end was a large straw mat. She threw off the mat. Below it was a trap door.

"It leads out of town," she said.

They climbed down a small ladder and entered a tunnel. It was a small tunnel, not more than six feet high and five feet wide.

"Wait," said Honeycomb. Behind the ladder was a shallow ledge with a lantern and flint sitting on it. She struck the flint, and after a few tries lit the lantern.

"Let's go,' she said.

The light revealed a long tunnel that wound this way and that under the town.

"What was this used for?" asked Dirk.

"Escape route for the townspeople. Pirates use to raid the town. As a little girl I found the trap door and explored the tunnels."

"Brave of you," said Dirk. A rat ran across the tunnel floor and disappeared around a bend.

"I had a little friend that would explore with me but he left with his father."

"Left? To where?"

"I really don't know. One day they boarded a big sailing ship and left. I was devastated."

Dirk followed Tom-tom and Honeycomb in silence, and watched the shadows on the tunnel walls dance as the lantern rocked in Honeycomb's hand. He never had many friends, as his dad had moved several times trying to seek his fortune. Boxer, carpenter, woodworker, merchant—he had kept the family provided for, but seldom in one place. His dad was a distant man, hard to love, yet Dirk had gleaned from him many things, the most important being the craft of woodworking and how to deal with people; yet he was a loner. Aeala was the closest friend he had; yet he'd known him only for a few days. Prior to that time he had been just another kanaka kid on the island; now he was special, very special, and Dirk determined to make good on his promise to rescue Aeala. He liked Honeycomb, was attracted to her forthrightness and her physical beauty. It was not the soft radiant beauty of Jessica or the exotic beauty of Miki, but a beauty born of trial and toughness—an angular beauty like the horizon at dawn. When he looked into her eyes he saw first steel and only then love and loyalty, and that love was not directed at him, but at Tom-tom, as it should be.

Honeycomb continued through the maze of tunnels and alcoves, always continuing in a southerly direction. Finally they entered a large room; the lantern light illuminated the room only dimly, but she made out the familiar tables and shelves at the far end engulfed in shadow. On the shelves stacked neatly were cans and on the tables bags and barrels.

"What are those?" asked Dirk.

"Canned goods. You know—food and some medicine, and some explosives."

"Explosives?"

"Yeah, black powder, lead balls, that stuff. The townspeople left it here in case they needed it in the future. We should examine this stuff for a moment before we continue."

"Why?"

"There may be stuff here we can use, or take with us on our trip."

"Right," said Dirk.

As she approached the shelves and tables Honeycomb spotted several bags and small barrels. She inspected them closely. "It's black powder and flints," she said.
Dirk noticed some of the cans with a bulge at the end. "Some of this stuff is spoiled."
Honeycomb looked up and nodded. A rat ran across the room and disappeared in the shadows.

"How much further?" asked Dirk.

"A mile or so."

"Let's get out of here," he said. "I hate rats."

They continued, with the way winding this way and that, but always toward the south. Water dripped from the ceiling and ran down the walls of the tunnel and green slime clung to the wet spots and water trails wherever they appeared. It was cool in the tunnel, and drafts of air occasionally swiped at them from unseen breaches in the walls or side tunnels. A black salamander slithered across a rivulet in the floor, its stubby legs churning as fast as it could, and disappeared in a side tunnel to the right.

"Did you see that!" exclaimed Tom-tom excitedly.

"Yeah, that was curious wasn't it?" said Dirk. He realized how much Tom-tom liked this experience.

"Tom-tom, you ever been in here before?"

"No. I never even knew it existed!"

Suddenly something flushed from the ceiling. Strong wings beat furiously, and a blur swooshed past them.

"What was that?"

"Bats," said Honeycomb. "They are all over the tunnel."

It was shortly thereafter that the first rays of sunlight breached the tunnel. Dust motes floated in the sunbeams casting tiny gnat-like shadows in the air. The smell of the jungle—the pungent odor of rotted foliage and wood—sprang at them like a predator on prey, but it was a good smell nonetheless, for it indicated a milestone of their flight.

"The trail to the mountains is about a mile that way," said Honeycomb pointing toward the coast.

Dirk was glad to be out in the open again; fresh air and sunshine were nourishment for his spirits. Directly above them floated dark cumulus clouds, but to the west, blue sky. The cloud moved fast toward the east, yet above it, high in the sky, strands of cirrus clouds moved in the opposite direction. Dirk took notice as they walked.

"Look at those clouds," he said. "The low ones are moving west, but the ones high up, east."

"Probably means it will rain," said Honeycomb. "When winds move in opposite directions the weather gets unstable."

"How do you know?"

"How do you not?" she said. "After you've lived on islands a long time you notice stuff like that."

They continued up the little side trail for fifteen minutes and passed a small brook with crayfish crawling about. It was not a very wide brook, possibly six feet across, but the water ran cool and clear and the crayfish lay at the bottom near the stones and rotting wood.

Moss and tall grass covered the ground on the sides of the trail and the smell of wetness and chlorophyll filled the air.

As they drew near the junction of the main trail it began to rain, not the fine mist of the early morning rain, but big, heavy drops that splattered and splashed when they landed. The day was warm and the rain made the air uncomfortable and humid. It stopped after a few minutes as the dark cumulus cloud passed to the east. There was a roll of thunder from the sea, then everything was quiet again.

"See what I mean? Unstable weather," said Honeycomb.

They turned left at the junction and continued their southward march toward the mountains. Tom-tom became distracted by all the wonders along the way—spiders' webs sparkling with raindrops, dark lizards that ran this way and that across the trail, a white-tailed rabbit that stopped on the boarder of the trail to munch on wild lettuce and fat beetles that crawled slowly in and out of the tall grass at the side of the trail. As they turned a bend in the trail, Dirk looked back and discovered Tom-tom was nowhere to be seen.

"Honeycomb! Hold up!"

He jogged back down the trail only to find Tom-tom off to the side under a small tree, picking the white and pink fruit. As he neared he got a better glimpse of the fruit. It was round and white with rose-colored streaks. Tom-tom munched on one and had half a dozen rolled up in his shirt.

"Mountain apples!" he said. "They're really good!"

Dirk chuckled, picked a few then bit into a plump one. Juice squirted out in a tiny jet. It was full of liquid and tasted sweet and firm. It exuded a fragrance like that of a rose.

"They're rose apples," said Honeycomb who had followed Dirk back down the trail. "They're quite good and full of juice."

He smiled and handed her a couple. "You sure know your island."

"It's been a long time since I've been this far away from the town, but we love the rainforest. Before my father died we'd come here often."

"You and Tom-tom?"

"Yeah, he was just five then. Why don't you take the lead? You must know the way you came."

"Good idea," said Dirk, and he turned and started back up the trail. It was about 1:30 p.m. when they reached Moko's cottage. Dirk thought about stopping by and telling him everything that happened, and then thought better of it. Perhaps it was better to involve as few people as possible. That way there was less of a chance of anyone getting hurt. They walked by the cottage without stopping, and into the vast grassy meadows beyond. The mountains loomed, shrouded in clouds, in the distance.

"We still have a long way to go," said Dirk, "maybe three or four hours."
The trail became steeper and switched back and forth for a couple of miles. Tom-tom grew tired and Dirk carried him in his strong arms. They entered the mists of the mountains and the atmosphere cooled quickly. Everything took on a steel tint, and wisps of cirrus clouds hovered above them, winding their way around the mountain peaks.

"It's not far now," said Dirk. "But there is a surprise coming up."

Honeycomb was exhausted. She had not slept much the night before and had been steadily hiking up hill for several hours, yet she didn't want Dirk to know how tired she was. She simply nodded and took a deep breath. They continued up the mountainside until the rocky outcrop loomed ahead. Dirk negotiated the narrow trail until it disappeared.

"We have to scramble up this rock face for a few yards,'" said Dirk, "then just up there is a fissure in the mountain." He pointed up the rock face to a shadow overgrown by shrubbery.

"Let's rest for a few minutes," said Honeycomb. "It has been a long hike."

Dirk glanced at her and realized she was exhausted. "Not a problem," he said. "Tom-tom needs to climb this stretch too. I can't carry him."

He set the sleeping boy on the ground. Tom-tom opened his eyes; the cloud of slumber still surrounded him. "Sorry, buddy. Got to put you down."
Tom-tom looked about, gained his bearings and took a rose apple out of his pocked and chewed on it. They sat there on the side of the mountain for twenty minutes and watched the strips of cloud float by.

"That's better," said Honeycomb.

"You ready to go?" said Dirk to Tom-tom.

The little boy nodded, the tawny hair shook up and down for a moment then a slight smile lit his face.

"Good, then let's go. You grab on to your sister's hand and I will lead us."

He took a deep breath and started up the rock face, carefully planting his shoes on the rock lips or into the small cracks of the face as he went. He grasped tightly onto Honeycomb's left wrist and helped her pull herself up the rough wall. With her other arm she grasped Tom-tom tightly and hoisted him forward as she struggled—fortunately he was not very tall or heavy. It may have been only ten minutes, but to Dirk it seemed like an hour before he grasped the fissure lip and heaved his left leg over the edge onto the path above. He panted, his breath coming in long gasps, but finally positioned himself so most of his weight was on the path instead of the rock face.

With one mighty heave he pulled Honeycomb's left arm, shoulder and breast over the lip and onto the path. He then grabbed her under the armpits and pulled her slowly up until Tom-tom's little arms appeared over the edge.

"Can you grab him with both hands while I hold you?"

She twisted to get her left arm in position but at that moment Dirks grip slipped. He desperately grabbed onto her blouse and held tight. She squirmed and struggled and managed to hoist Tom-tom up to safety.

"Hold on! I'll get you up!" cried Dirk. He grasped her hair then her upper arm and held on tight. Her weight stabilized and although his biceps burned he refused to give in.

"If you can get any grip with your feet do so, then shove forward."

Her legs trembled and skidded but finally took hold.

"Now!" he cried and heaved with every bit of strength he had left. Her body slid upward and onto the rock shelf. They lay on their backs panting for a couple of minutes before uttering another word.

"Are you guys all right?" asked Tom-tom, dismayed.

"Yeah, we're fine, I think. Give us a moment," said Honeycomb.

When the fire in their limbs cooled Dirk stood up and offered a hand to Honeycomb. She looked up at him and smiled then shook her tawny bangs away from her eyes.

"Thanks."

They all perspired freely and Dirk wiped his forehead on his sleeve.

"Come on," he said, "I have a treat for us."

They entered the fissure and immediately the sound of crashing water boomed through the chamber.

"Wow!" exclaimed Tom-tom as he spotted the falling water at the far side of the fissure.

"How are we going to get past that?" asked Honeycomb.

"Watch!" said Dirk pleased with himself. He walked through the cascade near the right side of the opening and disappeared.

"Dirk!" cried Honeycomb.

At that moment he stepped back through, drenched yet smiling. "On the other side is a big boulder. All you gotta' do is carefully step through. It is a bit slippery, so watch it." They joined hands—Dirk, then Honeycomb and finally Tom-tom—and stepped through the sheet of falling water. It was not burdensome or heavy but sheer and light and they stepped through into the brilliant daylight.

It took them only an hour to reach the beach where the others waited. Ka Mano was the first to spot them as he rocked in his chair on the porch of his cottage.

"The fellowship is broken," he said.

"Webster and Obie left – they were never really part of our group," said Dirk.

"Then it was a good thing."

"I think so, but Aeala is in jail. He killed someone in self-defense but they stuck him in jail anyway."

"Then you must tell the others and those that love him will help you rescue him."

"Yes, but I fear Webster will reveal our location and someone will come and steal the canoe. The fumes are getting worse on the other side of the island and many may want to flee."

Miki spotted Dirk and the tawny haired girl speaking with Ka Mano and jogged over to them from the beach where she was looking for crabs and sea urchins in the tidal pools.

"Dirk! How are you?"

"I am fine!"

"Who are these?"

"This is Honeycomb and the little guy is Tom-tom."

Tom-tom frowned. "I am a big guy. But I'm pleased to meet you."

111

"Honeycomb, Tom-tom – this is Miki. She is our kahuna healer and my friend," said Dirk, "and this is Ka Mano. He cares for this area. We need to gather our friends, as I have something to say."

"Tom-tom come with me," said Miki, "help call the people together."

Tom-tom's eyes opened wide he puffed his chest out and smiled briefly. "Let's go," he said.

"I see you've made a choice," said Ka Mano.

"Choice?"

"Yes, to save Aeala, and to do something about it—that you can do something about it."

Dirk was silent. He simply looked at Honeycomb.

"She will stand by you," he continued, "as long as you keep your vision in mind."

"Vision?"

Ka Mano laughed. "Yes, the island of the Emu. The same island that Aeala calls 'Āina Le'a Nui."

"That was just a dream… I think."

"Was it? Yet both of you had it."

"How do you know so much?" asked Dirk.

The old man puffed on his pipe. The smoke rose quickly, in long streaks, and dissipated in the late afternoon breeze. "It is possible to know without seeing, possible to know without proof."

"Well, I don't know what that means, but I feel I can trust you," said Dirk.

Honeycomb nodded agreement but said nothing.

"Are you going to leave right away?" asked Ka Mano.

"Yes, as soon as I speak with the others and get something to eat. I fear that Webster has intentions to steal the canoe and worse."

"Good, I will make you all some tea and cakes before you leave."

The old man stood up and headed for the front door.

"Thank you," said Dirk.

Honeycomb spotted Miki and Tom-tom marching toward the cottage with the remainder of the canoe's crew behind them.

In the distance on the edge of the beach was the double-hulled canoe, with its tall mast set against a background of blue. The sun, low in the west, spread a silver mantle over the far water.

"Listen up everyone," called Dirk. "This is Honeycomb and the big guy over there is Tom-tom. They are friends. Aeala was attacked, but he's all right. He shot someone in self-defense but has been thrown in jail. Webster and Obie have left us. I suspect they may betray us all. I am going back to rescue Aeala, but I need some help."

"I'm in," said Sumo immediately.

"I also," said Miki.

"Me too," said Jessica.

"I need only two. Too many will just slow us down and put people unnecessarily in danger."

Jessica sensed she was going to be the one left out. "Please. I want to help!"

Ka Mano opened the cottage door and exited with a platter of small cakes and a pot of tea. He placed it on the little table next to his chair and disappeared back into the cottage. In a moment the door again opened and he appeared with several mugs.

"Let's have some tea and cakes before you decide who shall go," he said.

They sat on the porch and Ka Mano poured the steaming tea into the mugs. The dropping sound of water gurgled for a few moments as each cup was poured, until Ka Mano was done with his task. He passed the mugs around and everyone received one along with a small dark-colored cake.

"Now," he said, "it appears Dirk and Honeycomb have the most information about Aeala and the town and we should listen to what they have to say."

Dirk hesitated for a moment gathered his thoughts and chewed on his cake. "I have a plan," he said. "It may not be a good plan, but it's the best I can come up with. We need to get Aeala out of jail and get off this island. I spoke to Aeala and we agreed it was not a good idea to stay here. The place is criminal—a real thieves world. Further, there is a live volcano that is throwing up brimstone and it is poisoning everything just like what happened on Pa'ai."

He hesitated. Honeycomb spoke. "I know you all don't know me but I've lived here my whole life. What Dirk said is true. It is not safe here and if there is a chance to leave then we must take it."

"But where shall we go?" asked Kaela. "There are no other islands."

"There is one," said Dirk.

Ka Mano nodded but said nothing.

"It is for Aeala to tell you, not me. What I have to do is rescue Aeala and bring him back. I need Sumo, Miki and you Honeycomb to come with me. The rest of you stay here and make ready to leave."

"But, I want to go," said Jessica.

Dirk shook his head. "I think it's best the way that I've laid out."

"Speak with Tom-tom," said Dirk to Honeycomb. "He needs to stay here with Kaela and the others. He should be safe with them."

She nodded and walked over to Tom-tom. Dirk looked to Ka Mano for direction but the old man was stone. He sat silently in his old chair and smoked his pipe. In half an hour the four of them were ready to leave.

"We should be back by dawn," said Dirk.

With soft goodbyes they turned and headed down the trail toward the waterfall as the sun sank low in the sky. Dirk felt alert and vigorous. He thought of Ka Mano's tea and cakes and smiled.

"How you feeling?" he asked.

"Surprisingly energetic," said Honeycomb. "Must be Ka Mano's tea."

"I was thinking the same thing," said Dirk. They quickly approached the waterfall and disappeared.

Chapter 17 – JESSICA'S CHOICE

There comes a time when one must find his own way, among the shadows and the light, among the lies and the truth, among his enemies—and his friends.
The Way of the Kahuna

Long tears ran down her cheeks, and she shook with frustration. She searched for someone to blame then thought better of it; blame was not a factor. She watched as the

four of them wound their way up the trail and disappeared into the mountains.

"You feel an obligation?"

Jessica turned and through her tears nodded at the old man. He slowly exhaled and the smoke from his pipe escaped in long fingers into the evening.

"Is it more than that?"

"I think so," she said. "I feel very close to him."

The old man rocked back and forth in his chair and it made a squeaking sound on the porch. The sun touched the horizon, red and fiery, and its light lit up the ocean.

"It is a nice night to change," he said.

"What?"

"It is a nice night to change."

"What do you mean?"

"Have you not been taught all your life to obey? Obey your elders and those in charge?"

"Yes, of course, but what does that have to do...?"

"It has everything to do with you. You want to help Aeala, but you have been told to stay here. The question is: are you going to change or not? Are you going to listen and obey as you always do or are you going to help Aeala?"

"Well, I... "

"If you are going to do something then you have to be someone."

"I don't understand."

"If you are going to sail a canoe then you first have to be a sailor. If you are going to fight a war then you first have to be a soldier."

She was silent and spun the thought around in her mind comparing it to her life and views of herself. The sun sank lower on the horizon and the red draped itself further across the sky and sea. She looked and saw a young girl rise from the depths; this girl was not like her—not soft or compliant, but hardened, grim and terrible, like Joan of Arc or an archangel. The wind howled, lightning flashed, great waves crashed on dark cliffs and the earth shook, but the warrior girl did not waver. In her gray eyes, the steel of purpose, and the strength, not of rock or koa, but of bamboo: bending but never breaking, swaying but always returning to its upright position. She stared, caught in the grip of the vision.

"Are there any explosives in the canoe?"

Jessica snapped back to reality. The old man, half his face lit by the setting sun, sat staring at her.

"Yes," she said, "how did you know?"

"It is not important," he said. "You go get it and bring it here."

She sprung from the porch and ran down the beach toward the canoe. The keg of black powder was tied securely in the starboard hull covered with a canvass. She loosened it and slipped the keg from its bindings. It was not heavy and she carefully lifted it out of the canoe and carried it back to the cottage and set it on the porch.

"Have you decided?"

"To go after the others?"

"No, to help Aeala. The others will do what they will do."

"Yes! I will help in any way I can."

"Good, then you will have to be a warrior, like the person in your vision, no longer a child."

"How did you know my vision?"

"It is not important. What is important is that you rescue Aeala and that you help each other in your endeavors."

"I will be whatever it takes to save Aeala."

"Good. Then get a lighting flint and take the keg to the cave. It is behind the waterfall about a mile up the trail. You will have to go under the falls so try and keep the keg dry. Once in the cave look to your left. There will be a small tunnel. Open the keg – just a small hole. Pour some of the powder on the ground – make a trail about thirty feet long and place the keg in the tunnel. Do not let any of the powder or powder trail get wet."

"Why am I doing this?"

"When they break Aeala out of jail there will be those that will pursue you back here. If you blow the cave… "

"I understand," she said.

"Good. Then get your flint, take some water and do what you must."

She spoke briefly with Kaela and the others then started off as dusk set in.

"Remember your vision, Keep it close," said Ka Mano as she passed him.

She smiled briefly. "I will."

As she approached the waterfall she could hear it roar. It thundered with a dropping sound that echoed through the mountain. She thought of the warrior girl she had seen in the vision—the courage, the integrity she personified. Jessica wondered if she could live up to the dream embodied there. Her mission was simple, she thought: take the powder to the cave, set it up in the tunnel and leave, but would it be that simple? And after she accomplished that, then what?

The moon was nearly full. It lit the trail and cast a magical glow upon the land.

Jessica recalled the pond she went to with Miki, the one filled with mana. As she approached the waterfall she felt the same thrill—not unpleasant. She felt neither fear nor worry about the mountains or what might lie within them, although she had never been there before. Ka Mano appeared to be a man of good will, and she trusted him. His judgment seemed accurate and reasonable. If there were dangers other than what he had mentioned, he would have told her.

The pond at the bottom of the falls roiled and foamed. To the left lay the flat boulder that he had mentioned—the one she would have to use to step through the falling water. She took a deep breath, shielded the powder keg with her forest cloak and stepped through. The cold water was a momentary shock, but less uncomfortable than she had anticipated.

The cave was utterly dark, and Jessica carefully lowered the powder keg to the ground. She checked her pocket for the flint striker and found it along with the cotton balls and rags she had brought. It took her many strikes but finally the cotton balls glowed with heat from the sparks. She gently blew on the glow and it finally burst into flame. She added the rags to the mix and the flames flickered then blazed. The inside of the cave was draped in shadow, and the light from the flames danced on the cave walls like thousands of glowing butterfly wings. She searched for more fuel and found some dried leaves and twigs that had found their way into the cave floor. This she added to the fire, and it blazed brighter. The tunnel was exactly where Ka Mano had described. It was only about four feet square and extended into the wall of the cave until it disappeared in the darkness. She examined the opening and found an old tar and rag torch lying on the tunnel floor. This she put to the fire, and in a few seconds it caught and blazed into a fiery brand. Satisfied, she secured the brand, picked up the powder keg and took it over to the tunnel. On the top of the keg was a tightly fitted cork that plugged the opening. It was a small opening not more than an inch in diameter and she struck the cork with a damp rock being careful not to cause a spark. After a few strikes the cork loosened and she pried it open with a twig. Instead of making the powder trail thirty feet as Ka Mano had instructed she trailed it almost to the opening on the opposite side of the cave fissure. She then took the keg back to the tunnel and carefully set it in there with the powder trail set in such a way that there was a continuous unbroken line of powder straight into the keg.

Her work done – she heaved a deep sigh and shuffled through the fissure to its opening on the far side. The vista before her extended for miles all the way to the sea. It was dark, with the nearly full moon in the sky providing plenty of light.

She spotted a light possibly two miles down the trail and immediately understood it to be Dirk and the others. However to the east another light flickered. Was there another trail in that direction? She did not know. She stood still for a moment and watched. The light from the east was moving toward her from the low lands up the mountain. It was easily two miles away and she suspected that from Dirk's location it was obscured by thick forest. She immediately thought of Webster and his potential for evil. It was not inconceivable that he would lead a party up the mountains and through the fissure to capture their canoe—and worse. She searched the shadows for a way down from the outcrop she was on and a trail to the east. She spotted the western trail; the one Dirk and his party took, but nothing to the east. She finally decided to slide down the outcrop and take the western trail and carefully search for a turn off to the east. The slide was rough and she scraped her thigh and buttock on the way down.

With only her gourd of water and flint striker in hand she set off down the trail. It was extremely steep at first and difficult to follow in the dark but her eyes finally adjusted and she started to make some headway. It was after about a mile from the outcrop when she first saw the turn-off. The east trail was narrow and faint but it certainly was there – cut from the foothills, partially hewn from rock and the earthen hillside. She followed it to a stand of palm trees that stood like giraffes in the night against the cobalt sky. There she waited in the shadows until she saw a lantern light in the distance. Garbled voices moved toward her as her heart thumped wildly with anxiety. Was it Webster with mischief on his mind? Was it someone else that she should fear? The footsteps tapped closer and she could make out the voices.

"How far?"

"Up ahead about a mile. There is an outcrop and a cave. It goes through the mountain to the other side."

It was the voice of Webster and someone else – a stranger. Aside from the two of them two other shadows walked the trail in silence. She immediately gave ground and circled abound the stand of palms and faded into the night. She then picked up the east trail and headed back up the mountain about a quarter mile ahead of Webster and his group. Her breath came fast and in gasps as she jogged on, in an attempt to beat them to the fissure where the powder keg lay. Fear beat in her breast. If they found Kaela and the others it would be an ugly scene. None of the boys were there to protect them. Perspiration gathered in drops on her neck and slowly ran down her back. She was still wet from the waterfall and the damp of that, along with the drops of perspiration chilled her. She made it to the outcrop ahead of Webster but could see his lantern in the distance. She scrambled up the steep rock however tiny chips of the cliff and gravel along its edges stopped her ascent and she slid back to the bottom. The lantern grew closer but she could not yet detect voices. She scanned the sides of the outcrop searching for another way up. To her right were several shrubs and a stunted tree. A shadow trail disappeared into this area and out of panic more than anything else she bolted toward it. Fortunately, a rock lip not more than a foot wide wound its way up the side of the outcrop. It occasionally disappeared but there was enough foliage for her to grab onto and pull herself up. As the lantern light approached the bottom of the outcrop she pulled herself up to the fissure opening. Loose gravel rolled down the cliff with a sliding sound.

"Who goes there!"

It was Webster's voice. He held the lantern up and its light danced menacingly across the cliff.

"It's probably just a rabbit or something," said the other voice.

Jessica scrambled into the fissure no longer caring if she was discovered. It was totally black and she stumbled and fell. The thunder of falling water echoed through the fissure. She searched desperately on the ground to find something to light to illuminate her way but found nothing. Finally she stripped off her forest cloak and attempted to light it but it was still damp. Footsteps entered the far side of the fissure where she had just come from and lantern light lit the cave. With that illumination she spotted the powder trail she had so carefully laid out only an hour before but she was only about twenty feet away from the tunnel where the powder keg lay. None-the-less in her fright she struck the flint striker three times and a spark fell on the powder trail igniting it. It sizzled and sparked and began crawling in two directions – one toward and one away from the powder keg.

"Jessica! Is that you?"

She looked up into the face of steamy face of Simon Webster. He reached out to grab her but she had the presence of mind to throw her cloak at him and obscured his vision. She rushed by him only to be caught by the shadowy hands of one of the others. She screamed and bit down on the hairy arm as hard as she could. It lost its grip on her and she rushed forward stumbling twice toward the mouth of the fissure. The cool air met her as she burst out of the opening and she immediately slid down the cliff face. The sharp rock scraped her buttocks and back but she landed on her feet at the bottom and immediately took off down the steep trail. Suddenly the blast roared from the fissure propelling sharp bits of rock down the hillside and collapsing the cave. Clouds of dust billowed into the night air.

Jessica continued down the mountain trail at a fast jog for several hundred yards before slowing her pace. Her back and legs smarted from the scrapes and she was covered in dust but she continued relentlessly down the trail in pursuit of Dirk and the others.

The realization that she might have killed Webster and his party seized her like the cold hand of Satan. She had not meant to kill them only to seal the fissure and prevent them from hurting Kaela and the others back at the canoe. She resolved she could not change the past and would do whatever she could to help Aeala and her crew to survive. If they had to take great risks and leave this island to search for another she would go. She would do whatever it took to help, as these people were now her family. The moon lit her way as she scrambled along the western path after Dirk and her friends.

The night was cool and she no longer had her cloak but she kept warm by continuing to jog slowly toward her destination. It may have been just a couple of hours but it seemed like an eternity before she reached flat land and spotted the silhouette of the town far in the distance. She estimated it would take her another hour or more to reach the town and she was now exhausted from her travels. She stopped at a small brook near the road for a drink and to wash her cuts and scrapes then continued onward.

It was well after midnight when she reached the town. Only a few lights were on and she was worn out from the hike. She had no idea where Dirk and the others were, but recalled that Aeala was in jail, so she would search for the jail AFTER she had found a canoe for them to escape in. The buildings stood like shadowy nightmares on either side of her as she slipped down the road trying to stay to the shadows so no one would discover her. A dog in the distance crossed the road, perked up its ears and barked a warning to stay clear. She approached anyway, and it scampered away under an adjacent porch. The buildings ended and were replaced by small cottages. The mouth of the road as it approached the beach opened up, and more cottages along the seacoast appeared. There was trash and an assortment of twisted metal and splintered boards on the beach, remnants of the great wave that had destroyed the opposite side of the island and drifted on the tide, flotsam and jetsam, to the beach before her. To the right, a long pier jutted out into the ocean near a small warehouse. Tied to the pier were several small outrigger canoes. Only one had a mast and she headed toward it to see if it was outfitted with sail. The smell of brimstone still hung ugly and acrid in the air. The canoe contained a sail rolled neatly in it and tied with coconut fiber line. She examined it closely and decided the sail was actually of matted material and not like the one on their canoe. Hopefully it would operate just as well.

Satisfied that she had found a suitable canoe she carefully took note of her surroundings so she would be able to find it again. The little warehouse was bordered on all sides by a boardwalk that stretched toward the west and off the boardwalk was the pier.

The seacoast extended westward for about a mile then disappeared in a stand of palm trees and boulders. Rectangular shadows along the beach marked the cottages and homes of the local residents.

She turned and looked back. The street lay quiet and deserted in the moonlight. It seemed reasonable that the jail would be a separate building near the center of town. Jessica turned and headed back up the road through town in search of such a building. She expected Dirk and the others would be found near there.

After a short hike she approached the marketplace. It sat dark and empty and ominous. Small shadows scurried this way and that. As she walked closer, she realized the shadows were rats searching for any morsels the market sellers may have dropped. They were big rats with pointed faces and long whiskers. In the shadows a cat slinked by, searching for smaller prey such as mice or lizards. She quickly skirted the marketplace, not wanting to deal with the rats or any other scavengers that may be about. She came upon a row of warehouses and, farther up the street, what appeared to be a hotel. There was a single light in one of the windows and she wondered who would be up at that hour. Beyond the hotel stood a large square two-story building, which was bordered on the right by a narrow street. She hesitated at the intersection of the two streets and searched for any signs of danger. Never having been in a situation like this before, she was tense and watchful, but everything was silent and empty.

Continuing straight would soon take her out of town, so she decided to turn right and follow the narrow street. As she did so she spotted the large sign over the door of the building across the street: *The Crow's Nest*. She continued down the narrow street and stayed in the shadows. Far ahead, she thought she saw something move. It was just a dark shade and it was only for an instant but she stopped still in her tracks, hardly breathing, while her heart pounded like loud drums. Perfectly still and cloaked in darkness, she stood one minute, two minutes and more, but nothing moved. The only sound was the low moan of the sea in the distance. Finally she continued down the street, even more cautious than before.

She passed a bakery. In the window, perched on shelves, were long twisted loaves of bread. The shop was dark, but in the rear a large cake and several pans of cookies sat all shrouded in shadow. For the first time that night she thought of her stomach and food. How nice it would be to have some of that bread, she thought. Suddenly, from out of the shadows, strong hands gripped her, one on the upper arm and the other over her mouth. Raw, searing fear coursed through her spine and body like lightning in a thunderstorm.

She struggled and tried to bite the hand over her mouth, but the hands and arms that they were attached to squeezed tighter, like a giant snake crushing its quarry, trapping her in their grip.

"Jessica? Is that you?"

She looked in the eyes of her assailant and relaxed.

"Sumo?"

"Yeah, it's me. But what are you doing here?"

"I came to rescue Aeala. I spoke with the old man, Ka Mano, and he thought it was a good idea that I come. I thought so too."

"He did – huh?"

"Yeah, and he thought it a good idea that I take the black powder in the canoe and bring it to the cave behind the waterfall. And then…"

"Okay, you're here and I am glad I found you. Sorry about the scare. We're going to blow the back wall of the jail and get Aeala out. I'm here to set a charge as a decoy. We'll blow this one and when the sheriff and his deputy come to check it out we'll blow the jail and escape to the mountains."

"No you can't!" said Jessica. "I blew the cave shut. There is no longer a path through the mountains. Webster and several others were on their way through the cave and to the beach where Kaela and the others are. I figured they were going to steal the canoe and worse."

Sumo's eyes grew round and wide. "So that was the sound we heard from the mountains."

"Yes, we can't get back by going through the cave. I did find a canoe by the pier. We can escape in that and sail along the coast and meet up with Kaela and the others."

"Okay. I'm supposed to blow this charge right now, so let me do that then we'll go to the jail and tell the others."

Jessica nodded. "Where did you get the explosives?"

"Honeycomb led us through a tunnel. They were stored in there."

"I have a striker," said Jessica. "You can use it to start the powder."

She handed Sumo the striker who struck it several times until the powder trail ignited.

"Let's go!" he whispered. "Follow me!"

Jessica dashed after him down the darkened street. The blast thundered and sent a tremor across the town. Sumo had set the charge in an open area so it would not harm anyone or property. None-the-less, it rattled the doors and windows of adjacent buildings and echoed through the town. It took them only a couple of minutes to reach the jail and they ducked behind its eastern wall just as the sheriff's deputy stepped out with his gun in hand. Luckily they were not spotted. Dirk and the others crouched concealed in the shadows behind the jailhouse.

"Jessica?"

It was Dirk. "What…"

"I came to help," she said brusquely. "The cave behind the waterfall is closed – I blew it shut so Webster and others couldn't get through and steal our canoe. They were on their way there and I had no choice."

"You did that?"

"Yes. I also found a canoe by the pier that we can use to escape by sea. I'm sure Honeycomb knows the way to the pier."

"Remarkable," said Dirk.

"Well done!" Honeycomb nodded. "I know the way."

"The deputy ran down the street toward my explosion," said Sumo. "Let's blow the jail and get out of here."

"Aeala, you ready?"

"No need!" he cried through the little barred window "The deputy left the key in his office. Just come and let me out."

Dirk raced into the office, unlocked the jail door and freed Aeala. "Hurry!" he said. "The deputy may be back soon!"

"Quick! Follow me," said Honeycomb. "The pier is only a short way from here."

Jessica looked worriedly at Aeala. "You okay?"

"Yeah - just fine," he said. "How'd you get here?"

"Long story," she said. "I'll tell you when things slow down."

They headed down an alley toward the beach. It was dark and muddy. A large rat ran across their path and disappeared into the shadows.

They emerged from the alley at a crossroad; to their right a small group of natives milled about talking and searching for whatever caused the noise. Honeycomb motioned everyone back into the alley and they disappeared into the shadows.

"We'll wait till they leave" she said. "The pier is up that way past them."

Long minutes dragged by. Shadows grew long as the moon sank toward the horizon. Finally the crowd grew bored and dispersed.

"Come on!" whispered Honeycomb. "Follow me!"

They crept down the road toward the beach. The pier lay over the water quiet and still. Adjacent to it floated several canoes.

"It's the one with the mast," whispered Jessica. "There is a sail inside."

Once on the pier Sumo untied the line and the group climbed aboard. It was a long canoe and they fit comfortably inside. There were six paddles and Aeala took up the rear position in the canoe. Miki and Jessica sat near the front with the others in between.

"Everyone - push off the pier and paddle on the right side," said Aeala.

The paddles dipped in the water with a plopping sound and the canoe slowly rotated counter-clockwise.

"Okay, we're clear," said Aeala. "Sumo, you, Honeycomb and Dirk paddle to port, the rest to starboard."

The canoe slipped silently through the water, around the pier and out to sea. The surface was calm and the wind came softly from the west. They headed southeast toward a point of land that jutted out from the coast. Coconut and palm trees lined the coast and their fronds, silhouetted against the sky, swayed gently in the breeze. The plopping noise of paddles into the water was the only sound.

"We're far enough away," said Aeala, "let's raise the sail.

"Good idea," said Sumo. "I'm tired of paddling."

They untied the sail and spread it out. The straw matted sail was difficult and heavy to work with, but after a short time they had it rigged and billowing in the breeze. The canoe shot forward, reaching in the wind, and sliced through the water with ease.

"Sumo, take the boom," said Aeala.

He did so eagerly and lined the bow up with the point of land in the distance.

"Thank you all for rescuing me," said Aeala.

"No problem," said Miki, "but what do we do now? The authorities will be after us and the brimstone smell is just getting worse."

Aeala looked fondly at the crew. "We are going to leave," he said.

"To where?" asked Miki.

"'Āina Le'a Nu'i," said Aeala.

"Where?"

"'Āina Le'a Nui."

"And that is?"

"It's an island to the west of Puna."

"How far west?"

"I don't know."

There was a silence on board the canoe for a long time. Aeala immediately began to doubt his vision yet it did not diminish; instead it burned brighter. Ka Mano believed in him—believed in it. His father had once told him that to navigate skillfully one must keep his destination firmly in mind and must believe in his own ability to find his way. The only problem was he wasn't even sure there *was* an 'Āina Le'a Nui. Was it possibly just smoke? Just a hazy quirk of imagination? He had seen it only in his mind, never manifest in the physical universe.

His uncle Ko had told him that illusion made solid *was* the physical universe; that the creative impulse of the gods *was* illusion, and it was the milk upon which the universe was nourished. He decided that in order to function at all he needed to rid his mind of doubt, and this could not be accomplished by figuring, or feeling, or even seeing—It had to be done by faith, and faith alone: faith in himself, in his dream and in his crew.

He called Jessica to the rear of the canoe and when she sat and looked up into his eyes he asked her for her view of his vision, his dream of 'Āina Le'a Nui. And her answer flowed like the breeze from the west, that she had been given a choice: not whether or not to believe in 'Āina Le'a Nui, but whether or not she believed in him. And she did. The rest was mere detail.

The breeze off the island filled the sail, and the canoe glided straight and true toward its destination.

CHAPTER 18 – KA MANO – THE SHARK

Everyone has a guiding star – whether it be in the heavens or in one's heart.
The Way of the Kahuna

As they neared the point of land that they had aimed for, a shark's fin cut the water to starboard. It then disappeared, and resurfaced ahead and to port of the canoe. Aeala watched, fascinated by the animal's movements. Suddenly he realized it was not just following the canoe but leading the way.

"Sumo! Change course. Follow the shark," said Aeala.

Sumo shifted the boom and Aeala dipped his paddle in the water on the port side and used it as a rudder. The canoe responded, with the bow turning toward port. Moments later, from the starboard side of the canoe, a boiling sound become apparent. Aeala scanned the surface of the ocean and where the point of land ended he saw just above water a dark thin ridge of rock extending out into the ocean. Tiny waves splashed over the rocks creating the sound.

"Sumo! More port!" cried Aeala. He dipped his paddle deep on the port side and held it still to help rotate the canoe. The canoe responded instantly, rotating toward the left and just escaping the treacherous rocks.

"Was the shark, no?" said Sumo.

"Yeah," said Aeala. "The shark saved us. He showed us the way."

The first streaks of dawn lit the horizon, as they turned shoreward toward the tiny beach where Ka Mano's cottage stood. The double-hulled canoe, the coconut palms, Ka Mano's home and the tall mountains behind all stood out, silhouetted against an indigo sky.

"Time to lower the sail," said Aeala. He and Sumo untied the lines that connected the sail from the mast and carefully rolled it up and bound it tight with additional line. The canoe slowed in the calm waters, and they broke out the paddles again and brought her to shore near the double hulled canoe. They pulled her through the foam and sand high onto the beach. Kaela and the others had rigged a lean-to between two coconut trees and lay fast asleep on blankets laid on the ground. Ka Mano had set up a hammock on the porch of his cottage and reclined there, keeping watch over the women and little boy.

"It is good to see you back safely," he said to the group, as Aeala and his crew approached the cottage.

"It is good to see you, Ka Mano. Your wise advice was put to good use."

"Oh? — As I recall, I told you the people in the town had no mana, yet you went anyway."

Aeala laughed. "Yes, I suppose you did. Do you know anything about a guide shark—a large black and white one? It has been guiding us since we left Pa'ai."

The old man smiled. "Be glad there are such wonders in this world and that you have a friend."

"Oh, I am very grateful," said Aeala, "but you did not answer my question."

The eyes twinkled. "We are known by the same name—and we both try to look after you."

"What are you going to do now?" asked Ka Mano.

"Leave," said Aeala. "Search for 'Āina Le'a Nu'i."

"'Āina Le'a Nu'i – land of great joy," said Ka Mano. "How will you find it?"

Aeala shrugged. "Head west."

"And, what will guide you?"

"A'a – the blue star."

"And when the sky is cloudy then what will you do?"

"I will use the sea swells to guide me."

"And when the sea is calm?"

Aeala did not know what to say so said the first thing that came to mind to see what Ka Mano would say.

"I will follow the shark."

Ka Mano smiled. "And if the shark does not show up?"

"Then I will follow my dream."

Ka Mano again smiled – this time broader and his eyes sparkled.

"Then you will find 'Āina Le'a Nu'i. Watch for the birds—they will tell you when land is near. Watch for driftwood and floating plants. Watch for clouds with green bottoms—it is from the reflection of shallow water and will whisper to you that land is near. But most of all, follow the vision and believe in it, for it is the purest truth there is."

"Will you come with us, Ka Mano?" said Aeala. "The volcano is poisoning your land."

The old man smiled. "This body is old and weak. It will not survive the trip. It would be a burden to you all. It is better left here. But yes, I will go with you. Look for the black shark. I will be there for you. You are a wise man, Aeala, and a great kahuna. The task now is to demonstrate it."

He went in the cottage and returned with a white, shell-lei. It was not a long lei and the shells were not large, but on the string between the shells was a large, white pearl that gleamed even in the early dawn light.

"Do not look too deep into its depths," said Ka Mano grinning, "for you may find yourself."

"I understand," said Aeala. "It is a compass to one's heart."

The old man grinned. "You are wise."

"And the light in the west you spoke of before we left for Port Ka'au, that was 'Āina Le'a Nu'i?"

The old man nodded. "You should sleep for awhile. You have a long journey before you."

Kaela brought them all some food: dried fish, onions and lettuce from Ka Mano's garden, and sweet potatoes which they had cooked the night before. Ka Mano steeped some tea that he said would help them sleep better.

Jessica sat next to Aeala in the shade as they took their meal; the others also gathered nearby.

"We were wrong not to take you with us," said Dirk.

"Yeah," said Sumo. "We thought you would just get in the way, but you may have saved us all. What you did was very brave – and very smart."

"We won't ever again underestimate your abilities—or loyalty," said Miki.

Jessica looked at them all and smiled. Aeala hugged her. "Thank you," he said.

They slept under the shade of the coconut trees into the afternoon until the shadows grew long. When they finally awoke they washed in the stream by the waterfall, then prepared to leave.

"Miki, I have some things for you," said Ka Mano standing on his porch. She walked over to the old man, whom she had grown to like in the short time they had been there. He took her into the cottage. On the kitchen walls were rows of shelves with all sorts of bottles, jars, open coconut shells and gourds sitting on them.

"Are you a Kahuna Laau Lapaau?" she asked.

"A healer who uses herbs? Yes – and more," he said.

"My grandmother was a Kahuna Laau Lapaau," she said.

He reached into a large clay jar and brought out a handful of dried leaves.

"This is for tea," he said. "If you cannot heat the water, just crush the leaves and let them steep in water for half an hour. It will bring strength to the crew and make them feel alert."

He wrapped the dried leaves in a ti leaf and tied it into a small bundle. He emptied a coconut bowl, which contained long silver fibers and wrapped them in a ti leaf also.

"This is for coughs and nose trouble. Again crush the strands and steep them in water for half an hour and it will clear up the trouble."

Finally he handed her a gourd. "In here are powdered roots. These are for cuts and infections. Just mix with water and apply to the area. It will help the healing.

"You are the healer of your people. You must care for them; observe them carefully for they may not know they are ill. Use your skills, but apply the medicine with moderation, for the body itself has wonderful healing power. And know that the spirit first suffers before it manifests on the body, so let them confide in you. That in itself is a healing technique."

"Thank you, Ka Mano," she said.

"Believe in yourself," he said. "You have much mana—much power and wisdom—and in your hands the health and happiness of the crew rests."

"I will," she said and took her herbs.

"Oh, send in Jessica and Sumo, will you?"

When Miki stepped out the sun was low in the sky and the breeze came out of the southeast. She spotted Jessica and Sumo loading food and water into the canoe.

"Jessica! Sumo! Ka Mano wants to see you."

"I wonder what he wants?" said Sumo as the climbed the porch steps.

Jessica shrugged and knocked on the door.

"Please. Come in," he said.

"Ka Mano," said Jessica, "I had to use the powder. I blew the cave shut. You cannot use that route any more."

He chuckled. "Haven't used it in years."

He set two steaming mugs on the table. "Tea," he said. "Sit. Drink."

They did and he pulled up a third chair from an adjacent room.

"I want to talk to you about your voyage," he said, "and about Aeala and Miki. Not everyone can lead. You both did a wonderful job in rescuing Aeala and caring for the group. However, on your voyage to ʻĀina Leʻa Nuʻi, out of necessity Aeala must lead, as he has the most knowledge of the sea. Miki will care for the crew. She has knowledge in healing the body and spirit. Sumo also has knowledge of the sea but he is not as comfortable in himself, and thus Aeala will make a better leader at this time. You two, although not in the position of power must back up your leaders and secure their positions of leadership. This does not mean you are any less than they, but there are only a few positions of power, and the remainder of the team must be subordinate for the team to function smoothly.

"You will be asked to do much more than you think you are capable of. You must have faith in yourself. Your own certainty is the most important quality you possess."

Is there truly a place called ʻĀina Leʻa Nuʻi?" asked Jessica trying to find some certainty outside of herself.

Ka Mano smiled. "The people here and at your home island are doomed. Does it truly matter if there is an ʻĀina Leʻa Nuʻi? To stay is death—to leave may bring life."

Jessica's doubts vanished. "We have no choice, do we?"

Ka Mano smiled. "You are all adults now, no longer children. In your hands you hold the lives and future of your group. You will learn the ways of nature, the foibles, and the beauty. Do not ignore the lessons. They may come when you least expect them. Be aware and open to knowledge."

They both nodded. "Thank you, Ka Mano."

They left the cottage in silence pondering what was said.

"He is a person of great mana," said Jessica.

"Of what?" smiled Sumo.

"Of great mana," said Jessica. "You know, full of that which life is made of. Knowledge. Goodness. Things like that."

When they got back to the canoe the loading and lashing had just been completed. Mia was playing with Tom-tom and Miki was searching the beach for seaweed.

Honeycomb walked over to Dirk and Jessica. "What shall we do with the canoe we commandeered last night?"

"I suppose we should ask Ka Mano to return it," said Dirk

"You think that's wise? They'll think he stole it."

"I'll talk to him about it," said Dirk.

Aeala and Sumo, silhouetted against the evening sky, spoke quietly at the bow of the double-hulled canoe.

Dirk walked over to them. "When do we leave?

"Soon as the sun disappears below the horizon," said Aeala. He pointed out to sea. The sun had sunk half way below the ocean. "See the light on the horizon," he said.

"You mean the glare on the water from the sun?"

"Yeah, when the sun gets low in the sky the glare becomes narrower. See; it looks like a triangle with the base closest to us."

Dirk nodded. "And?"

"And we're going to be sailing right into the triangle – right toward the setting sun.

"It's time to set the sail and say good-by to Ka Mano."

Dirk and Sumo climbed aboard the double-hulled canoe, unwrapped the sail and started to hook it up to the mast. Aeala turned to go to Ka Mano's cottage but saw the old man walking toward him.

"Be sure you note the direction of the wind well," he said, "and the angle of the ocean swells."

"I will, Ka Mano," said Aeala. "Will you return the canoe outrigger canoe for us?"

"I know the owner," he said. "He will be glad to get it back. I will explain the need for the canoe and why it was taken. He will understand."

"Thank you, Ka Mano. Thank you for everything."

"Remember, there is life after ʻĀina Leʻa Nuʻi. Your father is somewhere out on the ocean. There will be much to do, much to care for. You must have a big dream, for only in that way will you have the energy and courage to accomplish anything. Keep the vision and the dream clearly before you. It is your personal Aʻa, your own guiding star."

They hugged and in that touch mana from the old man were bestowed to Aeala. He could feel the strength and love as it flowed through is body and through his spirit. The remainder of the crew gathered and said their good-byes, several of them teary eyed as they left. Finally all was set and Dirk, Sumo and Aeala pushed the canoe off the beach and into the water. Aeala was the last to hop aboard.

"Remember your guiding star," called Ka Mano.

His words touched Aeala and the crew, and echoed across the sea and the vault of heaven. It was only a short time later that the shark's fin rose from the deep and silently cut a path through the water in a westerly direction before them.

Chapter 19 - A LOOK BACK

There is a season when one stops looking back; a time when the past no longer has relevance; and one turns his vision to the future. It is the way of the explorer – and the Kahuna.
The Way of the Kahuna

It was not very long before Aʻa (Sirius) was visible in the night sky. The blue star twinkled in the heavens above them like a guiding angel. Aeala made mental notes of its position, aligned the starboard bow of the canoe with Aʻa, then turned his attention to the angle of the wind as it came over the starboard stern. Finally he noted the angle of the swells as they intersected the port bow of the canoe. He stood at the steering paddle and sniffed at the sea breeze. For the first time in days it was fresh and clean and soft – the way it was before the great quakes. He envisioned Pa'ai, his home island, and its location in relation to their current position. Gradually his mind wandered, and the vision emerged of a beautiful green island surrounded by sandy beaches and green ocean. He saw the way, the path from Pa'ai to Puna to the green island itself. It was nearly a straight line, all three extending west with the green island far below the horizon.

"Aeala," called Sumo.

"Yeah, what's up?"

"This is going to be a long trip, no?"

Aeala sensed this was leading up to something else, as Sumo already knew it would be long.

"Yeah, it is," he said. "Two weeks, maybe more. I think we need to separate the crew into two shifts so some of us can get some sleep."

Sumo smiled. "That's exactly what I was going to talk to you about. I think I should be the leader of the second shift."

"You do, huh? And, why is that?"

He shrugged. "Because I know more about the sea than the others."

"What about leading?"

Sumo's jaw went tight. He furrowed his eyebrows. "I can take and follow orders," he said. "I have not done anything to harm the group. I feel my judgment is good."

"Then you feel you can lead?"

They both stared. A tiny v-shaped shadow was rounding the point. They watched for a long moment.

"It's a boat," said Aeala. "Someone may be after us."

"We should tell the others," said Sumo.

"No, not yet," said Aeala. "We don't know that that's what it is. No sense in causing undue worry. The sail is at the best angle to give us speed and Puna will soon be below the horizon.

Possibly if they are after us they will give up."

They watched closely as the shadow rounded the point and headed north up the coast.

"Maybe they didn't see us," said Sumo.

"If they are heading for Ka Mano's beach," said Aeala, "Webster or Obie must be with them. It is no longer in our power to influence the fate of those on Puna – not even Ka Mano's destiny. We must look ahead. Puna is no longer our concern."

Aeala again checked A'a against the starboard hull of the canoe – they were in perfect alignment. Sumo searched the water ahead of them. The fin of the shark cut the dark surface. Swells intersected the starboard hull at a slight angle, not enough to be a factor in their speed. The breeze had picked up, coming out of the southeast from behind the canoe, and created a fine chop on the ocean surface.

CHAPTER 20 – FIRE IN THE SKY

Fear is not ruler of the heart, but a cur dog in the night attempting to steal away that which is best in us.
The Way of the Kahuna

Miki sat in the rear of the port hull and watched A'a bob up and down in the heavens. She knew it was the motion of the canoe and not the star itself that made the motion, but she liked the view nonetheless. Ahead of her in the canoe was Honeycomb, slumped over and motionless.

"Are you okay?" she asked.

Honeycomb nodded faintly but said nothing. Miki reached for her medicine bag, pulled it up onto her lap and felt around for some ginger root. Her long fingers finally recognized the feel of the rough round root and she broke off a small nodule. The sweet smell of ginger burst forth from the exposed tear and scented the air for a moment before the sea breeze whiffed it away.

"Here. Take this," she said, and handed the nodule to Honeycomb.

"Thanks," she said and began to nibble on the root.

"It's spicy," she mumbled.

Miki sat in the rear of the hull and listened to the sloshing sound of the waves against the canoe. As she had nothing better to do, she paid attention to the sounds and smells of her environment: the sound of the breeze blowing across the sea, the creak of the lashings as they strained to hold the hulls to the crossbeams, the sound of the wind in the sail. At least they were dry, she thought, and in good health except for the seasickness. She dozed.

When she awoke, the nearly-full moon was rising. The direction of the wind had changed, coming now directly from the south, and she immediately recognized it. Her legs quivered as she stood, numb from her sleeping position. She rubbed them until feeling returned, then climbed onto the platform between the two hulls. Aeala stood aft on the starboard side, with the steering paddle in both hands.

"The wind's changed," she said.

"It's picking up," said Aeala.

He knew she would spot it soon enough and decided to mention it.

"We're being followed," he said.

"Where?"

He pointed toward the east. The tiny triangle on the horizon rose then disappeared below the horizon and again rose.

"Who is it?" she asked.

"Well, Webster or Obie or both are on it. They are the only ones that knew where we were. I first spotted the boat about four hours ago as it approached Ka Mano's beach."

"Do you think there are others with them?"

"Absolutely—probably with guns. But they have not gained much on us."

"Well, let's hope we can outrun and lose them."

Aeala nodded. "Let's hope so."

"Where's Sumo?"

"Sleeping. He's going to be head of the second watch come morning."

"Two shifts. Good idea."

"Yes, good idea," said Aeala with a shrug, "but as the head navigator even when I'm off watch I'll have to stay awake as much as possible."

Miki looked up at him her eyes questioning.

"I must know always where Pa'ai is. It is my orientation point. If I lose it, we're lost. I also track many stars as they rise and set. If I fall asleep for too long I could lose tract of their paths."

"How do you know where Pa'ai is?" she asked. "It has been below the horizon for over two days."

He smiled and slowly pointed toward the east. His finger hesitated and moved to the left another half inch. "It is there," he said. "I don't know how I know, but I can feel it below the horizon to the east. It's just that I'm afraid that if I fall asleep for a long stretch I will lose the location."

Miki nodded, and smiled at her friend.

They sat and watched the ocean as the canoe cut its way through the dark waters. The tiny triangle on the horizon continued to follow them, like a hound after a scent. The stars in the dome of heaven moved across the sky, some ascending, some descending and disappearing below the horizon. Aeala noted their movements. The wind picked up even further coming from the south.

"I think we need to let the others know," said Miki.

"You're right, of course. I just didn't want to worry them, but it needs to be done. I will tell them in the morning."

Miki sniffed at the wind. "There is something strange about the breeze," she said.

"Yes. There is the smell of rain," said Aeala. "A storm is on the way."

Miki turned pale. Aeala put his arm around her shoulder. "Don't worry. We'll get through it, and maybe the storm will help us lose whoever is following us. You should try and get some sleep."

"You're right. Mind if I sleep here on the platform?"

"No, not at all. I'll help you rig the lean-to."

"What happens when the storm comes? It'll blow it away?"

Aeala sniffed at the wind and gazed at the sky. "We have a few hours before the blow starts. It is not difficult to take it down."

He noted well his bearing then called Dirk over and handed the paddle to him. "Keep it close to the hull," he said.

He and Miki unwrapped the frame of the lean-to and set it up, then secured the straw mats over it and finally spread the waterproof canvas over that. The canvas had been soaked in fish oil and smelled, but it would repel water.

Miki grabbed a blanket from the starboard hull and climbed into the lean-to. It made her feel safe—like Aeala's tree house—and she soon fell asleep.

He went back to the steering paddle and relieved Dirk. He again checked A'a against the bow of the starboard hull and adjusted their course. Satisfied, he took a deep breath and said a short prayer. What was before them would be terrifying and difficult.

It was several hours later when he spotted the cloudbank as it began to move in from the south. Dark thick clouds low in the night sky advanced northward and brought the smell of rain with them. The substance of the wind changed from a cool sea breeze to an ominous wet wind, heavy with moisture. The surface of the sea turned angry as the wind whipped at the swells. It is time, thought Aeala, and called to Sumo and Dirk. They responded immediately, as if they had been awake, waiting. Jessica scrambled onto the platform from her place in the starboard hull and Miki crawled out of the lean-to and stood next to him.

"There is a storm coming," he said. "I will need you all to help with the canoe. Each must grab some line and tie one end around your waist and the other to something strong in the canoe. There are buckets and coconut shells somewhere in the hulls and I will need someone to find them and hand them out. Then some of you will need to bail if the canoe starts to fill with water."

He hesitated then continued, "I hate to say this, but if the waves get too big and the wind too strong we may have to swamp the canoe—let it float very low in the water and just hang on. This would prevent the wind and waves from capsizing the canoe. It would make it more stable against the wind and water.

"I will be holding the steering paddle steady so the canoe is at the correct angle to the waves and does not capsize. Miki and Jessica, I need you in the bow of the canoe as lookouts, one in the starboard and one in the port hull. Any extra big wave you see – cry out immediately and point in its direction. Sumo, Dirk – I need you on deck helping me with the steering paddle and sail.

The sail will have to come down when the storm really gets going, but we'll keep it up for as long as possible. Keep the others bailing with whatever they have to hand – any questions?"

They shook their heads. "Good. Let's get to it and ride this storm out."

The wind began to blow and the canoe creaked louder with the strain. Aeala was confident it was sturdy. He sensed the mana in its substance. He felt the presence of his father and his Uncle Ko in every binding and junction. Creak it might, but it would never break, for the spirit is stronger than any element, any barrier, love a tighter binding than any twine or rope. His father and Uncle and their forefathers had breathed life into this vessel and fitted it well. It would stay together; whether right-side-up or up-side-down—that was his responsibility.

The swell was steady from the horizon, but the crests of the waves were now seething with foam. The canoe pitched and rolled as it continued on its westerly course. Aeala strained at the steering paddle as the forces of the sea acted against it, trying to bend it to their turbulent will. Suddenly the sky flashed sheer white—the dark rain clouds hovered in stark contrast to the light—then all was dark again. Within seconds a loud boom rocked the canoe as if a cannonade from the heavens had been leveled at their portion of the sea. Someone from the canoe cried out in terror, but the sound was lost in the fury of the storm.

Honeycomb clutched Tom-tom tightly. His eyes flared with fear, and he trembled at the might of sky and sea. Her hair driven by the wild wind whipped toward her right shoulder, her faced exposed to the fury of the elements. Her stomach churned, wild and uncontrollable as the sea itself. Her own fear, dark and untamed, seized her like shadows from her most sinister nightmares. It raged within her, and she floundered like flotsam in a maelstrom. It was a fear like no other—unlike the fear of man or beast. It was much viler, the fear of dark elements and raging natural forces that threatened not only to kill her body, but to tear her soul to bits. Yet she hung on. Perhaps it was her little brother's need of her; perhaps just her own stubborn nature, but she clung to a small bit of herself until the maelstrom of her own fear passed. When she opened her eyes Tom-tom was still there in her arms and the huge waves dashed and dwarfed the little canoe, yet her own turbulence was silenced, and she felt she could now face whatever would come.

"Stay here!" she said to Tom-tom, "I'll be right back."

She untied her line, climbed onto the platform and saw Aeala and Sumo holding fast to the steering paddle trying to keep the canoe from overturning.

"Aeala!" she cried. "What can I do?"

Dirk was immediately by her side.

"It is time!" cried Aeala, pointing to the sail. "Take it down!"

A huge swell lifted the canoe upwards to its crest and it hung there on the top of the world for a moment. Again lightning flashed and revealed the dark mountains of water with peaks lathered by the wind. The canoe slid down the face of the wave into the trough. Honeycomb and Dirk held tight to the mast as spray swept over them like a cold relentless rain. Honeycomb clutched the sail, found the boom and held it steady. Dirk then lowered the sail using the olona lines of the running rigging. The sail itself flapped and twisted like a wounded bird but finally they were able to take it in and roll it up. Rain began to fall and in moments they were soaked through to the skin. Honeycomb shivered as she climbed back into the starboard hull and found Tom-tom curled up in a ball at the bottom of the hull.

"Are you okay?"

The little head nodded but the face did not look up from its position between the arms and knees. Suddenly the little body began to shake.

"What's wrong?" said Honeycomb, concerned.

"Nothing."

She then realized he had been sobbing but didn't want her to know. She hugged him for a moment.

"Don't worry," she whispered, "I was up there on the platform – it's not as bad as it feels down here."

He again nodded but did not lift his head.

"I'm going to stay right here with you until the storm is over," she said. Honeycomb then grabbed a gourd bowl and began bailing the rain and sea from out of the bottom of the canoe.

Mia sat in the port hull, her long black hair soaked by the rain and plastered to her face. She clutched Kako in her arms to keep him from barking and scurrying about. Her head spun from the motion of the canoe and she tried to steady herself by leaning heavily on the gunwale. She felt small and helpless in the storm and just wanted to find a safe, dry place to regain her bearings. An ache in her chest, a dark tightness, whispered that she missed her father – and although her mother had said he may have survived at sea her own hope was slowly waning. She missed her little room in the rear of the bungalow, the petite vanity and koa wood bed, the little mirror on the wall and the clutch of canvas dolls at the foot of her bed. And she missed her friends at school, sure that none had survived. For the moment she despaired, life seemed miserable, with the only good being her mother, her dog and her most unusual brother. She suspected she possessed the gift of prophesy but was reticent to communicate about it, much less develop it. Fear of wrong interpretation, fear of taking on too much, fear of being overwhelmed or assuming responsibilities far beyond her ability to cope—all of these haunted her thoughts. She had foreseen small things, things of little consequence—foul weather, a rock fall, a friend falling in love, a bounteous catch. Her friends had commented on it, but had not encouraged her to further develop it. In several instances her warnings fell on deaf and unwelcoming ears, so that her worst fear was asserting what she had soothsaid and the consequences of her pronouncements. She found it uncomfortable predicting little things, which came to pass.

Lightning flared again, but this time she caught the silhouette of a boat on a distant wave. For a moment fear coursed through her body, yet she could sense no malice from it. She stood up in the hull with Kako still clutched to her breast. Immediately she spotted Aeala staring down at her.

"It is okay, Mia," he said. "I've seen it too."

Relieved, she again sat and leaned her shoulder against the gunwale to steady herself. The wind howled and she closed her eyes to keep the elements at bay. Time, like a great flood, issued forth before her, penetrated the present and poured into the future, and the present and the future merged together as one. Chance and opportunity flowed through the present and into the future. She realized time was fluid and the future malleable, guided by the choices of men. She saw a giant pearl rise from the sea, gleaming with a soft light that lit the waters, turning them to emerald, to its left a giant bird, still as the palm trees at dawn and to its right a large shark with white belly and dark dorsal. On the horizon a small sail approached and when it drew near the pearl shimmered, dissipated and dissolved into a beautiful island with tall green mountains and gleaming beaches. On the beach stood the great bird, and in the shallows the shark. As the sail grew near Mia realized it was their canoe, *Ike Pono*, and in it the full crew.

The giant bird spoke to her: "You are *Kahuna Kaula*, the prophet, yet you hide your talent as a turtle hides its eggs in the sand."

He was familiar to her, but she could not recall where she had seen him before.

He laughed. "We met," he said, "before there was light, before there were worlds, when there were only gods. Our forms have changed, but our essences, never. You chose to leave and live with Men. But even with mortals you could not fully deny your heritage or talents."

From around its body a brilliant illumination emanated. The emanation rose up swirled in the sky and gathered into the form of a young man.

"I am Ka'ahele – the traveler. We once were alike."

Mia sensed there was much more. In his presence her fears, like a falling star, flared then burned to dust. In his presence there was only certainty, pure and innocent, unadulterated by Man or element. She breathed in his essence and was soothed.

"I will deny my insight no more," she said, "and endeavor to take my place among my people."

"And some day, when you shed the garments of this universe, we will meet again," said Ka'ahele.

Mia opened her eyes and again saw the storm. Lightning again flared hot and silver in the night sky, but she was no longer afraid. Where her fear had been, only the calm of certainty remained. She looked past the lightning, past the thick cloud cover, past the turbulence of wind and wave, and saw the edge of the storm and the calm beyond. She looked skyward and saw A'a, the guiding star, shining blue and bright in the heavens above. Thunder boomed, and her focus was again back in the canoe. But the storm was different, more familiar, less turbulent.

CHAPTER 21 - AEALA'S WAY

The noblest knowledge there is, is knowledge of the heart.

The Way of the Kahuna

Mia crawled onto the deck between the hulls. The waves, although still large, were no longer windblown or choppy. The sky was empty and quiet. She spotted Aeala near the rear of the craft, steering paddle between his arms and a frown on his face. As she rose and walked over to him he smiled.

"I think the worst is over," he said, "but we're lost. I cannot see the stars and I lost track of the angle of the swells due to the storm."

She went to him and embraced him but it was not the embrace of a young frightened girl but an equal filled with love.

"No, you're not. You must do as Ka Mano said. You can see without your eyes and find your way without the stars."

He hesitated, stared at her for a long moment as if seeing her for the first time.

"You are right, of course, but I still doubt."

"You have senses other than sight and touch," she said. "You have used them before; do so again."

So as not to pressure him further she turned and walked to the lean-to which had recently been re-attached after the storm and where Miki and some of the others were sleeping, and laid down under its canopy. Every so often she peeked out at him but he did not move. Instead, he stood alone amongst the elements like a great banyan tree, impervious to time and space and the elements themselves. She drifted off to sleep secure in her knowledge that he would find the way.

There is a moment when a child becomes an adult and realizes the metamorphosis, and there is a moment when a mortal realizes his place amongst the gods.—Mia had accomplished both that night, and slept soundly.

Aeala's mind expanded across space and time as if it were fluid, and when he looked about the sky was clear. A'a burned bright in the heavens along with other familiar stars. Clouds blanketed the ocean below, but Aeala saw through them as if they were gossamer. Directly beneath A'a was the canoe Aeala had named *Ike Pono*, and to the west below the horizon lay 'Āina Le'a Nu'i, its pearly light a beacon in the night. He did not know why it glowed then realized the moon had dipped below the horizon. Its light was what illuminated the island. The ocean night was beautiful from above, still and quiet and serene. For the first time in his life he realized what real freedom was, not only freedom from the elements, but also from the body itself. It lasted for only an instant, but long enough for Aeala to regain his bearings and certainty. The next moment he was back on board *Ike Pono*, hands on the steering paddle and the smell of salt air in his nostrils. The wind was out of the southeast and he checked the sail to ensure it was full. He moved the steering paddle slightly as *Ike Pono* ascended a tall wave. The canoe responded by rotating port. Aeala watched as the starboard hull shifted. Confidence permeated his being and he held the course, now certain of his way.

Dawn came softly, cool and overcast, the swells, still large, marched in straight lines from the horizon. Jessica was the first to wake, her clothes still damp from the storm. She noticed Kako lying in the bow of the canoe, eyes open. She reached for a can of fish to give to him. She recalled the sweet pastries served to her in the cafes of Paris before she came to the South Pacific, and smiled. What she would give to have one now! She dug out the contents of the can and placed it on a ti leaf then gently awoke the little dog. He gratefully gobbled up the food and licked her outstretched hand. She peeked over the gunwale of the hull. Aeala was still on deck with the steering paddle in his arms and she realized he had been there all night. She grabbed a water gourd and some dried fruit then crawled up on deck.

He stood highlighted against the sea and sky, as one, not of Man, but of Mana—*her* A'a, her guiding star, in this fierce realm of wind and water.

"Aeala. Here, have something to eat."

"Thanks," he said. He smiled at her.

"You look different," she said.

"How so?" he asked.

"I don't know," she said, puzzled. "Perhaps... I don't know. Different."

There was light about him, warmth that extended out and surrounded the whole canoe, strength without effort, purpose without reservation, but she did not know how to express it.

He looked into her eyes. "It is different now—I *know*."

"I'm not sure I understand," she said.

"Knowing is different now," he said. "Before I needed to prove to myself that I knew. I had to see, or feel, or hear or refer to something to be certain. I had to observe the stars to know our position, I had to hear your voice or see you to know you were near, but I don't need that any more."

She was taken aback for a moment by his words and aura. She needed the assurance and hope, for hers was exhausted, yet she didn't fully comprehend. He could see this in her eyes, and continued: "Our uncle Ko said that we were once of the gods and that each had a part in the creation of the world. In order to take part in this contest of life we had to forget that we were the authors of everything, and we did, but every once in a while we are reminded that we can simply know, without having to refer to anything as proof. He called it intuition or faith; my father called it *na'au*, knowledge of the heart. Do you understand?"

She nodded. Cool relief washed over her. Her body tingled for a moment as she looked out toward the horizon. Everything was sharp and bright; more real, more defined than it had ever been.

"Yes," she said, "I understand. And I feel it, too!"

He nodded. "I know that I am part of the creator and it is my task to attempt to live up to this—I don't know exactly how to say it—live up to the highest godliness I can."

At that moment she felt very close to him and close to everything about her—the sky, the sea, the canoe and the others. It was as if she were a part of it all and could sense the essence of everything about her. She understood the sea, cold and deep and very ancient, and the essence of Aeala, his goodness and his serenity. In some profound, mysterious way she knew these things, knew they were true, and had no need of explanation.

For his part, he plumbed the depths of the waters, sensing its energy and character. He was the fish and the sharks and the sea urchins and the sand below. He was the clouds in the heavens and the wind from the south. He knew their, oh, so ancient history and energy and character. It may have been an hour or just a few moments but he stood there on the deck of *Ike Pono* and was the essence of everything about him. He yearned to lead his life the way he felt at this moment, clear, pure, certain and powerful. He had approached this state before, felt its ecstasy, and tried to hold on, but it like the rainbow it vanished shortly after arriving, lingering only for a brief time, crisp and bright.

The crew stirred, still exhausted from a long cold night. "I'll take the steering paddle," said Sumo. "You eat and get some rest."

Aeala smiled and turned the paddle over to Sumo. Honeycomb stretched and crawled out from under the lean-to. Dirk peered over the port gunwale, sleep hovering on his brow.

They fetched large gourds, tied line around them and threw them overboard to catch some water to wash with. It was cold but refreshing, and although they had not slept well they felt alert, glad to be alive after the violence of the night before.

When all of the crew was up Aeala gathered them together on the platform.

"Sumo has something he wants to tell you," he said.

Sumo stood near the rear of the platform with the steering paddle in his hands the crew in a semi circle in front of him.

"I spoke with Aeala last night …" He hesitated, then started over.

"We are going to split up the crew into two watches," he said. "I am going to be the captain of one and Aeala the other. On my watch there will be Miki, my mother, Dirk, Honeycomb, Tom-tom and Emily. On Aeala's watch there will be the remainder of the crew. The captains will assign duties and each watch will be six hours long."

His round face broke into a shy smile. "You guys got any questions?"

There was silence then applause.

"Welcome, Captain Sumo!" smiled Miki.

Honeycomb looked at Dirk. "Glad we're on the same watch," she said.

He grinned. "Me too, but you better not get us lost!"

"Me?" she said, with mock indignation. "Never!"

He liked her smile. It was the first time he had seen her without care on her brow.

Aeala finished his breakfast then pointed out to Sumo the angle of the swell in relationship to their course and informed Sumo to wake him if the wind or swell changed.

"People on my watch – we have six free hours before we are on. Do with it as you wish but ensure you're ready to take over."

"How will we know when six hours have gone by?" asked Kaela.

"I have a watch," called Dirk. "It is 7:00 AM now – at 1:00 PM I'll let everyone know."

Aeala chuckled. He knew well by the sun and stars what time it was, but said nothing to Dirk.

CHAPTER 22 - SHADOWS FROM THE DEEP

Why do gods help man? Is it pity, or duty, or love? I think not – when they behold man they see themselves mirrored in his soul.

The Way of the Kahuna

Mia lay near the front of the deck between the hulls and stared at the sea. The sun, though it was obscured by a thick layer of clouds, yet shed its warmth all the way to the deck and helped dry her clothes. She tried to penetrate the dark surface and look into its depths, but the opaque waters blocked her view. The little canoe pitched and rolled with the tall swells and for a brief time the motion caused her mind to wander. She saw Ka Mano, the old man, as a black shark with pearly belly, a benevolent creature, yet around him swam large grey and green monsters, vicious sharks out for a kill. They surrounded him and the water erupted, frothy and crimson.

"Hey, Mia, What you doing?" It was Tom-tom looking down at her.

"I dozed off, I guess," she said.

Suddenly from the dark depths a scarred green fin cut the surface. Mia stared and below the surface swam the biggest shark she'd ever seen. She noticed its massive jaw, as it turned sideways by the starboard hull with huge jagged teeth and jet black eyes. She could feel its intent and could not bear to be anywhere in its vicinity.

"Shark!" she screamed and scrambled to her feet, grasping Tom-tom.

Aeala was the first to arrive and looked down from the deck. Its massive body circled first to the left of the starboard hull then disappeared and appeared again to the right.

"Miki! Throw me a paddle," called Aeala. He caught it in mid air and slapped the water near the shark. The whacking sound and force of the paddle did not deter the monster in the least. Aeala watched it circle then raise its head out of the water as if trying to leap onboard.

"It certainly looks evil," said Aeala to his sister.

"I had a dream just before this happened," she said, "but in my dream there were more sharks – many more."

"Stay away from the edges of the canoe – that should keep you safe," said Aeala.

"I think the dream was trying to tell me something, but it ended before it was complete."

Suddenly something jolted the canoe as if it were struck by a rock. The shark, thought Mia, she lost her balance and twisted toward the left. As she fell overboard she saw the giant beast under her, its dorsal fin scarred and ragged. She struck the shark and rolled off. It spun and dove startled by the contact.

"Grab the paddle!" screamed Aeala, extending the handle toward her.

She saw the knob and handle jutting out toward her face. The water burst near her as the shark surfaced ready to attack. She clutched the thick paddle and pulled her legs as close to the surface of the water as possible. Every muscle tense, her knees tucked to her chest, she quivered waiting for the jaws of razor-sharp teeth to snap shut on her body and tear at her flesh. Aeala heaved as hard as he could on his end of the paddle. Mia took a panicked breath expecting the brutal bite immediately. The paddle jerked furiously and she felt her arms and shoulders wrench skyward. Her legs shot out of the water and an instant later a loud snap and a burst of water as the massive jaws slammed shut, empty. She landed on the deck her lungs burning with seawater and her head spinning.

"Mia! You're bleeding!"

God no! She thought, and painfully gazed toward her legs hoping they were still there. A small patch of skin had rubbed off her outer thigh where the shark's side had scraped against it and the under-layer lay exposed – pink and bloody – but without tears gashes or gouges.

"I must have scraped against the shark's rough skin when I fell in," she gasped.

"That was close. Too close," breathed Aeala.

Mia looked up at him. "I fear Ka Mano, the old man at the beach, is dead."

"What?"

"I fear Ka Mano is dead. I saw him in my dream. I think someone killed him just moments ago, just before I fell in. I felt his spirit leave."

"I think the shark bumped the canoe and you fell in," said Aeala, "the rest…"

Her expression stopped him. "I am just glad you're okay. Miki will help you with the wound."

Aeala felt dread creep through him, afraid that his sister may have sensed the truth. He tried to feel Ka Mano's presence, but his perception was obscured by his own turbulence over what had just happened with his sister. He searched the depths but saw no sign of the shark, so he climbed back under the lean-to and fell into a fitful sleep, with shards of dreams surfacing but never completely forming. He awoke with the sun low in the western sky. He hopped up with a bound knowing his watch-crew was already on duty.

"Sumo, why didn't you wake me?"

"You needed the sleep. Besides, the seas have calmed and steering was easy."

"Has the swell angle changed at all?"

"No, we're still on course and sailing straight into the little house," said Sumo.

"Little house?"

"Yeah, you know – the glitter the sun makes on the water when it gets low in the sky."

Aeala chuckled. "You learn fast, don't you?"

"I'm the captain of the second watch. I have to." smiled Sumo.

"Give me a few minutes and I'll take over."

"Not a problem," said Sumo.

Near the aft of the deck was a small platform no more than a yard square and about four feet lower than the main deck. Aeala hopped onto it, grabbed a bucket hanging nearby, threw it into the water and pulled up a bucketful. He washed, relieved himself, and climbed back aboard.

"Ready," he said. "Is there anything else I should know about the course?"

"No, just that the seas and wind have been relaxing," said Sumo. "Your mother is standing lookout in the starboard bow and Mia in the port. Jessica is there." He gestured toward the front of the main platform where Mia had been when she fell over. "Robin and Mrs. Waha are cleaning the insides of the hulls or preparing food for the crew."

"Thank you – Sumo. It should be a good evening. You go and rest with the rest of your crew."

Aeala took the steering paddle and watched as Sumo climbed under the lean-to, exhausted, and was handed food and water by others in his crew. The sun was low in the sky and for the first time in days it was gold instead of red. He checked his bearings keeping the bow of the starboard hull in the house of the sun. He secured the steering paddle then walked up to the bow of the port hull.

"How is your leg?" he asked.

Mia looked up. "Oh, it's fine," she smiled. "Miki made a salve of aloe and honey and put it on there. Thanks again for saving me."

He smiled back. "My sister... For you, anything."

The rest of the watch was uneventful, with the moon rising in the night sky and A'a twinkling overhead. In his mind Aeala located his home island, traced his journey from there to Puna and on to their current location. It all seemed in order. They were on course as he had envisioned. He called the second watch to duty, except for Sumo whom he let sleep. When he finally turned the steering paddle over to him it was well toward midnight. The sky was alive with jewels of blue and silver and orange. Aeala slowly walked to the front of the platform and sat with his legs dangling over the edge. The bows made a soft sloshing sound as they rode high over gentle swells.

"Mind if I sit?"

Aeala looked up. It was Jessica. "No not at all." He smiled.

She sat with a cloak about her shoulders and the moonlight highlighting the right side of her face. How beautiful she looked, he thought, even with windblown hair and sunburn.

"It's so different tonight," she said, "so calm and beautiful."

"The sea has many moods," he whispered, as if not wanting the sea itself to hear.

"I was so afraid when Mia fell in today," she said.

He looked in her eyes and saw the softness and caring in them. It was such a change from the snooty girl that sat in front of him at the school a few days ago. Then again, they had all changed. They had come together with a single vision driving them onward.

"Look," he said and pointed to the water. The surface was a mirror of the sky above, with shards of light twinkling on the surface. Impulsively he leaned over and kissed her on the cheek. She turned her head and they touched noses for a moment. He gently put his hand on the small of her back and they embraced. Magic flittered about their bodies and spiraled upward into the heavens. Sumo at the steering paddle and Mia under the lean-to saw their silhouettes and smile.

The voyage continued day after day, with the wind coming at first from the south then from the northeast. The swells slid long and smooth under the canoe, low rooster tails jetting from behind the double hulls. Aeala was glad for the fair weather. The crew grew restless as the days wore on and Aeala and Sumo had to think up things for them to do on watch.

One of the chores was tending to fishing lines, which they threw off the sterns of both hulls baited with dried fish or the catch from the day before. Most of the catch were not longer than a foot, but the fresh fish made a welcome supplement to their diet. Miki and Kaela built a small barbecue out of a metal can and cooked the fish using wood from boxes they had brought along. The hot meals raised everyone's spirits.

On the tenth day as Mia stood lookout on the port bow she spotted the sandy hillock on the horizon. "Aeala – its land!" she cried, pointing toward the northwestern horizon.

Aeala at the helm gazed in that direction, but the glare on the water obscured his view. Finally he spotted the shadow and rise of the land on the horizon. The crew, all went to the starboard side to see, and Aeala had to tell them to move as the canoe listed from the weight. The wind was brisk and the sail full, so that it took only a few hours to make landfall.

It was a low island with sand dunes and coconut trees. There were several low hills draped in shrubbery and a small green lagoon. A spring bubbled from a gully in the hillocks and meandered slowly to the sea.

"This is perfect!" cried Honeycomb.

"The sky is clear and the air fresh," said Dirk with a smile.

Aeala looked at them. For the first time on the trip they were calm – the concern on their brows gone.

Mia walked over to him from the front of the deck, concerned.

"This is not 'Āina Le'a Nui," she whispered.

"I know," he said.

"Then you have to tell the crew," she said. "They think we have arrived."

He looked at her and nodded. "Let them enjoy this for a little while."

"Their hopes are soaring. Look at them. When you tell them the truth it'll crush them."

"I can almost see their minds," he said, "their hopes and dreams. These are strong people. These are good people. The truth cannot crush them. It will uplift them."

"Tell them soon," she said, "before they get accustomed to the comforts."

He nodded, but said nothing. He knew she had a gift, the ability to see into time and space and the souls of others, but he also trusted his own judgment.

They pulled the canoe onto a smooth sandy beach that gently sloped upward and culminated in a row of low hills. The crew jumped joyfully into the shallows and pulled the canoe onto the beach. Tom-tom squealed and splashed water on his sister. She picked him out of the water laughing and threw him a short distance where he splashed down in delight. Sumo jogged up the beach to the little creek and jumped into the fresh water. It was clean and cool, a pleasant relief as he washed the salt off his sunburned body and drank deeply of its sweet water.

Miki also sensed this was not their final destination, but she was glad to set foot on land again. She liked the soft sand and low-lying dunes, but she felt a sense of incompleteness about the place: a slight disappointment. If they were to start a new life, this was not the place. It could not support a large population; there was not enough food or land.

She dug her toes into the soft sand and wondered where she would find the courage to go on. It had been an arduous ten days. The violent storm had thoroughly frightened her and she had no idea how much further they had to go.

A flock of sea birds flushed from the shrubs on a low-lying dune, their wings and chocolate breasts wide and heavy in the morning sky. They were a species unfamiliar to her. She searched the beach for anything that may be of use and found pieces of smooth driftwood. She wondered how long they had been sitting there, for they were pearly white bleached by the sun. She came upon an empty conch shell half buried in the sand, its interior smooth and pink. There had been many of these on her home island and she knew the soft fleshy foot would make a tasty meal.

"Aeala," she called, "look!" She raised the conch shell as if it were a prize. He walked over to her and examined the piece then smiled.

"We'll go diving later and see if we can find any live ones."

"Aeala… I don't want to put a damper on our good fortune, but I don't think this is 'Āina Le'a Nu'i."

Aeala chuckled. "You're right, but we'll stay here a day or so before we sail on."

Miki smiled. It was not just she who sensed their voyage was not over.

"Look, driftwood! We can build a big fire tonight and have a hot meal!"

"Yes, and I spotted some crayfish and some bird's nests too," he said.

They unloaded canvas and blankets from the canoe and set up camp in the saddle between two sand dunes, which afforded protection from the wind. It was only a few yards from the creek and therefore no long journey for fresh water was needed. Aeala and

Sumo went diving for conch and crayfish while Miki and Jessica searched the coast for roots and wild vegetables.

Honeycomb and Dirk circled the island in the opposite direction, leaving Tom-tom to swim and play on the beach with Kaela and the other women. On their journey they came across green coconuts lying in the sand under trees.

"Must have been blown down by the storm," said Honeycomb.

"Why do you say that?" asked Dirk.

"Well, the green ones don't fall unless they're blown down - usually they dry up, turn gray then fall."

"You know a lot about this kind of stuff, don't you?" said Dirk.

Honeycomb shrugged. Her tawny hair bounced about and she smiled.

"I've lived on the islands all my life. I was not always a barmaid. I lived with my father on the seacoast for many years. He took me to sea often, and I learned the ways of nature."

"I didn't mean to imply you were *just* a barmaid," he said, embarrassed.

Honeycomb chuckled. "Don't be so self-conscious. I know you didn't mean that."

They continued down the beach until they came across a round globe lying in the sand.

"What is that?" said Dirk.

"I'm not sure," she replied. It looks like a round glass ball." The object was light blue and Honeycomb picked it up and examined it carefully. Netting surrounded it and there were tiny bubbles in the glass itself.

"It looks like some kind of fishing float," said Honeycomb. "The glass ball is used to buoy the net – let's keep it." She dusted off the sand and placed it in her shoulder bag. They continued down the beach and found several more of the globes—some blue, some green in varying sizes. They kept them all, figuring they could put them to some use in the future.

It was not a big island—less than three miles in circumference—and after an hour they met up with Miki and Jessica. The girls had a bag full of wild lettuce and edible roots. They looked rather pleased with themselves.

"I see you've collected coconuts," said Miki.

"That and these," said Honeycomb opening her bag to display the glass globes.

"Wow!" said Miki, surprised. "What are they?"

"We think they're floats from a net."

"And they were washed up on the shore?"

"Yeah, that's where we found them."

"Well, I'm sure we can put them to use," said Miki. "They're beautiful!"

The four of them walked back to the canoe together.

"It's not a very big island," said Honeycomb.

"This is not 'Āina Le'a Nu'i," said Miki.

"It's not?" Honeycomb looked wide-eyed and dismayed.

"No," said Miki matter-of-factly.

"How do you know?" continued Honeycomb.

"I've seen 'Āina Le'a Nu'i in my visions," said Miki. "This is not it."

"Does Aeala realize this?" asked Dirk.

161

Miki nodded. "I asked him about it when we landed. He also knew this was not our destination. He just didn't have the heart to tell everyone that first moment when we arrived."

"Well, I was thinking this island was kinda' small for all of us," said Dirk. "Can't say I'm looking forward to more time at sea, though."

Jessica and Honeycomb nodded. "It has been a long trip," admitted Jessica.

"Don't worry," said Miki. "Where we're going is not far, and Aeala knows the way."

"Does he?" muttered Honeycomb under her breath.

"Of course he does," said Miki. "Besides, Ka Mano told him how to get there."

She was not totally certain about her last claim but it seemed Aeala and Ka Mano had discussed it—or had they? She tried to put her own doubts behind her, but the whispers wouldn't sleep. The only thing she was truly certain of was her own vision, and that she would have to lean on.

When they returned to the canoe, Sumo and Aeala had not returned. Kaela and the others had strung a rope between two coconut trees and laid a canvas over it to create a lean-to. Jessica and Miki again wandered down the beach collecting driftwood as they went.

"Once we get to 'Āina Le'a Nu'i what will we do?" asked Jessica.

"We'll have to build houses and grow enough food to feed ourselves."

"How will we do that? We did not bring any seed."

"We'll find a way. There'll be native plants on the island. We can collect enough of them to cultivate. My mother, Kaela and Mrs. Ka know how to weave reeds into mats and rope. They know how to make clothes from tree bark. We'll do just fine."

Jessica appreciated Miki's optimism; it made her feel hopeful. "This is all unfamiliar to me," she said. "All of our clothes were made in factories. All we had to do was purchase them. Things were always provided; we never had to make them ourselves."

Miki nodded. "I understand, but we have to do what we have to do to survive. I suppose there will come a day when we meet up with a merchant ship—you'll have to make a choice then."

"What do you mean?" asked Jessica.

"Well, if a ship finds us you may want to go with them back to your original home. You know, go with your own kind."

"My kind? You and Aeala and Sumo and the crew are my kind.—You're my friends."

"I'm sorry," said Miki, "I just meant that given the opportunity you may want to return to your original home and, well, we wouldn't try to stop you."

Jessica fell silent as she contemplated the import of Miki's words. The great waves had wiped out her family and friends and left her an orphan; in fact, her whole way of life had been destroyed. The only *family* she had left was the crew. A tear rolled down her cheek and she brushed it away into the wind.

"I'm sorry," repeated Miki. "I just meant that your background was different than ours and we don't have the right to determine your future or decide things for you. Only you have that right."

The sun sank low in the sky. Blue turned to peach and gold, and the shadows of the coconut trees grew long on the dunes. Jessica and Miki had returned several times to camp with armloads of driftwood, which they deposited in a pile by the lean-to. They then took a dip in the creek to wash the salt and perspiration off.

Aeala and Sumo returned with bags of conch and crayfish, and roasted them on the fire. Sparks and flames rose high in the night sky, casting flickering shadows against the lean-to and sand.

"Let it cool for a few minutes," said Aeala to Jessica, as he handed her a plank of driftwood with wild lettuce and roasted crayfish on it.

"Thanks," she said, "it smells good!"

"It tastes like shrimp," he said. "You'll like it. The conch is almost ready – I'll give you a piece when it's done."

"I've never had this before," she said, delighted.

He sat down next to her on her straw mat and threw a blanket over her shoulders. Her face gleamed in the firelight and he thought how beautiful she was, despite these rough and wild conditions.

"Miki told us that this is not 'Āina Le'a Nu'i," she whispered.

Aeala quickly glanced at her. "She did, did she? And, what do you think about that?"

"I am weary of sailing, but this island is very small."

Aeala hesitated. "I should tell the whole crew. They have a right to know—but thanks for bringing it up."

"You can trust us," she said. "We believe in you."

"Thank you," he said in a soft voice.

"Do you consider me a foreigner?" she asked.

"A foreigner?"

"Yes, you know—different from you and Miki and Sumo."

Again he hesitated, spinning the thought in his mind. "I consider you my friend. You risked your life to save mine. That binds us. Not that it burdens you. On the contrary, it tends to free, for you will always have a friend to lean on. I feel you will always be a part of me, no matter where you are, no matter where you go."

Relief washed over her and she felt he was as close to family as one could be. It was a good feeling, a safe and secure feeling, in a wide and perilous world.

The moon rose in the heavens with strands of clouds crossing its width. Aeala sniffed at the breeze; there was rain in the air.

"We may get wet tonight," he said brushing himself off. "I'm going to collect some coconut fronds and lay them against the lean-to."

Sumo, Jessica and Miki helped him. Within an hour they had collected a pile of the fronds and laid them against the lean-to to keep wind and moisture out. They then bundled up in their hovel and fell asleep to the rhythm of the surf on the sand. It was early morning and still dark when Aeala awoke to the drum of rain on the makeshift roof. Cool mist, carried by the breeze, settled on his face and he brushed it away with his blanket. Jessica lay at his feet, her long hair draped about the mat. He thought of waking her to listen to the rain, but then thought better of it. The soft drumming of rain was like a song, low and melodious, the beat of many faraway drums. Gently, he drifted back to sleep.

He awoke shortly after dawn and looked out of the lean-to. It was still raining—a slow misty drizzle that silently settled over the island, enclosing everything in a blanket of silvery gray. He threw off his blankets and stepped outside. A cool breeze blew from the northeast and swayed the coconut fronds high up in the trees. He walked down to the canoe and checked out the hulls. There was much rainwater in them and he climbed aboard, grabbed a bucket and began bailing. He was just about done with the starboard hull when Sumo poked his head over the gunwale.

"Hey, Aeala – it's still raining. Why are you bailing – just going to flood again."

"Well – I think the rain is just about gone and it'll be fine in another hour or so."

"Oh, okay. I'll help bail. Let me get in the port hull."

Sumo disappeared for a moment then reappeared on the far side of the canoe. Soon water was flying out of the port hull and onto the wet sand below. Sumo worked fast, and when Aeala was done on the starboard side they finished the other together. Within the hour the hulls were reasonably dry and the rain ceased. They climbed off the canoe and waded in the foam that the surf threw up on the beach. The gentle murmur that the sea makes when the surf ebbs and flow whispered across the dunes.

"Hey, looked," cried Sumo. He pointed toward the eastern horizon.

Aeala looked up. For a moment the sea and sky were one, steel gray and misty. Slowly the line of the horizon took form; and on the edge was a small dark shadow.

"It's the ship that's been following us," said Sumo.

"I thought we'd lost it in the storm," said Aeala. "Let's get the crew up. We need to get out of here."

"They certainly are persistent," said Sumo. "It just seems odd that they would care that much about 'bringing us to justice.'"

"You mean bringing *me* to justice," said Aeala.

"Don't forget we 'stole' the boat—and broke you out of jail too," said Sumo.

"Yes, but it still seems rather strange that they would follow us into unexplored waters—especially since both Webster and Obie know that we've never been beyond Puna."

Sumo shrugged. "Perhaps they have more faith in you as a navigator than we realize."

"We may have to fight them," said Aeala. "I hate to think of it, but if they try to harm the crew... we may have to."

Sumo nodded. "We have one pistol and the machete. If need be we can make some spears. I will collect some rocks here and try to make spear heads."

"I think rocks are rather scarce on this island," said Aeala, "but check it out. And hurry—I want to sail in an hour."

"I had another thought," said Sumo, "you know those glass globes the girls found – we can crack them and glue the pieces to sticks – use them as clubs."

Sumo turned, veered off down the beach at a jog. Aeala hurried to the lean-to and woke up the crew.

Jessica awoke from a deep sleep and looked up at Aeala. She immediately sensed the urgency in his voice and shook off her sleepiness. In a few minutes she was washed and ready to go. She helped with the packing of the canoe and then drew fresh water from the creek and stored it in the jars in the rear of the canoe.

"It's serious, isn't it?" she said to Miki who was bent over stacking folded blankets in the canoe.

"Yes, I think we all assumed that boat had sunk or at least had lost our trail. But don't worry," she continued, "our canoe is faster than their boat. We'll lose them again."

"Thank you, Miki."

"For what?"

"For being so positive."

They launched within the hour with Aeala at the steering paddle and the sail billowing with a fresh wind out of the northeast. Suddenly a black fin cut the surface of the choppy water ahead of them.

"It is Ka Mano," called Mia, "here to lead us to 'Āina Le'a Nu'i!"

Jessica looked up at Aeala from the starboard hull, puzzled. He beckoned her to climb onto the platform close to him and as she did so, sunlight and a gust of wind caught her hair and rippled it like waves of grain in a field at dawn. For a moment Aeala stood there stunned by her beauty.

"Why does Mia call the black shark Ka Mano?" she asked.

Aeala turned away for a moment to break the spell. "Ka Mano means the shark. Ka Mano, the person we knew on Puna told us he could not come with us in the flesh as he was too old and would soon die. He has done so, but his spirit now resides in the shark."

"Do you really believe that?"

Aeala stared at the horizon. "Before we met the man that was Ka Mano, the black shark led us to Puna. At that time I felt it came to protect us. When we arrived at Puna, there he was in the flesh of the old man. Do you think it was just a coincidence we arrived at his cove on Puna? By his words he gave us hope, the fuel which fires great achievements."

Jessica said nothing but stared at the dark fin as it cut the surface of the water.

"He is now here to guide us to 'Āina Le'a Nu'i – and deliver us from our enemies," said Aeala. "He is now like the others—a shadow from the deep—but this one has come to help us. This I believe."

She put her hand in his and gave it a squeeze. The wind from the northeast, full of salt and mist, breathed its cool breath over the sea and whisked the little canoe onward toward its destiny.

CHAPTER 22 – 'ĀINA LE'A NU'I

One is but himself. To deny self is the path to death. To alloy ones certainty because of another's doubt is a sin equivalent to murder for it is murder of self.
The Way of the Kahuna

"Are you sure of the way?" asked Jessica. "We left after daylight and there were no stars to guide us".

For the first time since they had left the little island Aeala realized he had not used anything to direct them. Yet he was certain of their bearing.

"I know the way," he said simply. She looked at him and said nothing. His eyes were dark coals that glowed in the mist and spray and nothing as trivial as stars and tides was now needed to show him the way. The vision of 'Āina Le'a Nu'i burned brilliant in his mind and that was all he needed to guide them.

Aeala turned the steering paddle over to Sumo as the sun sank low in the sky. The watches changed with Miki and Dirk assuming their positions as lookouts on the port and starboard bows of the canoe. There was still a chop to the ocean surface from the storm that had hammered them that morning. Aeala, tired from the long watch, crawled under the lean-to and lay down. Jessica, Kaela and the others were there preparing dinner.

"You look tired," said Kaela, handing him a bowl of cold crayfish and conch.

"It's been a long day," he said. "In a few hours it will be sunset and Sumo will take some bearings. I'm sure we're headed in the right direction but it doesn't hurt to check."

He rested till sunset then checked the golden sphere as it touched the horizon. The port bow lined up perfectly with the setting sun. The swells, about three feet high, came out of the northeast with wide peaks and troughs.

"Note the angle of the swell," called Aeala to Sumo.

Sumo nodded in acknowledgement – a lone figure to the rear of the canoe.

The sky that evening was filled with low fluffy clouds; A'a peeked out between them and twinkled overhead. The dark fin of Ka Mano glided several yards ahead of the starboard bow and led the way west.

The cool wind out of the northeast dissipated late that night, replaced with a warm southerly breeze. Aeala awoke shortly after midnight and lay awake on the straw mat under the lean-to, reflecting on what Jessica had said to him. She was concerned as to how the group would interact once they arrived at their destination. Who would lead? Who would follow? Who would do what jobs and who might want to leave? Aeala had told her he would call a meeting as soon as they arrived, and work things out. For all they knew there would be others on the island, which would make their own arrival less difficult. He saw her concern, and he understood how much she wanted to fit in and make things go right. He liked that: the way she took responsibility for the crew and their future. He also understood the change in her from the time of the great waves till now, how her frame of reference had changed, how her priorities had changed. Then again, they had all changed; each taking responsibility for their share of the work and the voyage.

He stretched, stood up and walked over to Sumo. "Hey, how you doing?"

"It's good! We are moving fast and the wind has changed; it's coming out of the south."

Aeala looked about. The sail billowed in the wind and the canoe slid smoothly through the water.

"Give me a couple of minutes and I'll take over."

"No problem."

Aeala roused his crew, washed up and took over the steering paddle. He scanned the eastern horizon, that faint line between the waters and the heaven, but saw no craft pursuing them. He sighed with relief but knew they may not have lost their pursuers, who may have simply stopped for fresh water and food at the same island they had just left. He noticed Robin with Mia in the starboard bow, both scanning the western horizon and engaged in conversation.

He wondered what they were discussing, and realized how little he knew about Robin. He considered her just another foreign classmate, with different ways and ideas. A hint of shame passed through him as he realized that truly the way he looked at her was similar to the way Webster and the other foreign students had viewed the native kids. Why so much alienation, he wondered. Were people so different that they could not trust each other? Was there no common ground upon which they could stand and relate to one

171

another? He understood Webster was unique in his vitriolic temperament, but the others tended to discount the natives also. And he, Aeala, was similar but in reverse, for he was inclined to dismiss the foreigners as unaware and uninformed about the essentials of life.

And what *were* those essentials? He smiled at his own thoughts. The wind blew warm and gentle from the south, the heavens twinkled with thousands of tiny sapphires and the waters rose and fell in unhurried rhythm. He looked at his crew. These were the essentials: the living beings in his surroundings, the elements in his environment, a belief in the creator, the brotherhood between all, not just the human beings, but the brotherhood among life, the elements, the universe and the creator.

He gestured toward Robin to come near. At first she mistook the gesture, thinking it was Mia he was gesturing to. When Mia approached he smiled.

"Call Robin – will you? I want to talk to her."

"Really?" said Mia, as if this was something new and unusual, which of course it was.

"Yes will you bring her over?"

Mia gestured to Robin, who responded with puzzlement.

"What's up? Did I do something wrong?" she asked.

"No, no, not at all," said Aeala. "I just wanted to talk to you and thought this would be a good time."

Mia grinned, knowing her brother was feeling slightly uncomfortable in this situation.

"Oh, Mia," said Aeala. "Will you keep watch on the starboard bow."

Mia nodded and returned to her position in the starboard hull but kept an eye, every now and then, on them.

"How are you tonight?" asked Aeala.

"Fine," she said nervously, expecting some criticism or harsh word.

There was an awkward silence. "Well, I was seasick most of the trip but in the last few days that has gone away," she said.

"Has anyone shown you how to watch the horizon? Be a lookout?"

"Yes both Mia and Miki told me to scan the ocean at an angle. You know, use my peripheral vision and to shade my eyes when there is a glare on the ocean."

"They taught you well. Here. Take the steering paddle."

"Oh, I...I'm not sure I can."

"Of course you can. Here... take it."

Her hands were tiny, and they trembled, but she took the paddle. "Now just keep it steady," he said. "Notice the vibration as it slides through the water."

Timidly she did so then smiled. "I can feel it. It's the movement of the canoe through the water."

"That's right. The paddle echoes the movement of the canoe. It's like holding a friend's hand: you can feel his movement as he walks or coughs or... whatever."

She smiled again. "How do you know we're going in the right direction?"

He pointed to the sky. "See that star?"

"You mean the bright blue one?"

"Yes, that's it – that's A'a, our guiding star. We just follow it. As long as we're directly in alignment with it we're on course."

"Guiding star, huh? It once crossed my mind that we should have named the shark after the stars we followed."

Aeala chuckled. "Perhaps some day we will be the A'a of a new people."

"You mean the guiding star of a new civilization?"

He signed. "Yes, perhaps."

"We've all lost a lot," she said.

"Yes, I know."

"I think I understand now…" Her words choked in her throat, she did not know how to express herself. "We all had misconceptions. All us foreign students thought you guys were ignorant and worse. I realize that was not so. You have done so much for us."

"We also had… how do you call it? Misconceptions," said Aeala. "I was just thinking how mistaken I was in the way I looked at you all. But I think I understand now. Like you said, we all lost a lot and we need to help each other."

She nodded. A long tear ran down her cheek. "Thank you for asking me over. I needed to talk. I lost my dad and mom in the tidal wave. I'm still trying to deal with that plus all we've been through. It's been tough to deal with the voyage and the elements and all that. I am not familiar with it all."

"But you survived – and you've helped our crew survive also."

She nodded. "Thank you, Aeala, for your help and support."

He wanted to say more but was afraid he'd overwhelm her. She had enough to deal with as it was. "Well, I'm here if you—you know—need something."

She smiled. "Here, you better take this before I get us lost."

She handed the steering paddle back to Aeala. "I better get back to my look-out post with Mia."

Her slim form moved toward the front of the deck as if floating on vapor. Aeala felt warmth in his heart. He was glad he had talked with her, even if it was just a few words.

There was now more understanding between them, and she had left happier than when she had arrived. The night wore on, with the stars journeying across the heavens like geese in autumn.

Aeala at the steering paddle found it pleasant with the warm south wind at his shoulder and the long swells gently sweeping the canoe toward its destination.

Dawn unfolded in indigo and gold, and the watches changed with Sumo at the steering paddle and Miki standing lookout on the starboard hull. Aeala crawled under the lean-to too tired to eat, and lay staring at the ceiling. Jessica, her hair still wet from a chilly sea bath, sat down next to him and began combing out her long blonde hair. She wore a tan kapa shift with dark zig-zag markings that ran horizontally.

"Where did you get the clothes?" he asked, knowing full well whose they were.

"From your mom," she said. "She was nice enough to let me wear them after my bath. She also lent me her comb."

"I see," he said, "you look good in the shift".

Jessica smiled. "It's difficult to look good in the sun and wind."

He thought about saying that she always looked good, but decided against it as he figured it might make her feel uncomfortable.

She nibbled on some dried berries.

"Want some?"

"No thanks – I just want to get some sleep. It's been a long night."

"I know," she said. "I saw you talking with Robin. I'm glad."

"Why?"

"Well, I think she needed to know she was appreciated, and coming from you it just made it special."

"How do you know I told her that?"

"I could see it on her face after she spoke with you."

"I didn't think I had that much pull," he said.

"More than you know. We all look to you for strength."

Aeala looked up and stared into her eyes. They were soft and deep, like the sacred pool back at their home island. He kissed her on the wrist.

"I hope your faith in me is rewarded," he said. "I certainly do not intend to let anyone down."

He then noted well the canoe's heading, laid his head on his forearm and fell asleep, exhausted.

Robin finished eating. It was a hot meal of fresh fish caught the night before and seasoned with sea salt. Kaela was a good cook, but the true art was the making of the small cooking fire. Kaela had used a wooden box filled with sand from the small island they had left, and built the fire in it then roasted the fish in seaweed which she had collected from the island. This was a definite improvement from the previous tin barbecue which they had used as the sides had a tendency to overheat after prolonged use. Robin liked Kaela, her calm temperament, her caring nature and her wisdom. "He knows what to do," she would say about Aeala, whenever his actions were questioned. And she believed it, for she looked upon Aeala as a man, not a child. Robin wished her parents had considered her such, especially in the situation she was now in. She had been pampered her whole life, with servants to do all the menial tasks for her, and now she did not have any survival skills. She couldn't even make a fire. Her contributions to the crew had been bailing the canoe and keeping the supplies neat. Although no one had said anything, she felt she had contributed the least to the survival of the crew. After the talk with Aeala her spirits had lightened, and she determined to learn from the others and make herself more valuable to the group. She was aware that it would take some time and a lot of effort, but for the first time in her life she felt able to help, and that her contribution would be valuable. She had stood the last watch with Aeala and Mia and was also exhausted. Salt from the ocean spray clungto her skin and made her body feel sticky but she was too tired to wash. Instead she simply laydown on a soft bag of clothes in the port hull and fell asleep.

She awoke perspiring, with the tropical sun high in the sky. The weather had changed. It was warm on the ocean, and the wind from the south gave little relief. She grabbed one of the water gourds and splashed fresh water on her face then washed out her mouth. This done, she grabbed a towel and bucket and climbed onto the deck. Miki was at the steering paddle and Sumo nearby seated on a box.

"How is it going?" she asked.

"Good," said Miki. "We are moving fast with the wind."

"I'm going to take a sea bath," said Robin.

Miki nodded. "Good idea – the sea is calm."

Robin slipped over the rear of the deck onto the low bathing platform. She stripped off her clothes, hung them on a crossbeam, and reached down with the bucket for water.

It was cool but not cold and she was glad the sun was out while she was bathing as its warmth made the chore pleasant. When she was done she dried off her hair and wrapped the towel about her then climbed up onto the deck.

"Hey, you look fresh!"

It was Sumo. "Hi, Sumo. I need a favor from you."

"Oh?"

"I want you to teach me to navigate."

"Oh, good!" said Miki. "I can use a break."

"Why don't you get dressed and I'll show you what to do," said Sumo, his smile extra wide.

Aeala rolled over and opened his eyes. The sun was bright and he squinted until his eyes adjusted. The sun was in a position such that it was ahead of the canoe and he estimated it was late afternoon. He took a moment to observe the sail and the direction of the wind. It was still coming from the south and they were making good time. He estimated they were well over three hundred miles west of the island they had left. He scanned the sky for birds and the sea for debris but saw none – the color of the water was deep blue and thus, he concluded, they were still far from land.

He saw Robin at the steering paddle with Sumo close by. Jessica, Kaela, Mia and Mrs. Waha were still asleep under the lean-to. Jessica stirred.

"Jessica, wake the others – it is time for our watch."

She looked up and nodded. He noticed the skin on her nose was sunburned and peeling. He crawled over to the port hull and slipped over the gunwale and into the hollow. There were a number of coconuts stored astern and he grabbed one and opened it with his machete. He tried to drink the juice but in his haste most of it spilled out. With the point of the machete he dug out some of the meat and shredded it – the milky pulp he put in an empty can and took to Jessica. After she had washed up he smeared it on her nose and cheeks.

"That will help heal your nose," he said. She thanked him with a smile and went to the port bow to stand watch. He grabbed some dried fish to chew on and went to the stern to relieve Sumo.

"I'm teaching Robin to steer the canoe," said Sumo. "She got up early to learn."

"Oh, good – I'll continue the lesson."

"All yours, Captain," said Sumo.

"I'm glad you have an interest," said Aeala.

She started to turn the steering paddle over to him.

"Oh, no. You keep it. I'll give you instructions."

"Thanks," she said. "I'm enjoying this."

He checked the swell against the sun and noted the angle between the two. He decided it had changed just a bit, with the swell now coming at them from the east.

The image of his home island emerged in his mind and he instinctively pointed toward the east in its direction. He adjusted his pointing finger slightly to the north until a familiar feeling came over him. It was the feeling of home – a relaxed, calming sensation.

"What are you doing?" asked Robin.

"Pointing toward home," he said.

"How do you know that's the correct direction?" she said.

He wanted to say he saw it in his mind's eye and that he just knew but realized she wouldn't understand. "From experience," he said. Satisfied, she went back to gazing at the setting sun.

As night fell he pointed out the triangle the sun's rays made on the water and explained that *that* direction was west.

The dark fin of Ka Mano surfaced from the depths and Aeala told Robin to align the starboard hull with the fin. She did so; and as the disk of the sun began to sink below the horizon the bows of the canoe, like giant fins themselves, stood out in contrast for a few moments, silhouetted against the sky.

Jessica carefully, smoothly walked over with two steaming bowls of soup. "Fish soup. You guys hungry?"

"Thanks," said Aeala as she handed a bowl to Robin then to him.

He put his arm around her shoulder and kissed her on the top of the head. "I made it myself," she smiled, "with the help of your mom."

"It's going to be a beautiful night," he said pointing to the moon in the sky. "It has been nearly a moon month since we left our home."

"How can you tell?" asked Jessica.

"Do you remember that first night we all stayed in the tree house?"

"Yeah?"

"That night had a moon similar to this."

"I didn't notice," said Jessica, surprised he could recall such detail.

"We need to keep a close look-out the next few days—for birds, ocean debris, things like that," said Aeala.

"Are we close?"

He nodded. "There is a different character about the swells. I only noticed it an hour or so ago."

"What do you mean?"

"It's like an echo – the swells are echoing. They are bouncing off land below the horizon and a small amount of their energy is rebounding back toward us."

. . .Mia, in the port bow scanned the horizon. She too felt something had changed. She sniffed at the breeze. It still had a warm quality about it, although the sun was now below the horizon. She looked about, trying to sense the difference, but couldn't put her finger on it. She had felt this way before but couldn't get an exact recollection. She sniffed the breeze again trying to understand the disparity. Her ears tingled and her stomach felt very cold and empty. She closed her eyes for a moment hoping the sensation would pass. Instead in her mind, dark swells rose up and folded over upon themselves in a fury of foam and spray. The thunder of primeval force released, echoed. It was then she recognized the feeling. She linked it with specific incidents, the earthquake, the death of her grandfather, the old man, Ka Mano's death. It was a sense of impending danger. Slowly she returned to the real world and looked toward the rear of the canoe. The shadow of her brother, with Jessica and Robin at his side, stood silhouetted against an indigo sky. She climbed out of the port hull onto the deck and made her way toward her brother.

"Aeala, may I speak with you."

He could feel her intention and knew she had something important to say.

"Excuse me," he said to Jessica and Robin. "I will just be a moment."

They met amidships.

"Something is different," she whispered. "I sense danger near yet I am unsure of its source."

He nodded. "We are getting close to our destination, but I suspect it will take some effort to make landfall. Keep a close watch on the ocean; it may not be kind to us."

She kissed him on the cheek. "I will," she said, and headed back to her position as lookout.

"Robin, Jessica – I need you both in the starboard bow – I think we are getting close and there may be shallows. Keep a close watch on the surface. If you see any unusual movement let me know immediately."

"No problem," they answered and immediately headed forward to their lookout posts. Aeala, left alone with the steering paddle, pondered Mia's words. She had not mentioned the island, only the danger. He did not consider himself a seer, but a navigator – an ocean navigator. His sister apparently could navigate the future, but the way she delivered her warning unnerved him: "I feel danger near yet I am unsure of its source." The warning rang in his mind.

He sensed she was blind to crucial details but possessed a general perception of peril. He stared at the horizon and the dark waters about him and tried to extend his senses, but all he perceived was the moan of the wind and the sound of the sea lapping on the hulls.

It was two nights later when the roar began - softly at first like a cat's purr, nearly undetectable to the human ear but Kako the dog with his acute hearing picked it up and began barking.

"Mia, Jessica, Robin – be alert!" cried Aeala. "Kako has picked up something."

The waxing moon from behind a cloud slipped into view and cast golden glitter upon the sea. The wind was light and directly behind them coming from the east. Shadows wavered across the swells like ghosts in ones nightmares. Mia, with a lump in her stomach and her ears tingling, was the first to see the dark lines on the southwestern horizon. She stared, not quite sure of what she was looking at, and waited for it to unfold as the canoe grew closer. The purr turned to a moan, as if the sea were expending great effort and protesting all the while. The dark lines developed into mounds of shadowy water rising from the sea.

"Aeala! It's here!" she cried, scrambling out of the port hull onto the deck. The crew who had settled in for the night jumped up, startled by her cry.

"What is it, Mia? – I see nothing," said Aeala.

She pointed toward the horizon. "The sea has arisen – look! The waves out there – they're as tall as mountains!"

He stared into the night, then he saw. On the horizon, walls of water rose up as if pushed from deep down and folded in upon themselves with massive force. They crashed, spewing fury and foam upon the surface.

"I've seen it once before," said Aeala.

Mia stared at him, her eyes pleading for an answer.

"There are mounds under the sea. Some of them reach almost to the surface. When the deep ocean swells come in touch with them, the water rises high and they crash over – you know, fold in upon themselves. But these... they are gigantic!"

"We need to stay far away from it!" said Mia.

Aeala nodded. "Yes, but not so far away that we go completely off course."

"What does it matter if we go off course for a bit?" she said. "It'll topple the canoe over if we get close!"

Aeala pointed toward the moon and smiled. Mia and the others looked up into the heavens. Across the face of the moon flew a gull.

"It's a bird," he said. "I spotted it shortly after Kako started barking. It'll show us the way to land!"

They continued on their way, circumventing the giant breakers as they crashed and boomed in the distance, but soon found themselves in smaller surf; smaller, but nonetheless dangerous.

"There appear to be many shallow reefs," said Aeala. "I think it safest if we turn about and wait in deep water till morning."

"You're the *Kahuna Kilo Hoka*," said Miki. "We will do whatever you say."

"Yes, I am the navigator. But it is *our* survival, all of us; thus I consult with you all first."

The crew nodded. "We're with you," cried Dirk.

"Then untie the boom and come about," called Aeala.

"You mean turn the sail the other way?" said Robin.

Sumo and Aeala laughed. "Yeah, exactly."

They waited in deep water, Aeala at the steering paddle with the whole crew on watch each with paddles prepared to maneuver the canoe out of harms way if it approached too close. They drifted on the swells. Aeala attempted to guide the canoe with the steering paddle far away from the shallows and booming surf.

The stars moved across the dome of heaven and disappeared under the horizon. Dawn unfolded delicately from the east - indigo, violet, lilac, then rose and gold. The hazy first light revealed what they had heard the night before – giant breakers folded over on themselves trailing streaks of spray in their wake. North of the big breakers were lines of white water that foamed and roiled, indicating the presence of shallow reefs. Aeala gazed intently at the western horizon but saw no land; only the dark line between sea and sky.

He scanned the heavens and finally spotted the small dark dots he had been searching for: gulls.

Land! he thought, Land is near.

"Dirk, Jessica – help raise the sail," he called.

They immediately jumped to, and in moments the sail billowed from the mast. There was a jerk, then another, then finally the smooth sensation of wind caught in the sail, propelling them forward.

Aeala steered south and circumvented the turbulent sea, leaving it far behind. Finally he turned west again and followed that course toward a bank of thick clouds. The dark fin of Ka Mano surfaced and led them steadily toward the cloudbank.

Aeala felt relieved that Ka Mano had returned, and a warm, secure feeling enveloped him, like the arms of his father when he was small.

It was shortly thereafter that Sumo relieved him, but before turning the steering paddle over to his trusted friend, Aeala informed him of all the signs that he had observed. Less than three hours later Miki, in the port hull, peered through a break in the clouds and saw what they had been searching for. At first it appeared as a gray line on the ocean surrounded by mist, then as a dim pearly mound. She let out the cry: "Land! Land! Land!"

Aeala bolted from his sleeping mat, struck his head on the ceiling of the lean-to and rolled out onto the deck. The crew stood on the starboard side of the canoe shading their eyes and peering toward the horizon. Aeala stared in their direction saw the pearly mound mixed in with the fluffy clouds and sparkling sea. His head spun from the collision with the lean-to and he strained to get a better look. He noted that the bottoms of the clouds appeared greenish as if they reflected the color of whatever was beneath them..

"Over there," cried Miki in exhilaration and pointed north of the starboard bow.

Aeala followed the line of her finger toward the horizon and spotted a second mound rising from a cloud. This one was a misty blue and seemed to rise through the clouds as if floating on them. A rush of joy surged through his body.

"'Āina Le'a Nu'i!" he shouted.

Honeycomb and Jessica both hugged him.

"We made it!" cried Honeycomb as tears ran down her cheeks.

Mia walked over to him. "This is it, isn't it?"

"Yes," said Aeala. "This is 'Āina Le'a Nu'i."

"There is still danger," she warned. "We should not let our guards down."

Aeala nodded, although he thought his sister was being a bit too cautious. As they came closer the features of the island appeared. Tall cliffs and towering mountains draped in gray and green rose from the sea. Rain clouds shrouded the mountaintops, almost obscuring what appeared to be a bamboo forest. A peninsula jutted out from the north side of the island, and a bay, half visible from their location, waited invitingly to be explored. The sea at the mouth of the bay, instead of being deep blue like the rest of the water, was emerald, indicating a shallow bottom. The beaches were pearly, with white sand and red clay outcrops. It appeared a paradise except for a strip of white water that, as far as Aeala could discern, surrounded the entire island. He was familiar with the phenomenon – his home island of Pa'ai had a similar feature – but the portent of the white water was that shallow reefs existed just below the surface poised to rip apart the canoe and the flesh of any hapless mariner that fell overboard.

The wind blew out of the east. Aeala, with the steering paddle and sail, turned the canoe north toward the bay and looked for an opening in the reef. The whitewater was about a mile off shore. Beyond it Aeala could clearly see the land features. Dark lava rock jutted out and the sea met it in bursts of foam and spray. Two tiny beaches surrounded by coco palms and jungle awaited the strangers – on one a small stream flowed from the depths of the jungle to the sea.

"There!" pointed Sumo.

Aeala looked in that direction and saw what he was searching for: a break in the reef, an area of calm water. It was not more than fifty yards wide with breakers on either side but it appeared to be wide enough for the canoe to sail through.

"Everybody – hold on." called Aeala. "We're going through the channel and it may be rough."

"Stay close to the south side of the channel," said Mia.

"What?"

"Stay close to the south side of the channel. The current is moving in a northerly direction and will take us into the reef if you go down the middle."

Aeala was dismayed that he himself had not noticed this.

Mia smiled. "Don't worry. I am the *Kahuna Kaula*. I must know these things."

The prophet, thought Aeala. He still had difficulty conceiving his little sister as such,

yet she had been right in every instance since her encounter with the green shark when

she had fallen overboard. He had a difficult time conceiving of any of them being

kahunas, as the title spoke of great wisdom and years of training. But, out of necessity,

they each had to assume the duties; for they were the only ones—the last kahunas.

He turned the canoe about and headed north toward the channel. The wind picked up

and the sail billowed forth like a giant winged bird. It was as if the canoe rose out of the

water and skimmed the surface. The hulls whined as they cut through the water. The dark

fin of Ka Mano surfaced ahead of them and sped through the channel into the calm water

shoreward. Aeala on the steering paddle approached the left side of the channel. He

watched the foam and spray surge as the strong current caught the canoe in its line of

force and propelled it forward toward the reef. The water seethed from rock and coral just

inches below the surface. Suddenly it was no longer the channel or the fierce current

Aeala was responding to but the spirit and power and skill of hundreds of ancient *Kahuna*

Kilo Hoku each with the special talents of the navigator, each with the intuition and will

to find their way, to navigate through calm and storm and dire elements, to command

oneself and one's crew through any crisis be it on sea or land or in life itself. The Foam

and spray exploded about him, a wave lifted *Ike Pono* and dropped the bow nearly

capsizing it. The current caught the stern and swept it to port. Without thinking Aeala

stepped to his right and plunged the steering paddle deep into the water off the starboard

hull, held the flat of the paddle perpendicular to the hull and shouldered the force of the current as it strained to dislodge the angle of the paddle. It was more than his own strength that held the paddle that instant, but the strength of all the brave mariners that had ever ventured out into the unknown and through the power of spirit alone conquered the sea. *Ike Pono* came alive, swung back into the channel, but suddenly the steering paddle snapped with a sharp crack, jagged rocks and coral only feet from the port hull. Aleala's heart sank in horror envisioning *Ike Pono* crashing into the rocks and breaking up. He watched helpless as the port hull neared the churning water. But the canoe had already been set in motion by Aeala's actions, already in a turning mode, already revolving toward starboard It continued to rotate as if pushed by an invisible hand. A small wave rebounding from the under water reef caught the stern and propelled into the bay. Aeala went limp stunned by this stroke of good fortune.

"Sumo! Grab me a paddle!" cried Aeala. "The steering paddle…" He lifted the handle of the fractured paddle in the air.

Sumo disappeared into the starboard hull for a moment then two paddles flew from the lip of the canoe where he had disappeared and clattered onto the deck in front of Aeala.

"Perfect!" Aeala shouted.

Sumo's head popped out of the hull with a big grin on his face. "That was some sailing you just did!"

Aeala was glad someone appreciated it although he knew it wasn't *only* him that had a hand in the maneuver. They glided into the mouth of the bay, the water green under them, and discovered a pearly-sand beach that stretched for about a quarter of a mile. Near the far end a stream, wide and gurgling, met the sea.

"Sumo, Dirk! Get some paddles and help us in," called Aeala.

They turned to, and in a brief time the canoe approached the pearly beach. A gentle jerk as the bows of the canoe met sand heralded the end of their voyage.

Tom-tom was the first over the side, and let out squeals of joy as he waded to shore. Kako barked with excitement as the others slowly disembarked and waded in. Aeala was the last over the side and slid into the water up to his waist. The water was cool and pleasant and although the sky was cloudy over the island the air was still pleasantly warm. He pushed and shoved the rear of the canoe forward as Sumo and Dirk pulled on the bow-lines. The hulls slid smoothly onto the beach and sank in the sand.

"Come on – let's do a little exploring," said Miki.

"Okay, but lets stay together," said Aeala.

They headed south on the beach where a rocky promontory loomed before them. It was composed of jagged basalt from an ancient lava flow that descended from a tall mountain to their right. The promontory was wrapped in green with boulders and dark outcrops of the volcanic rock protruding through the tangled groundcover. The mountain was entwined with long strands of gray clouds that wrapped around and through its peaks. Stands of pine and hardwood dotted the ridge and face of the mountain.

"Look!" cried Mia, pointing toward the upper beach near a grouping of shrubs and tall grass. Animal droppings littered the damp earth and nearby, large footprints pockmarked the sand. She carefully observed the features of the print – three pointed toes and a rounded heel. The prints were sunk deep in the sand indicating the animal that they belonged to was heavy.

"Bird prints," said Aeala staring intently, "big bird prints! I think there are emus here!"

"Emus?" said Mia.

"Yeah. Moko, a man we met on Puna, told us about them. He had a few near his home. He said they were brought there by a sailor from an island far off—probably this island."

"They are big and run on two feet," said Mia.

"You know of them?"

"I saw one in a dream," said Mia. "They are a good sign."

Aeala nodded. "Come on. Let's see what else is around here."

"There appears to be a faint trail up there," said Miki, pointing to the base of the promontory.

"Trail? How could that be?" said Honeycomb.

"Perhaps we are not the only ones here," said Miki.

"Or whoever was here before has left," said Aeala.

They continued around the base of the promontory, carefully following the rudimentary trail until they rounded a high wall of basalt. Another bay opened up in front of them.

This one was smaller than the one they had just left, but its waters were green and translucent. They descended to the foot of the promontory, the trail winding down to the beach below, and traversed the beach. On the far side the faint trail, overgrown with ferns and low-lying shrubs, disappeared into the jungle beyond.

"Let's follow it," said Mia staring up at her brother with intent eyes.

He considered her suggestion and countenance. "Do you sense something?"

She shrugged. "I felt an urge to follow."

"Well, we do have time – the sun is not yet high. What do the rest of you think?"

"Sure! Sure! Why not?"

They turned toward the jungle and headed inland. The verdant canopy bristled with life. Colorful birds chirped and whistled, squirrel-like animals scampered through the branches and flying insects buzzed about in the shadows. The forest was damp and steamy, and dripped moisture from its trees and giant ferns. Just as Aeala decided entering this tangle of vegetation was not such a great idea, Mia turned to him and pointed toward a break in the undergrowth.

"There!"

Aeala peered through the shadows and vines. A large opening in the jungle loomed in the distance. He smiled at his sister.

"You were right," he said. "Let's go check it out."

They slogged down the damp trail with Aeala in the lead swinging his machete to and fro clearing the trail as they went. The clearing was wide encompassing many acres. The grass in the area grew low, less than knee high, and in the center of the clearing stood an ancient city enveloped in vines and moss. Layers of mist suspended in the damp air shrouded its walls and towers.

'It's ancient!" said Mia. "Can you feel the mana?" Her voice was a whisper, her face lit with awe. Wide stone steps swept upward to the first floor which was surrounded by a low wall, its sides adorned with carved stone animals – jaguars, parrots, turtles, and sharks.

"It looks like a temple," said Aeala, "or a palace."

Tom-tom squealed with excitement and headed toward the steps at a run with Kako barking at his heels.

"Stop! Stop!" cried Honeycomb. "It may be dangerous up there!"

Her voice rang across the clearing like a church bell through streets and alleys. Tom-tom pulled up at the steps to the structure and looked back. Honeycomb ran ahead of the others to catch up to him.

"Let's wait for the others," she said, "it may be dangerous to enter alone."

"I'm sorry," he said. "I just got so excited."

The others caught up, and with Aeala and Sumo in the lead they ascended the stone steps to the first landing. Large stone columns held up a white limestone outer ceiling. The front entrance was an enormous opening, bordered on either side by tall stone slabs set upright with a massive cross-beam of thick stone. It was intricately carved with images of vines, animals and people. Aeala cautiously entered and looked about the interior, which was entirely in shadow.

His eyes took several minutes to adjust to the dim light and as they did, he found himself in a room with two halls leading forward into the darkness. There near the back of the room was a staircase leading to a second floor. Near the front of the room sat a low oval planter, its sides of stone and overgrown with weeds and vines. At the center of the planter was a structure of hewn white stones that appeared to be a dried up fountain.

"What is it?" whispered Sumo.

"It appears to be the foyer to whatever this structure is," said Aeala.

The floors were muddy from the dirt and fine mist that surrounded the area, and Tom-tom slipped and nearly fell as he scrambled toward the staircase.

"Take it easy, Tom-tom.—It's slippery," said Aeala. "Let's go up, but be careful."

The group followed searching this way and that for any signs of danger or objects of interest. As they approached the second floor Aeala spotted a torch mounted in the wall.

"Did anyone bring a flint?"

Jessica dug into the bag she had brought and pulled out a striker.

"Good thinking," said Aeala, "I would have never thought to bring one."

He lit the torch. It smoldered at first, and only after blowing on it for several minutes did it burst into flame. In front of them on the second floor stood a large altar, it also made of white limestone. In its center protruded the top of a smooth pearly stone.

"It appears the altar was built around the stone," said Aeala, fascinated with the piece.

"This is a temple, isn't it?" whispered Miki.

"I think so," said Aeala, "but no one has used it in years."

"What is that?"

"I'm not sure – but it appears the altar was built around it."

"It's what you saw in your dream," said Mia.

"My dream?"

"Did you not have a dream on Puna, when we were with Ka Mano?"

"Yes, of course. But I never told anyone."

"I know," said Mia.

"But you know of it because you are the prophet?" said Aeala.

Mia nodded. "I do not know exactly what your dream was—only that it is connected with this."

"It was about a beautiful pearl. I dreamed a great kahuna placed the pearl about my neck. He told me there was much more to navigate than just the sea, that I was a navigator of life and much, much more. I looked in the pearl and saw the world, the universe and then myself. This stone is the pearl. It is the pearl he was speaking of. This is the center of our new world, and it is up to us to create a new life, a new civilization. In my dream I put the pearl about my neck, but now I understand. I have always carried it with me. When I assumed the responsibility for this group I donned the pearl in spirit. It is not a piece of jewelry or even an object, but solid mana; a symbol of sacred responsibility."

He looked upon the stone in the center of the altar and it appeared to glow—but not the glow of mere white light. Instead it shimmered with iridescent colors. Again he beheld images of the island, the world, the universe and much more.

"Thank you, Mia, our seer. We are all strengthened here. We will survive—and grow."

When he looked up at the group their faces glowed with the same light as the stone. Time stopped and space grew limitless. It may have been just moments or eternity – finally Aeala stood.

"Let's go," he said, "We will bring everything in the canoe here."

As they descended to the first floor he knew that there was one other place he would have to visit before they headed back to the canoe. He turned down one of the halls and came upon a stone door.

"Sumo, Dirk – help me," he called. "I think it opens inward."

They pushed and slowly the heavy door swung inward. In the torchlight they beheld chiffon-like sheets of cobwebs hanging from the ceiling and behind, an arsenal of weapons – spears, stone axes, clubs, bow and arrows and bamboo shields.

"How did you know this was here?" asked Dirk.

Aeala shrugged. "I just knew."

"Yeah, but how?"

"I don't know. It's just that awareness comes easy these days. Must be all that navigating we did the last few weeks, believing that we knew where we were headed."

"Whatever, it was a good trick whatever you did cause we needed weapons," smiled Dirk.

They examined the weapons carefully. Some, such as the long spears and axes were too heavy to handle. After wielding and testing they decided on short spears and tomahawk-like clubs. Miki and Kaela selected the long bows with arrows and Mia simply took a long knife made of sharp volcanic glass bound on one end by what appeared to be lizard skin. Aeala, Sumo and Dirk donned the bamboo shields which they strapped on their backs for carrying.

"Are we all set?" asked Aeala.

They all nodded. "Yes, yes."

"Good then lets head back."

The sun set as they rounded the promontory and followed the shoreline into the bay where the canoe lay. Mist from the ocean rose skyward in long strands like fingers fluttering in the wind. Aeala stared at the eerie scene then at the others. It was then that he noticed Miki, her attention fixed on the horizon. She began to point then dropped her arm.

"What?" said Aeala.

"It's the dark sail."

Aeala stared a long time at the horizon until he finally discerned the tiny shadow against the rapidly darkening sea.

"It's the boat—those that have followed us from Puna."

"Then we will have to fight," said Dirk.

"It appears so," said Aeala. "If they have pursued us this far they certainly seek revenge. It's best we hide in the jungle near the canoe. Perhaps we can surprise them."

Darkness set in quickly and when they reached the canoe the stars were already glittering in the heavens. They unloaded the canoe and placed the contents in a secure area just off the beach.

"We need a plan," said Sumo.

"Ambush," said Aeala. "We'll follow them till they land and surprise them."

"Shouldn't we at least talk first," said Jessica.

"I think it's pretty plain what they want and talk will just prolong things," said Aeala.

Jessica turned away, neither agreeing nor disagreeing, but stood silent near the others.

"Brother, we need to speak in private," said Mia, her dark eyes calm yet severe.

The reaction of the two unnerved Aeala. "Come. Follow me," he said.

They walked down the beach together in the dark. The small ocean waves broke on the sand causing the water to foam.

"I don't sense evil from the boat," she said. "I have been trying for days to sense their mood and in the last few hours, even more so. But I can't sense evil. Perhaps your plans are too harsh—at least to start with."

"I am only trying to protect the crew. It seems the most reasonable way."

"Reasonable? You mean you don't want to make the same mistake you made on Puna."

His body grew taut. Anger flared from within.

"What exactly do you mean?" He stared into her eyes. They were no longer that of a little girl. She looked back, placid yet determined.

"That first night in the bedroom above the tavern, when you were attacked, you don't ever want that to happen again."

"It was not my fault. Dirk left the door unlocked, and ..."

"You were the leader. You should have foreseen such an occurrence. That is the responsibility of a leader—to see that all risks are avoided."

"You mean if I had warned Dirk beforehand I could have avoided killing..."

She looked at him, not accusatively but with understanding, and said nothing further.

A storm welled up in Aeala as he confronted that part of his past. He had the killing of Willie well justified, for he had never considered prevention of the attack on himself as an option. If he could have prevented them from knowing he had money on his person, if he had simply told Dirk not to leave the room that night, perhaps the whole incident wouldn't have occurred and Willie would still be alive and they wouldn't be in the situation they were now in. Tears welled up in his eyes. He had seen too much death in the last few weeks and imagined even more—the death of his own father and those of his friends' as well. When he looked up long tears ran over Mia's cheeks.

"You thinking of father?"

She nodded, trembling. "There has been so much death in the recent past. I just don't want there to be any more."

"We will find another plan," he said, "perhaps I will have to go back and stand trial."

"You can't do that! You'll never get a fair trial. And the volcano may blow up and kill everybody."

"We have gotten this far. It won't end badly," said Aeala.

"How do you know?"

"You're the prophet. Look at it, at the future."

She turned away toward the sea. It was serene with a twinkle of moonlight on its surface. "I think we'll survive," she said. "It just does not make sense that they would come all this way for 'justice' or even revenge."

"Unless they were following us because they thought we knew where we were going."

"Well, didn't we?"

He laughed. "For awhile there I doubted myself."

"Maybe, like us, they are just trying to survive—to get away from the volcanoes—and they followed us because they reckoned we knew the way."

"I would like to believe that," said Aeala, "but I think it's unlikely. We will prepare to defend ourselves and if it is unnecessary—all the better."

Mia nodded. "I think that is best."

They returned to the others who were huddled together in the dark.

"We will fight," said Honeycomb, her eyes fiery, her voice trembling.

"Hold on – we should find out their intentions first," said Aeala.

"But we'll lose the element of surprise," said Miki. "And we need that. They're bigger and stronger than us."

"How many bows do we have?" asked Aeala.

"Two," said Miki.

"Three!" said Tom-tom proudly raising his bow in the air.

"And arrows?"

Miki looked at Kaela who clutched the other bow and a quiver of arrows. "About twenty."

"That's plenty," said Aeala. "We'll have three archers hidden close by, and if there is no way to avoid a fight I'll say 'Sorry!' bold and loud which will be the signal to fire. I'll drop and roll in the sand to get out of the way of the arrows."

"What if we miss?"

"Then pull out another arrow and step closer. Sumo, use the pistol. Dirk, use Tom-tom's bow."

He saw Tom-tom suck in a breath, ready to protest. "Give him a tomahawk club to replace it."

Dirk handed Tom-tom the club. A grin broke out on his face and he handed the bow over to Dirk.

"I'll need some arrows," said Dirk solemnly.

Miki handed Dirk some, as did Kaela.

"They'll make landfall by the early morning so some of us should get some rest," said Aeala.

"I'll stay the first watch," said Miki.

"And, I," said Jessica, her voice trembled.

"Okay - but short watches – two or three hours. I want to be on watch when they approach."

They spread out their blankets in an area sheltered by shrubs and trees and laid down to sleep. The echo of the surf and the chirp of crickets sounded softly about them.

Aeala watched as the two girls settled in next to each other on the ridge of a shallow sand dune overlooking the beach. How brave they had been on the long voyage and now on the eve of battle, he thought. He recalled tales his Uncle Ko had told him about famous battles and bold warriors, but he had never understood the true essence of the warrior. Courage was not a trophy that one acquired—it was not like a pearl or turtle shell or gold coin. It was caring for those that one was trying to protect. It was caring so much that one would risk his own life for the preservation of his friends. And yet it was even more than that.

It was what Jessica had done when she went alone to help save him from jail. It was what Dirk had done after he had been released from jail: returning with help and rescuing Aeala. It was a firm, steady and unyielding love for one's fellows.

The night wore on and Aeala dozed. He dreamed of drifting in the double-hulled canoe alone on a dark sea. He grieved for his father and cried his name, which seemed to echo forever. Slowly the waters moaned. The sea foamed and boiled then gyred toward the heavens. The shades of thousands churned and swirled in the depths below and out of the center of the vortex the spirit of Kulo arose.

"Father, I miss you. Sometimes I feel lost, blind, without a guiding star."

Kulo looked surprised. "I have been with you always, my son, in your heart, in your thoughts and in your dreams."

"But I need your guidance. There is so much I don't know."

"Aeala – you are the *Last Kahuna*. You *are* the guiding star. And others need you now. You must take your place in the heavens and on the earth."

"I do not understand. I am not a bird. How can I take a place in the heavens?"

"The land, the waters, and the heavens are bestowed by the same creator. The essence of these are not separate, but one. And you must believe in yourself, for the creator is within you."

Kulo Pa'au then smiled lovingly at his son. The waters fell silent, dark and deep. Kulo Pa'au slowly disappeared back into the depths of the dark sea.

"Aeala – they're coming." It was Jessica's voice. He looked up into her eyes. They were fire.

"Where?"

"There," she said pointing out to sea where the waves swept over the coral reef. "They appear to be searching for the channel to the bay."

He nodded. "I will wake the others."

CHAPTER 23 – THE FINAL JOURNEY

ust act, not just talk or think in order to survive. He must act—brave the elements,

the rigid ideas of the fearful and yes, if necessary brave the gods themselves.

Way of the Kahuna

Sumo lay on his back and looked up at the stars. He knew that his sleep would be brief and restless. For a moment he envied the girls for at least they had something to distract their attention. He, on the other hand, tossed and turned on his straw mat, flicked his blanket this way and that then again stared at the heavens.

His thoughts gravitated toward the battle to come. He envisioned Simon Webster with hatchet in hand advancing forward, eyes like blood. He saw One-Eyed Jackson, a ghoul in the night, swinging a machete as blood flew from the blade. And he saw others, grim-faced and merciless, stronger and more skilled in the art of war than he, approaching relentlessly in the dark. He frowned, rolled over and looked out to sea. Like long fingers reaching toward heaven, mist slowly rose from the surface of the water and unfolded there above. It was not a heavy vapor but a fine sheer shroud that allowed the stars to peer through.

He clutched his war club with the glass ball chips to his thigh and felt the sharp shards as the dug into his skin.

He recalled a fight he once had at the school where he was thrashed soundly, not only physically but emotionally, by an older boy; where he fell humiliated in front of his schoolmates, and to this day he wondered if he had quit too soon. Perhaps if he had persisted the outcome may have been different. He did not like to think about that incident, for the mental hurt was still raw and with effort he pushed the vision away. He resolved this night would be different. He would stand and fight, kill if nec[...] whatever happened he would stand his ground, fight fiercely for his new ho[...] friends. As he relaxed, the cold barrel of his pistol touched his ribs and he sh[...]

Dirk leaned against a boulder at the edge of the jungle where the little party [...] camped and held Honeycomb in his arms. They had grown close during the voyage an[...] leaned on each other for encouragement and inspiration as well as physical support. Early in the evening he abandoned the notion of sleep and resigned to just rest his body till things came to a head. The bow that Tom-tom had surrendered lay in the sand nearby. He was familiar with the weapon—had trained with it early in life—but never in battle.

His stomach ached, not from anything physical, but from the need to confront the unconfrontable. He feared the next few hours and stoically admitted to himself he was scared, but the need to protect those he loved burned much more brightly than fear. He would stand and fight. He looked at Tom-tom wrapped in blankets, his head in Honeycomb's lap, then at her hand clasped in his own. No way, he thought, no way would he not fight; no way would he falter. He sniffed at her long hair and smelled the aroma of coconut oil and salt and felt the aura of her spirit about him.

He then surveyed the others and understood in his gut the true meaning of a group, that they were all striving for the same goal and working with each other to accomplish it—and that goal right now, of course, was survival.

Mia slept peacefully next to her mother as the fog rolled in toward shore. She had resolved to believe her intuition, the future would unfold as it would and she would meet the challenges as they developed. She did not feel the boat headed their way was a threat, but it heralded the beginning of challenges yet to be faced. And there were key decisions

...t would carve out the future of their little group. There was much she did

...d about time—how she could glimpse the future yet not fully predict it.

...s as she had been told; we make our own future, and the individual

...de sweep destiny this way and that, like coco palms blowing in the wind.

...lt there was more to it than that. Certain individuals controlled the paths that

...re traversed; certain endowed individuals channeled the many through the chutes

...time. And what were these individuals endowed with, that enabled them to bend the

future? Mana? Wisdom? Simply a gift from the gods? That was what she did not know,

that was what she struggled with, for she knew her brother was endowed with the gift and

yet he was impetuous—a conqueror instead of a caretaker—and what the group needed at

the moment was the latter, not the former.

"Mia, Kaela the rest of you. Wake up—the boat is near."

The words, though soft, echoed through the little group as trumpets sounding a call.

They gathered on the leeward side of the little dune where Jessica and Miki had stood

watch and waited for Aeala to speak.

The words sliced like hot iron. "Everyone here? Listen up. I will go to the beach and

draw them in. Sumo—you stay right here behind the dune. You have the pistol, right?"

Sumo nodded. "Good. Dirk you'll be to my left. Dig a shallow hole. Not too deep –

one you can kneel in but still shoot the bow. You'll be maybe 30 feet away from where

I'll be standing.   Miki – you and Kaela will be standing to my right, there, hidden by

the boulder. The others will be behind the boulder with whatever weapon you have.

Again the key word is *sorry* – either *I'm sorry* or just *sorry*. When you hear it, it's time to

send in the bullets and arrows. I will drop to the ground and roll. Fire as many arrows as possible then come in with whatever hand weapons you have. Let's make it

deadly. That is the only way."

Mia choked on her own saliva. "Wait! That's not the only way. You told

something different earlier," she blurted. "They may not be hostile. We have

that also. If not, we could make a terrible mistake!"

Aeala appeared to brush off her words. She sensed the conqueror, not the care

him.

"If that be the case then the gods have graced us," he mumbled, unconvinced, and

turned toward the jungle.

"Sumo, help me collect wood for a fire. It will draw them to us."

Miki and Jessica also went with them and soon a big pile of wood stood on the beach

a few yards from the water. Jessica handed the flint striker to Aeala and he struck the flint

with iron. A few sparks fell on the coconut fiber Aeala had prepared and upon which he

blew gently.

A tiny coal glowed like cat's eyes in the dark and in moments flame burst forth. There

was scarcely a breeze and the flames soared directly upward into the night. He fed larger

branches into the flames until the fire burned vigorously spitting and crackling on the

sand. As he stood to stretch his back Mia approached face aflame.

"You will not start a fight if it's not necessary," she said. Her words stung.

He looked at her taken aback. "Yeah, that's what I said."

"But you didn't mean it."

He hesitated then turned away.

turn away! This is too important to be ignored!" Again her words cut like

agger at her side.

everything necessary to protect this group. No more, no less." He could feel

knife through him.

he time comes, remember your humanity as well as your courage."

ed at her. Her eyes were steel, shining like hot starlight. She certainly was not

girl of a month ago.

odded. "I'll remember."

he crawled forward moment by moment. The dark triangle that was the sail of their

er's boat grew larger. Aeala noted that they had found the channel and the sail was

trimmed for reaching as the wind came from their port side. Aeala felt a soft hand

h his waist and looked down. It was Jessica. She slipped her arm around his waist.

"I believe in you," she whispered. "Your judgment. Your intentions."

"I know," he said, gently, and kissed her on the top of her head.

"It is time!" he called to the crew. The dark shadow that was the boat was only a
couple of hundred yards off shore. The mist obscured the boat for a moment then it
appeared again, dark and silent, in the starlight. He glanced around. The bonfire burned
about forty yards from the water, which lapped at the shore; a gentle shore-break
tumbling into foam and spray. Forty yards, he thought, yet it seemed the longest voyage
of his life.

The boat drew closer and Aeala was able to distinguish several silhouettes on the
deck. They began to lower the sail; the momentum of the boat drew it still toward shore.
Aeala started toward it tomahawk in hand. He glanced back – everyone was in their

proper place ready for battle. He reckoned it would be quick and bloody wi

their pursuers stopped by the initial bullets and arrows. He would handle th

quick and deadly blows of his weapon. The boat made landfall with the bow

the wet sand. Aeala moved forward cautiously in the dark.

"Aeala is that you?" It was a husky male voice, which Aeala instantly reco

Obie Crats. Fury rose in his breast! Webster's sidekick had pursued him all this

this after leading his companions to Ka Mano's cottage where they very likely k

old man. He had witnessed the boat turn from its course into Ka Mano's beach ar.

could only imagine the scene that took place there. Had it been Obie that took Ka N

life? He clutched his tomahawk tighter and headed at a run toward the silhouettes, fi

bursting forth like lightning in a storm. Three of them had jumped overboard to secu.

the boat and were up to their waists in water. It was now that they were the most

vulnerable as they could not maneuver deftly in the water. Aeala raised his weapon, hi

mind aflame.

Mia stood near the boulder on the beach in tears, her certainty torn asunder, her

thoughts confused. She felt her brother's fury and suddenly realized she was the only one

to stand against it. As Obie's voice echoed over the beach she also recognized it. Like

reflections of moonlight on a calm sea, images of her father and others rose in her mind.

Suddenly she realized the truth and the true horror about to face them.

"Aeala! No!" she cried.

She burst forth from behind the boulder and headed for the shore. Dirk, startled, stood

up in the hole he had been crouching in, bow drawn, arrow aimed at Obie's heart. Sumo

d Mia away from cover and vulnerable on the beach took off at a sprint

ouettes, pistol raised and cocked, club in the opposite hand.

is that you!" A voice from the sea echoed.

t is I!" she screamed.

pped in his tracks only yards from the defenseless Obie. "Obie? Father!"

eala. It is I, and Mr. Ka and Mr. Waha."

! Miki! Your fathers are here!" cried Aeala.

dropped her weapon and broke into tears as she ran toward the surf and foam.

stared sheepishly at the weapons in his hands then dropped them to the sand.

. .

took over an hour for the joy to die down. They piled driftwood on the fire until the

es soared high and appeared to touch the stars.

'Tell us about your journey," said Mia. Reflections from the flames danced in her

es as she sat on the sand with her legs folded beneath her.

Kulo smiled at his daughter and tears ran down his cheeks. The flames lit the right

ide of his face and the lines in his weathered cheeks creased deep as he began.

"We should never have left that morning. It was raining, and the waves on the surface

f the ocean marched in, in a strange fashion, as if something in the dark depths had

cracked and shook the water above. However, we had only a small window of time to get

to Puna and back, before the fishing season began. We were totally unaware of the

quavering earth and great waves to come. The trip to Puna, although rough and slow, was

uneventful, but it was only hours after we made landfall that the great waves struck Puna.

It was terrible, but we were fortunate to avoid the fury and escape to the other side of the island. We stayed the night in a tavern, quickly picked up supplies then left.

what we would find when we arrived back at Pa'ai. It took us only two days

but the devastation was overwhelming. We searched the bungalow and tree ı

found no one – you must have left just before we arrived.

We did meet a party at sea in one of uncle Ko's canoes. Several of the people

badly injured and we gave them food and water before continuing on to Puna. ı

Jessica, your father – I believe – was one of the injured."

She gasped and put her hand over her mouth to squelch a shriek. Her hands clu

Aeala as if she would never let go, then tears welled up in her eyes and ran down hı

cheeks. She was silent as Kulo continued.

"We saw the canoe ruts in the sand near the pier and reckoned you must have hea

for Puna. We tried to stay the night in the bungalow but the fumes were so bad we sh

off and spent the night sleeping in the canoe at sea. The trip back was slowed by the

winds.

When we reached Puna we found Obie who told us that Aeala had killed someone and

had escaped from jail. He confessed it was not Aeala's fault, that he had acted in self-

defense, but nonetheless Obie and others went looking for Aeala's canoe on the other

side of the island to steal it. An explosion stopped and injured them and they never made

it to the canoe. He told us he was very sorry for betraying Aeala and would help us find

him. We sailed around the island, and with Obie's help found Ka Mano who helped us.

He told us that you had all left looking for 'Āina Le'a Nu'i and in order to find it we had

to follow A'a west. We did. On our way we occasionally spotted the canoe but it would below the horizon. We had faith in what Ka Mano said and followed A'a.

re here tonight."

ked up at Aeala. He realized how truly vulnerable she was – alone with no

r off land. Yes, she had friends; but friends from a different culture, with

iefs and a different way of looking at the world. He held her closer, resolve in

er told you this before, Aeala," said Kulo, "but I have brought you up to be a

r with the hope that someday you might choose that as your calling in life. As an

brought you to the tidal pools on Pa'ai and had you play in the water to teach you

the nature of the ocean and tides—the feel of the waves, the rhythm of the winds.

you were older we went to the mountains and I showed you the stars and pointed

he important ones that moved about in the heavens. Do you remember?"

Aeala nodded.

"I took you to the seashore and had you feel the wind as it blew to teach you the ways

f the wind.

would have you sail and swim in all conditions, calm and stormy, to teach you the

mperaments of the sea. These things had to be experienced, sensed; by simply telling

ou they could not be learned. Do you understand?"

Aeala nodded.

"So through experience I taught you the ways of the winds and seas. But there is one

thing I could never teach you other than by example, and that is courage. That is making

a decision and carrying it through. Man must act, not just talk or think in order to survive.

He must act—brave the elements, resist the rigid ideas of the fearful and yes, if necessary brave the gods themselves. I see that you have learned that lesson well. It tc

courage, not only yours but that of all of your friends, for all of you sail inte

unknown waters with faith as your only compass. We shall build a new civil

a just and prosperous civilization – and reach as far as we can toward the star

As he looked into Aeala's eyes, Aeala saw the pride and love his father hac

And, Kulo from his position near the roaring fire saw not a child but a fine your.

filled with integrity and courage looking back at him with the gleam of starlight ı

eyes.

EPILOGUE

Mia awoke early and sat up on the soft straw mat in her chamber in the temple. The

little window facing east showed no signs of morning's first light. She arose and threw or

a forest cloak to keep out the early morning chill. Something was different, it was as if sh

had lost something. A vacuum drifted through her. She descended the staircase to the maiı

foyer then exited the high temple door.

The crew had cleared the trail to the beach in the past few weeks and she scurried

down it expecting to discover the source of her irritation. As she d the beach the moon sank low in the sky and A'a twinkled blue in the heavens.

diately noticed that the canoe with its twin hulls was missing. Two deep tracks in

marked where it was pushed out to sea. She stared at the eastern horizon and there

he silver moonlight was the silhouette of a triangular sail. She let out a deep sigh

lked to the water's edge where she dipped her toes in the sand and foam.

"Safe trip," she whispered. "May the gods sail with you."

She stood there for another moment, sensing keenly the morning chill and the wet

and between her toes. As she turned to leave, Jessica shuffled down the beach toward

her.

"What's the matter?" she said. "I saw you leave the temple and thought it odd."

"It's Aeala. He's gone to find your father."

"Why? Why didn't he tell anyone?"

"Because he loves you and didn't want you along as it would put your life in danger in

the open sea."

"He's out there alone?"

Mia nodded. "Pray for him, to your own god."

"I will," said Jessica her eyes misting.

"He is the last *Kahuna Kilo Hoku*: the last of the master navigators. Our father will

never again voyage far from home, and his Uncle Ko hasn't been seen in three years. If

he perishes, so does the lore of the canoe navigators, for they were the last three. He

needs your prayers. I believe your god is very strong and will guide him."

Long tears ran down Jessica's cheeks. "I love him too," she whispered.

The tropical breeze sighed over the lonely beach, and the foam and spr

tumbling onto the sand, rose toward the heavens.

JT THE AUTHOR

nneth Sereno was born in the Territory of Hawai'i on the island of Oahu in 1948. In
he Sereno family moved to Upcountry Maui where they lived below an extinct
no, Mount Haleakala, on the rural semi-alpine slope overlooking the isthmus of
okama'oma'o with Kahalawai (West Maui Mountains) on the far side. He attended
wai'ian Public schools while surfing, fishing, and hiking in his spare time, where he
ew to appreciate and love nature and the elements peculiar to Hawai'i.

In the late 60's when the Viet Nam war raged elsewhere, he attended Maunaolu
College and the University of Hawai'i and studied Religion and English. In 1968 when
the Pueblo Incident occurred (North Korea seized the USS Pueblo) he joined the navy.
After spending several years sailing around Boston Harbor on a navy tug he was
discharged (the Viet Nam war was winding down).

He continued his studies in Religion, Philosophy and History while sailing around the
Iberian Peninsula and later the Caribbean. In 1986 he moved to California doing an
assortment of trades and professions. The dream and obligation to contribute to his own
culture always burned bright and thus led to the writing of *The Last Kahuna*, a spiritual,
adventure novel about growing up in the South Pacific (in the 1890's).

Proof

16291746R00114

Made in the USA
Charleston, SC
13 December 2012